D0818220

The Final Arrangement

By
Annie Adams

HA CASS COUNTY PUBLIC LIBRARY
400 E. MECHANIC
HARRISONVILLE, MO 64701

0 0022 0450176 7

The Final Arrangement © 2013 Annie Adams
All rights reserved

This book is licensed for your personal enjoyment only.. The book contained herein constitutes a copyrighted work and may not be reproduced, transmitted, down-loaded, or stored in or introduced into an information storage and retrieval system in any form or by any means, whether electronic or mechanical, now known or hereinafter invented, without the express written permission of the copyright owner, except in the case of brief quotation embodied in critical articles and reviews. Thank you for respecting the hard work of this author.

This book is a work of fiction. The names, characters, places, and incidents are products of the writer's imagination or have been used fictitiously and are not to be construed as real. Any resemblance to persons, living or dead, actual events, locales or organizations is entirely coincidental.

Cover Art © 2012 Kelli Ann Morgan / Inspire Creative Services

Interior book design by
Bob Houston eBook Formatting

ISBN-13: 978-1482314489

Dedication

This novel is dedicated with love to the real Aunt Rosy and to all the strong women in my life, past and present.

Acknowledgements

The journey to writing this book only began because of the encouragement of my dear friend, L.L. Muir, without whom I would still be one of those people who is going to write a book someday.

Many thanks to readers and friends in the URWA and to Alabama Heather, Texas Linda and Idaho Julie. Thank you to Lieutenant Atkin, Sergeant Joseph, Sergeant Dixon and all the fine folks at Layton City Police Department for answering my many questions and for keeping a straight face when hearing my scene ideas. Any mistakes or inconsistencies within this novel pertaining to police work are of my own making. To my flower friends and my mortician friends, thank you and don't worry—you are not in this book.

Thank you most of all to J.D. for everything!

CHAPTER ONE

There was nothing unusual about the beginning of the day they found the Vulture dead. I arrived at work at two minutes to nine, which is completely usual. Rosie's Posies, a flower shop, opens at nine a.m., and I am not an early riser. I'm not Rosie either. My name is Quinella McKay, Quincy to anyone who knows what's good for them. I'm Rosie's niece.

I took over my aunt's flower shop in northern Utah when she decided to travel the world. It happened to be at the same time that I needed a job. And a car, and a life. I got two out of three—the white zombie delivery van didn't do much for the getting-a-life part.

So there I stood that morning, struggling to unlock the front door. Nothing unusual about that, either. The ancient key was so ground down that part of my daily ritual included doing the unlocking dance while cars buzzed past on the busy intersection in front of my corner shop.

The hot exhaust belching from commuter cars accentuated waves of heat broiling off of the asphalt of the parking lot. Just before I finally muscled the key far enough to tumble the lock, I heard the phone inside the shop ring. The hand not turning the key held a giant Coke; another of the regular props in the opening dance, and off of that same arm dangled a tote bag. The bag was big enough to carry a small child and weighed about the same. Something at the bottom of it vibrated and chimed in alternating syncopation with the phone in the shop. It sounded a lot like my cell phone ring-tone. Using the key as a handle, I pulled the door open and stumbled into my store.

A wave of heat slapped me in the face as I continued in. The acrid smell of dried leaves and stems hung in the air. Apparently the air conditioner wasn't working properly— not unusual at all. I let the bag drop to the floor, probably crushing the cell phone and sprinted to the telephone on the back wall of the design room, the drink clutched in one hand. I tripped over a potted azalea left too close to the walkway but managed to keep my precious elixir of energy from spilling while I regained balance.

I slowed just long enough to put the drink on the design table then finished the race to the phone counter. I lifted the receiver and croaked out, "Rosie's Posies, how may I help you?"

"Hi, Quincy," Danny Barnes said in a chirpy voice. He was my nearest competitor and oddly enough, one of my closest friends. "Sorry to call in the busy morning but *O.M.G.*, have you heard?" Years of conditioning made it impossible for anyone brought up like Danny or me, as Mormons in Utah, to utter the phrase "Oh my God." This just wasn't done. One could say, "Oh my gosh," "Oh my heck," or even go as far as to say, "Oh my hell," when provoked, but never the forbidden phrase. Given the choice of either saying it or slamming my fingers in the car door, I'd choose the latter. The discomfort would be shorter lived.

"Did I hear what?"

"Oh this is big, this is so big, My Fair Lady. You haven't heard about Derrick?"

"Derrick—oh, you mean, flower Derrick, Derrick the hated, Derrick the Vulture?"

"Yes, yes that Derrick."

"What, is he selling flowers to all of the wedding reception centers in the state now too?"

Derrick Gibbons, the Vulture, had been responsible for the near death of my business, about a year before. Mysteriously, he emerged as the sole provider of all sympathy flowers to mortuaries in the entire area. At the same time, the flow of referrals from said mortuaries stopped coming my direction, which obliterated half of my sales.

"I haven't heard anything. I just got here." I glanced up at the clock on the fresh-grass-green-painted wall. "In fact, can I call you back later?"

"No! You have to hear this!"

"Wow. Okay, you were telling me about Derrick..." I wedged the phone between my chin and shoulder and switched on the nearby computer and printer.

"They just found him—at the mortuary—dead as a doornail."

"What?"

"I know! Can you believe it?" Danny asked me as if we were gossiping about something as mundane as the ugly arrangements at Joanne's Flower Basket.

"Wait...what?"

"No, it gets better. They found him—on display—in a casket—in the chapel—just like it was a regular viewing. And—are you ready for this—there were flowers on top of the casket."

"You are shitting me!" I forgot my customer language filter.

"I know. A fully arranged casket spray right there on top of the casket. I am stunned. I'm stunned! Absolutely speechless," he lied, seeing as how Danny has never been speechless a day in his life.

I absolutely *was* speechless for a moment.

"Danny, you're being totally serious right now. You're not joking?"

"I am not joking!" His voice increased in pitch at the end of his sentence sounding like an old-fashioned train whistle.

As I stood at the phone counter, I thought I should be feeling some kind of sadness, or at the very least feeling sorry for the Vulture. But the only thing I could think of was his overly tanned face lying in a casket with pasty, two-shades-too-white mortician's make-up spackled on.

"Danny, how do you know any of this?"

"Well, you didn't hear it from me, but, I sent my delivery driver to the mortuary early this morning to pick up a rental piece we used for an arrangement a week ago that we need to use tonight for an enDerrickment party. You know, the pillar with the cherub holding the bowl that I use for my waterfall design collection?"

For Danny, unwinding a good piece of gossip was an art form not unlike creating a beautiful one-of-a-kind floral masterpiece. A complicated design that must be carefully crafted, each stem thoughtfully considered before being placed, each detail delicately, yet purposefully described. I could just see his hands waving and imitating the flow of water cascading from the top of a cliff to the ground below while he talked.

"Isn't it ironic that we used the piece for a funeral one day and now we're using it for a wedding?"

"Danny! Dead Derrick—casket spray—mortuary—remember?"

"Oh, sorry. Anyway, my driver went to pick it up, and there were cop cars and flashing lights everywhere. So he calls me on the cell and says they've got the place blocked off and there's no way he's getting in. So I called the mortuary to tell them it isn't bad enough they have to whore themselves out to Derrick the Vulture, who doesn't even own a shop in our city, but they also have to inconvenience me and my staff and my customers by keeping my property hostage. I told them I would send them a bill to cover the delivery charge of having my driver return repeatedly, and that they would be charged a fee for every hour I am delayed in retrieving my property." He stopped talking and I heard the rush of air he sucked into his depleted lungs.

Of course I knew about one third of what he had just told me was the actual story; the rest was Danny's usual flourish.

"The secretary apologized for my inconvenience and told me there had been an accident. So, I called my brother and asked him to give me the scoop."

Danny's brother was a county sheriff's deputy, and at six foot three, weighing in at about three bills, he was Danny's polar opposite. While the sheriff brother spends his days off hunting and camping, the florist brother barely breaks the six-foot barrier, is very trim and put together, and he wouldn't be caught in public with as much as a wrinkle in his shirt or a hair out of place. Danny would rather die than wear camouflage.

"What all did your brother say?"

"Mostly what I've already told you about them finding the Vulture there at the mortuary in the coffin and the flowers. He really shouldn't have told me anything. That's why you didn't hear it from me."

"Were they his?" I knew Danny knew exactly what *they* I was talking about.

"Kevin doesn't know a tulip from a daisy, so I doubt he would know who made the casket spray. Besides, aren't you curious about how Derrick got there? I mean, I think he was processed and prepped like one of their customers."

The other line on my phone started ringing.

"Dang it! I've got to go, Danny, I'll call you later."

As much as I would have liked to gossip all day, I needed to run a business. I punched the button for the other line before Danny had a chance to reply.

"Rosie's Posies, how may I help you today?"

"Oh, so you *are* there?" My mother's voice rang with the usual guilt-imposing tone.

"Hello, it's good to hear your voice, too, Mom," I said

sarcastically. I grabbed my apron from a nearby hook and looped it over my head, while juggling the phone receiver. "Did you just call my cell phone?"

"Yes, I've tried to call you four times at the shop, but you won't answer your phone. How do you expect to get any orders if you won't answer your phone?"

"Mom, I don't know why you keep saying *won't* answer my phone. You know that the shop doesn't open until nine, and I've taken the extra precaution of adding a voicemail service to my phone so that people can leave a message." I sighed. "But you knew that already."

"Well, that's why I called your cell phone."

"I just couldn't get to it, Mom." I held back the next heavy sigh welling up in my throat. My relationship with my mother would probably be classified as dysfunctional by a mental health professional. At the very least one could call it strained. I decided however, that it wasn't worth ruining the day to fight with her. "Sorry, I guess I woke up on the wrong side of the bed this morning."

"You've got that right, missy. Anyway, I called to ask if you've heard your sister's news."

My heart sank. "Which sister?"

"Sandy. They just asked her and Rick to be the nursery teachers at church."

"Oh, really? Well good for them. I was afraid you were going to say something about Allie."

"Why? What have you heard about Allie? What's wrong?" Her voice filled with panic.

"Mom! Nothing. I haven't heard anything. Calm down. I just worried when you said something was going on with one of my sisters."

"Well, of course you assumed the worst with Allie. I don't know why you have such a problem with Brad. He is a good man, Quincy Adams McKay. You should go to the single adult ward at church. You'd be lucky to find such a catch. You're never going to find one with the life you're living now."

Ah...yes, she'd taken the gloves off. She'd used my middle name, and slipped in a dig about going to church. Or in my case, not going to church. She didn't come out directly and *accuse* me of not going to church. Instead, she used the time-honored method of most mothers, which was passive-aggression with a pinch of guilt mixed in for good measure.

"Mom, you know why I don't like Brad; I used to be married to one of his kind, remember? You know, the guy that used to knock the shit of out of me for a hobby?"

"Language, Quincy! You always have tended to exaggerate. I am sorry that your husband wasn't always easy to get along with, but we all have our faults. Brad is a returned missionary, and he has a good job..." Just as Mom started her repetitive trip down the denial river, the other line on the phone started ringing.

"Oh, sorry, Mom..." The phone rang again.

"She's hinted they might go ring shopping soon..." Another phone ring.

"Mom, I've gotta go—the other line is ringing—Mom—I'll call you back." I hung up fully aware I would have to pay for it later. She probably hadn't yet noticed I wasn't on the phone anymore.

I punched the button for the other line hoping I hadn't missed a customer.

"Rosie's Posies, this is Quincy." The refrigeration unit on top of the walk-in cooler started up with its loud whirring.

"Hello, this is Betty Carlisle—I'm a volunteer with the hospital gift shop."

"Oh hi, Betty."

"I just thought you might want to know that we are out of arrangements in the cooler."

"Out?"

"Out."

"Okay, we'll bring a cooler full as soon as we can."

"All right, dear. Bye."

This was more like it. July isn't exactly the greatest month for florists. It's even slower than January, which is horrific for sales except for the fact that it's funeral season. Not a term used with customers, but a common part of the vernacular in the business. I allowed myself just a moment of indulgence to think about where the mortuary would send its customers now that Derrick had fallen victim to funeral season in July.

My pulse quickened as I itemized the increasing responsibilities for the day. My glances at the clock became more frequent as I hoped my helpers would arrive sooner than planned. The radio I had switched on earlier no longer played background music; instead it was screaming car commercials. Sweat began to pool on the back of my neck, and along my hairline.

Where was that Coke? There had been far too much action already without taking a hit. I grabbed the cup and perused the order bins on the wall, dragging cold liquid comfort through the straw, making every sip count like the final pulls on a last cigarette.

After organizing the daily orders and the hospital list, I ducked into the walk-in cooler to get more flowers and greenery and relished the relief it offered from the summer heat and the inadequate air conditioner. The whirring of the fan pushing air inside the cooler played tricks on my hearing, making it sound like the phone was ringing. I ignored the phantom sound. Then I heard it ring again. I popped my head out of the cooler and realized both lines were ringing.

"Damn it!" Saying it out loud seemed to help. Arms full, I used one foot to close the door while balancing on the other leg, then walked over to the design table, attempted to put everything down quickly without breaking any stems and rushed to the phone.

"Rosie's Posies, how may I help you?" My voice sang out with a tone of warmth and enthusiasm—from where it came I don't know.

"Hi, my name is Roger; may I speak with the person who makes the decisions about the phone bill?"

A scream rang out within the walls of my skull. "She's not here right now," I lied, while hardly restraining the fury in my voice.

"When would be a better time for me to reach her?" Roger—if that was his real name, tried to sound friendly and helpful.

"I don't really know, just between you and me, she's kind of unreliable. I couldn't really give you a time, I never know myself."

Painfully, yet mercifully, the other line kept ringing. I didn't want to risk letting the voicemail pick up and lose a potential customer because I had been speaking to Roger.

"Oh, there's my other line, it's probably the boss calling to say she's not coming in."

"It's okay. I'll wait while you check." I had to give Roger extra points for trying. Unfortunately for Roger, I neglected to hit hold. Oops.

I answered the ringing line. My ear started to throb.

"Rosie's," I answered sharply.

"Is the owner there?" A deep male voice asked.

"I am not interested!" I fired back. "I'm really busy right now and you guys have already called me this morning. Talk to Roger over in the next cubicle."

"This is Detective Arroyo with the Hillside City Police Department. I'm looking for Quinella Swanson."

Ugh. I closed my eyes and leaned my forehead against the wall.

"This is Quincy," I corrected. "What can I help you with today?"

"Ms. Swanson, do you know a Derrick Gibbons?"

"My name is Quincy McKay. Swanson is my *ex-*

husband's name. And yes, I know Derrick—well I know who he is. I mean was. I guess that should be was, shouldn't it?" My cheeks started to burn like they always do when I jumble my words.

"Why would you say *was* Ms…McKay?"

A cold burning started to churn deep in my stomach. A three-alarm fire burned across my cheeks. Danny's admonition not to tell anyone echoed inside my head. His brother could lose his job if they found out he'd leaked the story. I had just broken the unspoken code of the florist.

If there's anyone who knows all of the gossip in town, it's the florist. Any florist knows that when they hear something juicy, they keep it in the vault. Danny was going to kill me.

"Ms. McKay, I need to speak with you about a few things. How long will you be there today?"

"I…all day as far as I know. But…"

"I just need to ask you a few things, so I need you to stay put.

"I'm sorry, Officer…"

"It's Detective."

"*Detective*; I was just wondering why you would need me to stay here. Not that I plan on going anywhere, but can't we just talk over the phone? I mean, I don't really know anything about Derrick anyway."

"No. Like I said, don't go anywhere."

"Detective, I'm trying to run a business, and I've got a lot to worry about right now. It doesn't really work for me to stay here all day, waiting. Isn't it possible just to do it over the phone…now?"

"Somehow I knew you would be a pain."

"Excuse me?" He was very unprofessional. "Is there a problem here?"

"Should there be a problem? Is there something you're not telling me?" He sounded like a detective on a bad TV show.

"This conversation is getting weird. I don't know why you're talking to me in that tone and I really don't know what I could tell you about Derrick." I swiped my hair out of my face and tucked it behind an ear. "If this is about the parking lot thing yesterday…"

"What parking lot thing?"

Oh, crud. "Never mind. Nothing. I'm just flustered by the way you're talking to me. I don't like your accusatory tone, Officer. I haven't done anything wrong."

"It's *Detective* Arroyo. And my tone is the least of your worries right now. You were the last person seen with Derrick Gibbons while he was alive."

"Whoa. Exactly what are you saying?"

"I'm saying don't go anywhere."

Then, there was nothing but silence.

I stood immobile after I hung up the phone. A knot inside my head, consisting of hundreds of thought threads all pulling in their own direction resulted in my inability to do anything but stand there, stunned. Meanwhile the cooler motor clanked on again and the radio blared.

What a bizarre phone call. And what kind of idiot cop calls ahead, thus tipping off a suspect? Of course, I wasn't a suspect. Was I? This had to have been a joke. But, I didn't know anyone that would pull such a mean prank. *Wait a second*—the ex-husband. His relatives were virtually half the population of Hillside; he probably had connections at the police department.

I looked down at the caller ID. It said Hillside City Police on the screen. If it was a joke, someone could get in a lot of trouble just for helping my ex get his jollies. There had to be another explanation, but I didn't have time to think about it. Maybe it involved Danny's brother. But worrying about the jerk cop and his weird phone call would have to wait. I had things to do and if Detective Arroyo wanted to talk to me about Derrick, or for whatever reason, he would have to do it around my schedule.

If Arroyo really was a cop, I would probably be regretting the fact that I almost let slip about my little tiff with Derrick. I hated him even more now dead than when he was alive. I thought back to the night before, when I had gone to deliver a puny little planter basket to the mortuary. We bumped into each other and I ended up falling down on the asphalt after he pushed me. Derrick walked away as if nothing ever happened and there were no witnesses to the altercation. Or at least I thought there weren't any witnesses.

"Okay," I said out loud, "Enough time wasting." The day was melting away as if the heat outside had an effect on the passage of time. I picked up the phone receiver yet again. I called Cindy, my assistant floral designer, who wasn't scheduled to come in until noon.

"Hello." The disdain in Cindy's hello indicated that she probably saw the shop number pop up on her caller ID.

"Hi Cindy, I am so sorry to ask this, but can you please come in early?"

She responded with a long, intentionally drawn out sigh.

"How early?"

"As soon as possible."

"Why?" She sounded like a whiny teenager arguing with her mom.

"Some last minute stuff has come up." I didn't want to mention the slim possibility of the police showing up. "The hospital called and we've got to get a full load over there soon."

"Wuhl, isn't Nick supposed to be there?"

Nick was my delivery driver. He'd been working for me for three weeks. So far he'd only been late four times, but he eventually shows up, which is better than the previous two drivers.

I glanced up at the clock and couldn't believe what I saw. "It's past ten already! Cindy, I just need to know if you can come in or not. Nick doesn't do arrangements, and we've got a lot of stuff to get done." Why should I explain anything to her anyway? I was supposed to be the boss.

"Hhhhuh," she exhaled forcefully enough to collapse a lung. "Okay, I'll guess I'll come in."

"Thank you so much, I really appreciate it."

"Yeah." The phone went silent.

"Be happy you have a job, you little troll!" I said to the receiver after I replaced it in its cradle with a little extra force.

I walked over to the radio and turned off one of the background noises. At least I had control over something. As I picked up my knife, I heard the familiar sound of the phone, and stuck the knife in the pocket of my apron as I reached for the receiver with my other hand.

For the next twenty minutes I fielded phone calls, which actually consisted of orders for the day. Now the heat was on—both outside with the weather and inside with the sudden onslaught of business. I returned to the design table and worked in between glances at my watch and the front window, worried it might be the police, instead of my helpers who would come through the door first.

Finally Nick walked in the door. Nick Wilson was twenty-two years old. A good enough looking guy, but he disguised it with a lazy demeanor. His slouch just shouted out, "I dare you to ask me to move any faster."

"Hey, Nick."

"Hey, Quincy. How's it goin'?"

"Well, it'd be goin' a lot better if my driver had been here at ten."

"Oh yeah, sorry."

"I'm sure you're all broken up about it."

"Huh?"

"About being late, I'm sure you just feel terrible about being late."

"Oh. Yeah." He had no idea what I was talking about.

"I was being sarcastic Nick. You need to be on time from now on."

"Oh." Pause. "K."

I wasn't going to hold my breath on that one.

"Since I don't have time to finish making all of these before you leave, I need you to go to the front display cooler and grab a thirty-five dollar arrangement. Then write the card and take the arrangement to Fairview."

Nick stood in place for a few beats while I watched for signs of cogs turning in his head. He looked up at me and I pointed toward the front of the store. His synapses finally fired up and he ambled in the direction of the cooler. While on his way, the front doorbell chimed. Cindy's blond hair filled the doorway and framed a giant pair of metallic bug eye sunglasses. The glam glasses only distracted me momentarily from the thing that would cause a stress-invoked heart attack before I turned thirty.

Cindy is what you might call well-endowed. She wore a tight, white, scoop-necked tank top, which was too short to cover her belly button ring. Her cut-off denim short-shorts were too low riding to conceal the jewelry either. As she begrudgingly swanked her way back to the design area, I noticed Nick had a new purpose and pace to his step as he followed her while holding an arrangement.

As she approached the design table where I stood, I tried to assemble the correct words. I had to say just enough, but not too much. She had to know she couldn't wear that to work right?

I must deal with this employee in a firm, but friendly manner. That's what Aunt Rosie had written in her shop instruction manual. As I tried to come up with something profound, Cindy reached the design table, but made a sharp right turn to the wrapping counter where she liked to stow her purse; she was obviously avoiding speaking to me for as long as possible.

"Hi," I said with questioning intonation. I had decided

to wait to speak with her privately about the dress code, after Nick left. That was, until I saw the view from behind when she crouched to put her purse under the counter. Not only was her lower back tattoo obscured slightly by the hot pink thong, but the shorts had a three-inch wide hole under her right butt cheek.

All thoughts of friendly firmness disintegrated.

"Are—you—kidding—me?" I said.

"What?" She said innocently as she stood up.

"You cannot seriously think you can wear that to work in my shop."

"What's wrong with it?"

"Yeah, what's wrong with what she's wearing? It looks pretty hot to me," said suddenly-not-slouching Nick.

"Nick! Aren't you supposed to be doing something? Besides, you can't talk about how hot your co-worker is."

"So you admit I look good." Cindy said, glowing.

I thought my head might explode.

"You know if you had only come in wearing the tank top, which shows the most cleavage as is possible while still maintaining the laws of physics, we might have been able to have a little talk. But the tattoo framing thong and the rip-in-the-ass jeans are just a bit over the top."

"Whoa, when did you get a tramp stamp?" Nick said.

"Nick!"

"Dude, you probably shouldn't show your ass though, that's not proper," he said, with a straight face.

"Proper?" I turned my attention to Nick. "Aren't you the guy that wears his pants so baggy that an old lady called the police and complained about being flashed when a young man matching your description got into a van in front of our store?" Things were totally out of control at this point. "By the way, have you bought a belt yet?"

"Hey, I was just trying to help." Nick said, surprised at my lack of appreciation for his words of wisdom.

"You can help by getting that delivery to Fairview and

getting back here to take the hospital cooler stuff."

"Okay, I'm going."

He picked up the arrangement he'd left on the table and reached for the van keys on the hook on the wall.

"Nick, the card!" He hadn't written the card yet.

"I'll do it." Cindy declared, and then walked over to the little rack on the front counter displaying the cards and envelopes that are usually enclosed with a flower delivery. She proceeded to pick up a card and pen, then lean down on the counter to write, causing her butt to protrude behind her and thus be prominently displayed to both Nick and myself so that we had a bird's eye view of the ensuing rip, which resulted in a now, six-inch tear.

I glared at Nick, daring him to say a word. A look of fear passed across his face. He walked over next to Cindy, and looked straight up at the ceiling with his hand held out until Cindy placed the card filled envelope in his palm. He then marched with intent toward the back door and the parked delivery van that doubled as my personal vehicle.

"Cindy," I said wearily, "if it were just the cleavage-fest tank top, you could cover up with an apron. But you can't wear those shorts. At the rate they're ripping you'll have a fully exposed cheek in about thirty seconds."

"Well you're the one that called and asked me to come in early. I'm doing you a favor by being here," she said indignantly.

"Exactly what kind of favor is it that you're doing for me? Doubling as an on-staff barfly? And what does coming in a few minutes early have to do with what you're wearing?"

"I didn't have any other clean clothes."

"Well next time do me a favor and wear something with stains all over them will ya? It'd be a lot better than this."

"Maybe there won't be a next time. There are other jobs out there you know."

"You're right, Cindy. There are a lot of jobs out there.

But the only ones where you're allowed or encouraged to dress like that have descriptions including words like, johns, pimps, street, and walking."

My sarcasm seemed to break the tension and Cindy looked up at me trying to suppress a smile.

"Okay, I shouldn't have worn this to work. But you don't have to be such a bitch, Quincy. You could have just told me to go change." She turned her head away, embarrassed to show the emotion beginning to well up in her face.

Employees aren't supposed to talk to their bosses like that. But, a boss probably shouldn't tell their employee they are dressed like a prostitute. I'd let the stress get to me and snapped. It hurt to have Cindy call me a name like that, though. But, I couldn't let her know it. I turned my heated face away from her.

The two of us stood there, three feet apart looking in opposite directions, both knowing we had breached employee/employer etiquette but not wanting to admit it.

"Cindy, you just caught me off guard. It's been a stressful morning." I felt very un-confident and none of the usual snappy comebacks came to mind.

"Not everyone is as perfect as you, Quincy." She said calmly without sarcasm.

I heard a sniffle, and turned my head toward her. She carefully wiped away tears so as not to smear her eyeliner. The sniffles kept coming as she maneuvered around the store. So maybe I really was a bitch. But I was a bitch who had orders to get out the door. I needed Cindy's help.

"I'm not perfect, Cindy. Far from it. I'm sorry I didn't handle this well." I really did feel guilty for talking to her in the way I had, especially in front of someone else. "Well, we don't have time to send you home, but I have my gym bag in the car. You can wear my warm-up pants and a t-shirt." I tried to think of a compliment to help smooth things over. "You know, you really are lucky. If I had a figure like yours I'd want to show it off too."

"Thanks." Cindy replied. "I'm sure your pants will be a little long," she said with a make-lemonade-out-of-lemons voice, "but they'll fit. I feel bad though—I'm definitely going to stretch the chest out in your t-shirt. Sorry."

"No problem," muttered the B-cup.

CHAPTER TWO

We survived the morning madness and the early afternoon ran smoothly. No sign of the unprofessional detective—he sure seemed in a hurry on the phone earlier. Nick returned and left again with a full vanload. Cindy and I made several bouquets to fill our orders, and we even had time to make speculation arrangements to put in the front cooler for sale.

As we placed the last mono-botanical arrangement of fuchsia gerbera daisies in the cooler, I heard the back door slam against drywall, and then the pounding of feet.

"Quincy!" Nick was almost breathless after blasting through the store.

"What's wrong?"

"I was just in a hit-and-run." He sounded genuinely upset. But in the short time Nick had been employed by me, he had already proven to be quite a storyteller. Coupled with that, my sister Sandy's husband grew up in the same neighborhood as Nick, and Sandy knew all of the dirt about Nick and his infamous reputation. Her "helpful" warnings about Nick were reminders of my inferior abilities to run the business, thus keeping her superiority intact. This of course only made me want to believe in Nick all the more now, despite my better judgment, if only to prove my sister wrong.

"A hit-and-run?"

"Yeah!"

My shoulders dropped and I looked for the nearest seat when I realized Nick was serious. I reached to my forehead and drew my hand down my face as if it might help swipe the stress and frustration of the day out of my head. I took a deep breath and sighed. "Tell me what happened."

He pointed as he said, "I was at the intersection right there. I was turning left onto Main Street, and just as I went to get into the left turn lane, this truck hit me on my side and then passed me on the left and turned left in front of the cars coming straight and took off onto the freeway." He said it all without stopping for a breath.

"Where did it hit on the van?" I asked as I started toward the back of the shop.

"On my side in the back."

We arrived at the van. A small dent dug into the rear panel and poppy-red paint streaks overlaid the dent like brush strokes, just behind the rear wheel.

"Nick! It looks to me as if you just didn't look in the mirrors and ran into someone."

"Quincy, I swear I looked. It was a red pick-up truck. I saw them in the rear view mirror when they were behind me."

I looked at him with a puzzled expression.

"Far behind me, Quincy. There is no way I would have hit them if they hadn't sped up. I swear."

"You said them. There was more than one person?"

"Yeah, I'm pretty sure, 'cause when I looked over after the truck hit me, I saw them passing me. It was two guys. They were looking at me, shaking their fists and yelling."

"What did you do after they passed you?"

"I waited until it was my turn to go through the intersection, and then I tried to follow them, but I was too far behind. I saw them get onto the freeway."

What else today? I took a deep, cleansing breath, and exhaled as slowly as I possibly could. "Okay, Nick. Let's go call the police."

Nick busied himself with sweeping and taking the garbage out to the dumpsters while we waited for the police to arrive. His newly found work ethic led me to believe he might have told the truth about the accident.

Cindy had gone home promising to wash and return my clothes the next time she worked. I attempted to get some much neglected paperwork done while waiting for the police, but I found myself staring into space at my desk, thinking about what I would say to that jerk detective when he arrived. I thought of several different ways to tell Detective Arroyo how I would be talking to his boss about the way he had talked to me over the phone. Of course I would need to get the hit-and-run taken care of before I berated him.

When he questioned me about Derrick, I would tell everything I knew about him, which was pretty close to nothing. Just that he took over half of my business with absolutely zero design skills and the highest prices for flowers and then treated me like garbage when I saw him in person. The detective said I was the last person seen with Derrick. But I didn't think anyone knew about our recent altercation, nobody else was there. He must have bragged to someone about it afterward. Big tough man knocking down an unsuspecting woman. He had probably changed the details of the story to whomever he talked to.

"Quincy, he's here." Nick called.

The ball in my stomach returned after I stood up and saw the navy and white Crown Victoria parked directly in front of the shop. Not exactly good for business to have the cops parked just outside the front door.

I made a quick dash to the bathroom in the rear workroom to do a once over in the mirror over the sink. As I fluffed up my hair and checked my teeth for foreign bodies it occurred to me I was doing something my mother would do. I shut the light off and returned to the design room.

I gasped as soon as I saw our visitor. How could this guy possibly have been the jerk on the phone? It didn't seem karmically fair. The officer in the front of my store wore a uniform that fit just right over a body which was obviously toned and hard underneath the taut navy fabric. His physical presence alone commanded my attention, not to mention the gun in the holster at his waist, along with all of the other objects on his belt. He must've been six-four. Tall, even by my five-nine standards.

"Hi," I said as I approached and extended my hand. I didn't know if it was proper procedure to shake hands with the police in this situation. I was on autopilot; this officer's good looks were distracting.

"Hi." His return handshake was accompanied by a smile. The gesture was firm but not a bone crusher. They say you can always tell a lot about a person by the way they shake your hand. He displayed strength, along with thoughtfulness for another person, and handsomeness. I could have imagined it, but I thought his gaze lingered an extra beat as our eyes met.

This was decidedly different than I had imagined after this morning's phone call.

"I think I spoke with you earlier today on the phone?"

"Um…I don't remember talking to you." A look of confusion spread over his amazingly handsome face. "I'm Officer Cooper. Are you sure it was me you talked to? I'm here about a hit-and-run call that came into dispatch."

"Oh, sorry, I guess I spoke with a different officer this morning." Relief. "Yes—hit-and-run. That would be Nick's department." I called Nick's name toward the back of the store. He had become scarce after announcing Cooper's arrival.

"So, are you the manager here?" Cooper asked.

"You could say that. I'm the owner, actually," my

cheeks heated up at this, for some reason.

"And you were involved in a hit-and-run?"

"No, it was my driver, Nick, who seems to have disappeared."

"Okay. Well, let me get your information down and then we'll find Nick and talk to him." He unsnapped his front shirt pocket and my knees got weak. My palms were sweaty and I think I may have drooled a little. Then he pulled a tiny notebook and pencil out of the pocket.

"So your name is Rosie?"

"No, my name is Quincy. The business is named for my Aunt Rosie, the previous owner."

"Oh, that makes sense. So, Quincy," he looked down at me and smiled, "is that your full name?"

Ugh, the name.

"Quinella Adams McKay. Q...U...I...N..." I spelled it before he had to ask me to.

Nick returned, looking furtive.

"Nick," I said, "this is Officer Cooper. Tell him what you told me."

Nick began his tale and I listened in.

"So you're saying that this car hit the rear driver's side as you were getting into the left hand turn lane?" Cooper asked.

"Yes," Nick replied.

"Well," Cooper paused slightly, the pause proclaiming doubt, "let's take a look at the car."

I asked if Nick needed to be present while looking at the damage. He didn't, so I directed Nick to stay inside and stack the clean, dry buckets.

We made our way to the back parking area. Walking next to Officer Cooper made my insides feel all fluttery. I hadn't experienced that feeling in a long time. It was like I was a teenager sneaking outside the back door of the house with a boy.

I led Officer Cooper to the van. The remnants of red

paint disturbing the shiny white rear panel of my Chevy Astro mini-van, along with some ten-inch-long gouges just above the back driver's side tire were still there.

Cooper took what seemed to be too quick a glance, and then scrawled some things down in the tiny policeman notebook.

"Okay, I think that's about all I need," he said.

"That's all?" After watching and reading so many crime dramas, I wondered if there shouldn't be more of an investigation, perhaps the CSI squad should be called in.

"Is there something else...?" His eyes brightened while he paused to look at me before putting the notebook back into the little shirt pocket. Maybe the pocket wasn't so small; he just filled out the shirt so well it seemed impossible something could fit into the pocket.

"I—no. Just—I'm really hot." I noticed a smile quickly spread across his face.

"Yes," he said.

"I meant it's too hot out here..."

"Yes—hot—out here. It is hot out here," he said.

I couldn't stop being a moron. He had a hypnotic quality that kept me from making sense. My brain synapses were somehow being blocked by good looks.

"Let's go inside and maybe I'll remember what I was going to say about you." I gave my head a shake to try and rattle the confusion away. "I mean—what I was going to ask you."

"That's a good idea."

As we made our way back into the store, I realized Nick hadn't told Cooper about the drivers of the truck.

"Officer Cooper, Nick told me about two guys driving the truck; I noticed he didn't give you their descriptions."

While he looked at me intently as I asked, his expression changed to apprehension after I finished talking.

"Let me be honest with you, Mrs. McKay..."

"It's Miss and it's Quincy," I interrupted.

"Sorry, Miss Quincy."

It was his turn to blush.

"I'll tell you what. I'll write up the report of what Nick told me and what I've seen, and we'll see if anything comes up. But I have to say..." he spoke carefully while the corners of his eyes wrinkled as if it were painful to tell me, "I really don't believe Nick. The way the damage looks on the car, it seems like he just didn't check his blind spot and wants to cover it up."

Now I know I didn't really believe Nick at first when he told me about the accident, but something about having Officer Cooper assume Nick's guilt just rubbed me the wrong way. Maybe because he was agreeing with my older sister.

"Officer Cooper..."

"It's Alex, and no officer—please," he said.

His dark brown eyes warmed as he offered the personal detail. The warmth melted my insides for a very short moment until I realized again why he was there. There was a purpose for the police being here whether I called him officer or not and we needed to stay focused on the current problem.

"Okay—Alex. I realize Nick probably has a reputation that makes it difficult to listen to him objectively, but please base your report on fact and not assumptions."

The tilt of his head along with raised eyebrows indicated perhaps I had extended my boss duties a little too far.

"I'm sorry. I'm not trying to tell you how to do your job. It's just—I think Nick is telling the truth about this one no matter how it looks. I feel it in my gut. Believe me—I know Nick is no saint."

His expression softened slightly but he rolled his eyes—I think he thought it went unnoticed. "Okay, I'll take down a description of the guys in the car just in case. But I'll tell you right now, it's doubtful you'll be anything but disappointed."

"Why would I have any reason to be disappointed? If you do your job I'm sure there won't be any reason at all for me to be disappointed."

"Listen, Miss McKay, I don't tell you how to do your job, so how about you go ahead and let me do mine? This isn't my first day, you know. I was actually trying to help you out by saving you a little grief. If you stopped trying to be the boss for a minute you might be able to appreciate that fact." His hands braced tensely on his hips, above the cop tool belt.

"I'm sorry." I mumbled. What had Cindy called me earlier? I guess she was right. "Please forgive me, it's been a stressful day and I didn't mean to be rude."

"It's okay. I understand. If I ever need help interrogating a criminal, I might just give you a call. Let me give you my card. This is a direct line to reach me if you ever need anything, except if you want to boss me around." He handed the card to me and winked.

"Thanks Officer Cooper. I…"

"It's Alex," he said softly.

I felt my face heat up. "Alex, thank you. I hope I won't ever need to use it. No offense."

"None taken. See ya."

He left and I felt butterflies flutter up just about everywhere they could.

CHAPTER THREE

The end of the workday couldn't have come soon enough after the day I'd just had. Although, I did receive a nice reward in meeting Alex Don't-call-me-Officer Cooper. I didn't know what had happened to Detective Arroyo and I didn't care.

I pulled the van into the driveway next to my Victorian cottage on the corner. Due to a frugal choice made by my grandmother, it's a cottage rather than a gingerbread mansion like the Painted Lady houses in San Francisco. Grandma was a widow with nine children to take care of. The top levels of those brick Victorians got drafty in the winter, and being the sensible woman my grandma was, she had the second level removed from the house. Sure it would be more crowded down below, but the closer proximity of all the people inside would make everyone warmer and decrease the heating fuel needs even more.

Grandma left the house to me when she died. She passed away just before I left my ex-husband. I had lived with her during the summer right after high school and for the couple of semesters I went to college before getting married. Everyone in the family was surprised after the reading of the will. Her attorney told me she had arranged to change it about two weeks before she died based on a premonition. I had never told her of the things that were happening with my ex-husband.

She saved my life when she gave me that house. I had no money and nowhere to go. Home wasn't an option. My father had moved to another state to get away from my mother. He left under the auspices of a lengthy tour with his bluegrass band, "The Salt Flat Lickers." Frankly, I couldn't live with her either; she refused to remove her head from the sand regarding the topic of my abusive husband.

My usual "coming home" routine included a thorough visual security scan of the entire property. The first and most important step was to take a look around as I drove up to the house, checking to make sure nobody was lying in wait. It was a habit I learned as soon as I moved in. For about a year, chances were good either my ex or one of his many, many relatives would be waiting there or had already been there and left. Being related to polygamists held perks for the ex such as a seemingly endless pool of extra people with nothing better to do than lean over the front fence and stare at me from a few yards away or leave nasty little calling cards. Nothing specific, just a dead rat or bird on the porch or blobs of spit dripping from the back door. I liked to refer to them as the Housewarming Gifts. I kept a whistle on my key chain and a canister of pepper spray in my bag just in case someone was waiting for me with one of those gifts when I got home one night.

Of course I had no desire to cook anything when I finally left the shop. I stopped at the Bulgy Burger drive through before heading home. I cut the security inspection short when the aroma from my burger reminded me I was ready to devour some junk and drown out the resulting malaise and grease after-burn by making my own hot fudge sundae. Somehow I always seemed to have the ingredients for those on hand.

After a swift change into my nighttime uniform, consisting of a Han Solo t-shirt, cut-off pajama pants and knee-hi tube socks with the requisite tangerine colored stripes at the top, I sat down on the couch to eat my Bulgy

Junior Burger with a side of tots and fry sauce. Just as I reached for the remote, the phone rang. The caller I.D. said it was my sister Allie's cell phone.

"Hey, Allie."

"Hi, Quince."

"What's up?"

"Oh nothing. I just thought I'd call and see what's going on." I knew right away something was wrong. My sister never called me just to chat, and her usual bubbly, enthusiastic voice was strained and flat.

"Um...nothing going on here, I just got in. How about with you?"

"I was just calling to say hi," she said. Okay, something was seriously wrong.

"Allie, where are you?"

"I'm in my car."

"Where is your car?"

"I'm parked in front of Mom's house." My heart dropped. Call it intuition or experience, but I knew she must not have wanted to go into the house because our mother would have been able to see something Allie didn't want her to see. Allie didn't realize I understood all too well what kind of guy she was dating.

"Do you want to come over here?"

Her voice cracked. "Yes."

"Okay, come over. We'll watch a movie. I'm making hot fudge sundaes." I knew right then she didn't need me asking what was wrong, what he'd done, or why she didn't want to go into Mom's house. It would probably be obvious in about seven minutes when she got to my place.

She came to the back entrance. I opened the door and became sick inside at what I saw. She had a red and purple goose egg with a cut on her left temple. Her jerk boyfriend hadn't been as crafty as my ex. Mine always kept the blows to the head within the perimeter of the hairline—that way the bruises couldn't readily be seen.

I got a bag of ice and a hot fudge sundae for her. "Allie, I know how you got that, and you don't need a lecture about it or him. But I am telling you that I'm not going to let it happen again. We're not going to let it happen again. And that's all I'm going to say about it right now. Let's watch a movie."

She smiled and nodded her head. Then we ate too much ice cream and watched the movie. Allie crashed on the couch before the flick finished. I hated to move and wake her up, so I turned on the local TV news.

Suddenly, a non-specific shiver chilled my spine while the hairs on the back of my neck stood up. I looked up, muted the TV, and listened. I heard nothing and returned to the news. Just then, a shadow climbed up the wall behind the TV set. I turned to the big picture window behind us. Through a gap in the curtains, I could see the shadow growing taller with every flicker.

I shot up from the couch, knocking a spoon from the ice cream to clang and rattle on the hardwood floor. I ran to the front door, then fumbled before I unlatched the deadbolt and the lock on the doorknob. The front door opened to a fifteen foot long sitting porch running half the length of the front of the house. At the other end of the porch was a column of flames licking the bead board ceiling. My breath stopped short at the sight of the orange monster in front of me.

I always keep a small fire extinguisher in my kitchen upon the advice of a smart lady at my bridal shower. "Have a fire extinguisher in your kitchen," had been a lot more useful than "never go to bed angry." Next to remaining alive and intact, it was the best thing that ever came out of my marriage.

After retrieving the extinguisher from the kitchen, I ran back to the front door, grappling with the pin. I aimed the nozzle at the base of the fire and squeezed the handle. After the loud swooshing noise was gone and the white cloud had disappeared, the orange tower at the end of my porch had been replaced by a black, charred, stinky pile.

I stood, arms dangling at my sides, the extinguisher still hanging from my fingers. I was too stunned to do anything else. Allie appeared at my side and gently slipped the extinguisher out of my hand. She put her arm around my shoulders and we stood there and cried, our shoulders shrugging together as the let down from the adrenaline rush set in.

After a quick inspection and pause to sniff the air, Allie and I determined that someone had left a flaming bag of poop on my porch. We returned inside the house and both sat on the couch. Neither of us spoke for a long time. The house was still and quiet; Allie must have turned the TV off when she woke. With elbows on knees and head in cupped hands I tried to make sense of what had just happened, including trying to wrap my mind around a murder, a hit-and-run and now a fire on my porch, all in one day.

Allie broke the silence. "This has to be Brad."

"The guy just doesn't do anything subtle, does he? I mean, I guess he could be worked up enough to do something like this. I know he's jerk enough for sure, I'm just not sure it's his style. His MO seems to be more secretive, at least from what I've seen—or not seen before."

"How did you know he was doing things before?"

I snapped my head up and looked at her. "Allie, I know how he works. I lived through it with one just like him. And it isn't to their benefit to have visible proof of their handiwork, so that everyone in the world can see what sick, demented, psychos they are. Although, he wasn't too careful on your forehead this time."

"I really did fall down the stairs, Quincy."

I looked at her with an "oh-give-me-a-break" expression.

"That is, after he slammed me into the wall and pushed

me."

"I don't believe I have to say this yet again today, but we need to call the police."

Allie grabbed my arm and looked at me with fearful eyes.

"Quincy, we can't call the police. Brad told me if I ever called the police, he would kill me and I believe him. Even if he didn't do this, Quincy you cannot call the police. Please, Quincy! Don't call."

My sister had been terrorized by that monster, and he was probably feeling extremely pleased with himself and the power he had just wielded over the both of us. He was in control now, or so he thought.

"Allie, I know you're scared right now, but we can't just sit here and take it and pretend that nothing happened. And who knows? Maybe it wasn't him. Maybe it was a bunch of teenage boys with nothing better to do."

I looked up at the clock, it was only nine-thirty. I had an idea. I retrieved the business card Officer Cooper—I mean Alex—had given me. When he'd given it he said, "If you need anything, call me."

Well I needed something, so I called.

CHAPTER FOUR

The butterflies that had made acquaintance with my stomach earlier in the day came flying back when I heard Alex's knock. I opened the door to a perfect pair of jeans with a man poured into them. He wore an un-tucked, cornflower blue, button-down shirt that made his brown eyes look like melting chocolate. Heat flashed up my neck and I swallowed hard while I felt my heart beating in my chest.

"Hi, Alex. Thanks for coming over so soon. I realize it's late." I waved him in to the living room hoping he hadn't noticed my unintentional impression of an excited cartoon character with eyes springing three feet out of her head accompanied by the sound of an old-fashioned car horn.

"It's not late. Besides, I wouldn't want to miss my chance at seeing the aftermath of a flaming bag of dog excrement. You don't see too many of those anymore. Classic old school prank. Anyway, its way better than sitting home alone watching TV."

"You seem pretty impressed."

He shrugged. "I can't help it. I'm an adult male and therefore I'm impressed by juvenile behavior. It's the rule of the Stooges."

Allie walked in from the kitchen.

"Alex, this is my sister Allie."

"Hey Allie, nice to meet you." He shook her hand and then looked around the room. At which point she looked at me wide eyed mouthing the word "Hot!" while his head was turned. I gave her a quick glare.

"So, not that I mind it, but why call me instead of the on-duties at the station? What makes me so special?" I could feel the heat from the blush from my sternum up to my scalp. He looked at me with a crooked smile, and while I couldn't be one hundred percent sure, I think he smiled at me knowingly, having seen Allie's tactless miming.

"Well you did tell me to call if I needed anything."

"Absolutely. I meant it."

"Okay." I couldn't help grinning like a fool.

The three of us sat down and we filled Alex in on as many details as we could. We told him about our suspicions concerning Brad. I didn't know Alex well enough to know if I could trust him, but Alex was the best alternative we had short of doing nothing at all.

"This Brad guy sounds like a real prize. But I'm not completely sure he's the one who did this."

"You're not?" Allie said.

"There's been a lot of vandalism going on lately, especially in this part of town and we think it's the same group of kids that's been doing it. What I can do is check tomorrow to see if anyone else has reported anything similar in this neighborhood. Kids tend to be stupid and hit more than one house. I bet we'll find them out soon."

Allie nodded her head in agreement. Alex had a calming influence about him, but I wasn't so sure he was right.

"What if it wasn't a bunch of teenagers? What if Brad is out there right now watching us?" I asked.

Allie glanced at me with pleading eyes. Her mouth straightened into a taught single line. She turned to look at Alex. "He can't know we called you," she said, "he told me he would kill me if I ever told the police. He's probably still outside watching us."

"He won't know I'm with the police. I'm fairly new to this area, and I don't think I've been here long enough to pop up on his radar. I'm not in uniform, and I drove the Scout over. I only bring her out on special occasions. I don't ever drive her to work. He'll probably think I'm here to see you, Quincy. That is... if you're not already with someone."

My cheeks felt like I was standing next to a bonfire. "Uh, yes. I mean no. No, I'm not seeing anyone, currently." It could have been his eyes, or the cleft in his chin, or those broad shoulders, but something about him put me under a spell whenever he was near.

"Well I just wanted to make sure...for your sister's sake of course."

"Of course. Yes then, I'm single."

"Good. This will be perfect then."

"What will be perfect?"

"I'll start coming over periodically, just in case this guy is crazy enough to be watching your place." He turned to Allie. "He'll think I'm Quincy's new boyfriend. Does Mr. Psycho have a job?"

"He's a stock broker in Salt Lake, so he works all day," Allie said.

"Good, so at least he'll be occupied during the day. I'll have my buddies who are out on patrol drive by the house occasionally just to check on things. Like I said, there's been some vandalism in your neighborhood lately, so a police drive-by won't be too unusual."

"Oh my gosh Alex, are sure you want to do all of this?" Allie asked.

"Yeah," I added. "Why would you do all of this for us?"

He stood to leave. "Well I get a new girlfriend out of it, so that's a pretty good pay-off." He looked at me with a hypnotic smile and winked. My face must have looked like a beet with large green eyes.

He started toward the door, and I looked at Allie and jerked my head to the side, indicating she should go with me to see him out. She sat on the couch and pretended not to see me. I followed Alex to the door.

He stopped in the small alcove leading to the front door and said quietly, "Don't worry about the fire tonight, Quincy. I don't think your sister's boyfriend did it. But I'll help you and Allie however I can. That includes helping you fix the damage to the porch."

"You don't have to do that. I'm pretty handy. I'm a real do-it-yourself kind of girl."

"Yeah, I kinda gathered that the first time we met. But we want to keep up the charade in case the low life really is keeping tabs. I'll call you later to see when I can come help *you* to fix it. Does that sound empowering enough for you?"

I gave him a sarcastic scowl. "Alex, there is one more thing I should probably tell you before we pretend to get too involved."

"What is it?"

"I think I might be tangled up in…well there's a slim chance that I'm kind of… considered to be a suspect in a murder."

"Oh, is that all?" He swept the air with his hand as if being a murder suspect was an insignificant detail.

"Alex, I'm serious!"

"I know a little bit about the case you're talking about. I wouldn't worry about that too much. Trust me." His eyes could have hypnotized a snake charmer.

"Okay, if you say so." I realized then that I would believe nearly anything he said. He had a way of making me feel all warm and cozy and safe without knowing anything about him.

He stood in the doorway for a moment without saying anything.

"Is…there anything wrong?" I asked.

"Oh no, nothing at all.   I was just waiting for a goodnight kiss from my girlfriend." He wore a mischievous grin, and had a twinkle in his eyes.

"How about a goodnight kick in the pants?" I offered.

"I'll just take the goodnight part."

"Okay then, goodnight, Alex."

"Goodnight, Quincy." He began to leave but turned back. "Oh, one more thing."

My heart leapt to my throat. "Yes?"

"*Love* the socks."

I went to bed with the taste of mortification on my tongue.

CHAPTER FIVE

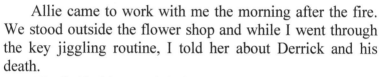

Allie came to work with me the morning after the fire. We stood outside the flower shop and while I went through the key jiggling routine, I told her about Derrick and his death.

"Well if this Derrick is dead, who's going to sell flowers to the mortuary now?" Allie asked.

"You, dear sister, are brilliant. I bet if I jump right on this, I could catch them before they make a decision."

"But didn't you say you would never do business with Hansen Mortuary again? Oh, and won't it look kind of desperate for you to go swooping in like a vulture when the body is barely cold?"

"Funny you should use that description. I'm just trying to take advantage of an opportunity. Things have changed, and I'm adapting. Besides, I'll admit that I'm easy...when it comes to flowers. Not with men, but flowers."

I finally felt the lock tumble and we made our way inside.

"Speaking of men," Allie said as we filed into the shop, "Alex is a hottie. And he's hot for you."

"Whatever."

"Are you kidding? He hardly looked anywhere but at you the whole time last night."

"You don't know what you're talking about." Why did my face feel like I was sunburned after a day in the Wasatch

Mountains? "Besides, I don't need a man in my life. If I learned anything from my marriage it was that I don't ever want to be in another one. You're so lucky things didn't get worse for you with Brad, Allie. Maybe you'll find someone else, but I'm not willing to endure what I suffered with Randall ever again."

"Don't say that. You should give Alex a chance. You two would be great together."

"What do we even know about the guy other than he looks *fantastic* in a pair of jeans? Besides, what if he turns out to be just like Randall or Brad? Everyone said how great we'd be together, and look how great it was?"

"Quincy, not all guys are like that."

"With our experience, I don't think we're the best judges of men."

"You're probably right," she said.

We spent the next twenty minutes re-orienting Allie with the store. She used to work for Aunt Rosie in the afternoons after school. Rosie always said Allie was the best designer she'd ever had. As we made our way around the shop, a couple of orders were called in for the day. We started filling those when Cindy arrived for her shift. Surprisingly, her outfit was nondescript and almost *appropriate*. Must have been an off day. She looked at Allie with a suspicious glare, posturing at the sight of a new designer. Every shop seems to have its pecking order. With any new arrival, the hens start ruffling their feathers and the clucking usually happens behind the new bird's back.

"Cindy, you've never met my sister Allie, have you?"

She relaxed slightly and her demeanor became less vicious. "No, I didn't know you had a sister."

"I have two actually. Allie used to work here. Long before I did. She managed the store for a while."

"Nice to meet you." Allie went over to Cindy and shook her hand. "I'm here to help you out. So feel free to tell me what to do. I'm pretty rusty." Allie had a way of melting the ice faster than anyone I knew. It was one of her many talents.

"Sure. We could get the standing orders out together." Cindy got the recipes out for the arrangements and began directing Allie on which containers to pull.

As the two of them worked and laughed together, I figured I could work on the sales end of the business.

"Cindy, would you be cool with me leaving for a couple of hours?"

She shrugged indifferently.

"Nick should be here soon. Oh, and I guess he'll need a van to drive." The Astro van was my only mode of transportation. When Nick first hired on, I told him the van was my baby and that he should drive it like he would drive his own car. That's what made me so angry with him when I thought at first the hit-and-run was just a Nick-and-run.

I borrowed Allie's car and left the two of them to bond over horrible boss stories. Allie is the little sister in the family, after all, so they had something to which they could relate.

I drove to Danny Barnes' shop first. I paused to look at his exquisitely designed display window before entering the store. A panel of luxurious black and white damask fabric hung in the background. In front of that, a crystal curtain rod hung from the ceiling on which were attached staggered lengths of multi-shaped, faux diamond garland. Some of the lengths almost touched the floor. In front of the garland curtain three arrangements of permanent botanicals in hot raspberry and shocking lime colors spilled into one another for the focal point. It all must have cost a thousand bucks.

A person couldn't help but be jealous of a place like his. As soon as you walked in, all five senses were tempted. Fragrance filled the air, not only from fresh florals—which I was no longer able to distinguish due to working with them all of the time, but from scented candles and room sprays. Beautiful classical music floated through the background, and vignettes in every square foot of available space contained an array of gifts of every variety, grouped by color and theme.

Danny always told me I shouldn't be jealous, that I had a lovely shop. He was right, I did have a lovely shop, but it was hard not to leave his place feeling just a little bit small-time. Of course sometimes it was a great place to get some inspiration, which was precisely the point of my visit.

"Hello Lola! What can I get for you today?" *Wait for it,* I thought.

He didn't disappoint, singing the famous song from a Broadway play.

"Hi. I'm here to ask you something."

"Anything for Lola."

"Let me preface this by saying that, given the time frame, and the nature of the question, I'm feeling a bit like another vulture swooping around the road kill right now."

"Yes…" He said with interest.

"Is it too soon do you think to find out…"

"Oh my heck!" His interruption startled me a bit. "You want to know who's doing the flowers for the mortuary!"

"Well, yeah. Is it wrong for me to wonder? Is it completely diabolical and disrespectful?"

"Of course it is, and it's also smart. You're just lucky you beat me to the punch. Otherwise I'd be knocking on the mortuary door right now. You'd better hurry up before someone else gets there first."

"So I guess you don't have any idea who would be next on the list of providers?" I asked.

"No, but I would drive directly to Greg Schilling's office right now. Don't call ahead, his secretary screens the calls."

"Okay, I'll get going."

"Oh, and Quincy," he said, "don't you dare offer to give them a cut. You see what they have in mind and talk them down from that. They're not in a position to play hardball with anyone right now. They were just caught with a dead florist in their mortuary, and they don't have anyone to replace him."

It's become standard procedure for a florist who receives a referral from the mortuary to let the mortuary keep a certain percentage of the flower sale to cover the time and expense of the consultation service the mortuary performed instead of the florist. How much had Derrick been giving them, I wondered?

I drove to the mortuary directly from Danny's shop. Rather than use the front door, I parked in the back and used the floral delivery entrance. It really bothered certain morticians to have florists inside the rest of the mortuary. In fact we were always treated pretty much as second class citizens by the Hansen morticians, especially now that they didn't rely on us to make them look better. So I was going to make sure and do things just the way they wanted, no matter how ridiculous it might be.

There were only two "civilian" vehicles parked. The first; a black Lexus I recognized as belonging to Linda Schneider, the secretary. The other was a sunflower yellow Hummer H2 that I had never seen parked there before. I made my way into the flower room, being careful not to let the door slam behind me so as not to tick-off any noise-sensitive mortician. As I walked through the room toward the rear corridor of the mortuary, noises spilled from the hall. I stopped walking and listened.

"Oh Doug…we can't do that here…you're so bad," a female voice said in a halting, breathy tone and then giggled.

"C'mon, babe no one else is here. We've got the whole place to ourselves."

"But what about the security cameras?"

I recognized the voice now that she wasn't panting. It was Linda.

The male voice replied, "I turned them off when I got here. I planned it all in my head while I drove. First I turn off the cameras, and then I come in and find out if you're wearing a certain present that I gave you."

"Why do you think I sent those two new grave-diggers to pick up that headstone down in Filmore?" Linda said. "I knew you'd have to come pick up Mr. Clark if they weren't here to do it."

"So the answer is yes?" he asked impatiently.

"Wouldn't you like to find out?" she teased.

The muffled sound of a screaming rock band came from the same direction as the two lovebirds. The sound grew louder and repeated itself. A specialized ring tone on a cell phone.

"Hello," the male voice answered abruptly. "What?" He let out a huge sigh. "Why do I have to go?" He paused to listen. "What about Gaylen?" Another pause. "Fine. I'll be there soon." The volume of his voice changed. "That was Greg, he says I've got to go out on a call."

"Well, what about Gaylen? He's supposed to be on call." Linda's voice dripped with desperate disappointment. I knew as secretary, she did all of the scheduling of employees, check writing to vendors, appointment setting for Greg Schilling and pretty much managing the place for the guy who was called the general manager. She would know who was supposed to be where and when.

"He was out doing that rural funeral and one of the hearses broke down," said the man. "I've got to cover for him until he gets back. Sorry babe. I'll call you when I'm done. Maybe I can come back before the creepy twins get done in Fillmore."

Linda sighed. "You better go now. We can't get found out. If you don't get going, they're gonna wonder where you are."

"Okay," was the boyish reply, "but can't I get a little sample before I go?"

I had probably already started to blush, but now it felt like I had walked into an X-rated movie, waiting in the lobby for my eyes to adjust to the darkness. I heard a sound like flesh being spanked and then a squeal of delight; from Linda I hoped. Then I heard some pitiful good-byes in baby talk. As I fought to keep down my breakfast, another sickening thought struck me. I stood in the middle of the path to the nearest exit.

I fled through the door to my left, which put me in the garage of the mortuary where they kept two hearses and a backhoe. Today they also kept a gurney with a thick, black plastic bag with all of its space completely occupied by *something*.

Dress shoes clacked on the linoleum floor of the flower room. The mystery man was coming toward me.

I looked for the nearest thing to hide behind. I spun to my right and tried to make it to the nose of the nearest hearse.

The footsteps were getting loud enough to be just outside the door. I was out of time. I wouldn't be able to explain why I was where I was, when I was, and it would look like I had been doing nothing but listening in. Okay maybe I *had* just been listening in, but come on, who wouldn't have been a little curious? Linda couldn't find out what I had overheard. She would be embarrassed, and I would lose my golden gossip contact within the otherwise impenetrable fortress of silence of the Hansen mortuary.

The only thing close enough to provide some cover was the gurney and black body bag. I took the turn a little too sharply and my pivot foot slipped on the concrete floor. I fell forward with arms locked straight out in front of me. Both hands landed dead center on the bag, the right hand sunk down into a soft area that didn't give much resistance, the left felt like it landed between two rigid poles.

I froze in place. Then I looked to my right to face my discoverer and I noticed the black bag hadn't quite been zipped up all the way. I could just make out a mouth and a nose. *Mr. Clark I presume.*

This was bad. Looking down at the placement of my hands, I surmised that not only would I be caught—a possible murder suspect lurking in the dark—after listening in on someone's afternoon tryst, but I would be caught groping the private parts of a formerly eighty year old man, after listening in on said afternoon tryst.

I heard screaming rock music at the entrance to the garage.

"H'llo. Yeah I'm still here. Wuhl it's a good thing I didn't leave yet. Is it in the office? Okay I'll bring it."

The sound of shoes scuffing the linoleum diminished, and I knew he was headed back into the hallway and toward the opposite end of the building. I whispered to Mr. Clark, "I don't think this is going to work out. It's not you—it's me."

I tiptoe-ran into the flower room and out the back door. The H2 was still there, obviously belonging to lover boy. If he was headed toward the office, I had just enough time to jump in Allie's car and drive up to the front of the building as if I were just arriving. Hopefully, if I timed it right, Lover Boy would be headed back to his Hummer as I arrived at the office to speak with Linda.

My plan worked. As I entered the foyer of the mortuary main hall, the Hummer sped through the parking lot toward the road. I could see Linda making adjustments to her clothes as I approached.

"Hi, Linda!"

"Oh," she let out a half shriek. "Quincy, you startled me."

"I'm so sorry, I didn't mean to sneak up on you."

"No, no, you didn't. I guess I was just distracted. What can I do for you sweetie?"

"Well actually," I lowered my voice, "I'm just going to get right to the point because I know I can trust you. I was wondering, with everything that's happened with poor Derrick, what is the mortuary going to do about flowers?"

Linda stopped the vigorous hair fluffing and smoothing.

"Quincy, I am so glad you're here. I need to talk to someone. I know you'll keep this top secret anyway, but you can not tell anyone what I'm gonna tell ya." Her mouth made a straight line, while her eyes seemed to bore holes into mine with her seriousness ray beams.

"Of course. You know me, Linda."

"I do. It's just that, things are crazy right now. I mean not just with Derrick and everything, but it's been that way for at least six months and every day has gotten worse. There's something going on around here, and I don't know what it is. And that's what scares me. I'm usually the only one who knows everything that's happening in this place, but Greg Schilling's been keeping something from me and it just feels weird."

"What do you mean *weird*?"

She turned her head left and right, as if looking for any lurkers. "Let's go sit down in my office," she whispered.

I followed her lead and we nearly snuck across the lobby to her office, which was in plain view of anyone who might enter the mortuary.

Linda paused at the entrance and looked from side to side again. Then she closed the office door, which she had never done before.

"Well first of all, you'd think they'd feel really bad for Derrick. I mean they dealt with him every day with his flowers and all. But it almost seems like they're kind of relieved more than anything."

"Huh," I thought out loud.

I wondered why they would be relieved. He had to have been giving some great incentives like a percentage of sales. Maybe he had even been giving gifts to the morticians. Who wouldn't want the flow of free perks to keep coming?

"You said it's been about six months. What started to be different six months ago?"

"It was gradual at first, but Greg told me we should try to use Derrick's shop for referrals. As you know, Quincy, I told him that you are the one I like to recommend because you've always done such a nice job for me and my family."

"Thanks," I said. I did know this and appreciated it.

"So for a while, when someone would call from out of state, or if I was here when a family would call and ask for a florist's name, I would tell them yours. But Greg started getting kind of grumpy about it. Then about three months ago, he says that I was not to recommend anyone else but Derrick's shop or I would lose my job. It made me so mad. That flower guy was an idiot and his arrangements were either dead or falling apart half the time. I didn't want to give my personal guarantee on his crappy job. So I says to Greg, I should type up a memo telling everyone that it's company policy, and that way when someone complains, I can quote the company policy and tell them my hands are tied."

"Well I know you still call me so he must have changed his mind on the firing part," I said.

"Oh no. I could still get fired. If they found out what we were talking about right now I would be in so much trouble. But I still tell people to call you when nobody else is around. Piss on him. I run this place and he has the nerve to tell me I can't write a memo?" Anger smoldered in her eyes.

"Why couldn't you write a memo? That seems weird. A memo would be a good idea."

"I don't know why. But he went nuts about it. He said he didn't ever want me to write any of it down. That it was important I didn't."

"Well since we're on the subject of Derrick, how much of a discount was he giving?"

She leaned forward nearly jumping out of her seat.

"That's the thing, Quincy! He wasn't giving them anything! I know, because I'm the one that writes the checks to you guys."

"What? No discount? For all those referrals?"

Generally when a family goes to the mortuary, the mortician recommends a specific florist for whatever reason. They will say to the family, "I recommend Quincy. Go there and pick out the flowers and have her send us the bill." So, I would then meet with the family, make the flowers and deliver them, then send a bill to the mortuary, minus the 'discount' that they get to keep for having advertised my business for me.

"He's got to be giving them something, Linda. They don't just recommend him out of the kindness of their hearts. Greg Schilling hasn't paid for a flower arrangement for his wife's birthday or anniversary since I've been in the business. All those things were always given to him as incentives. There's no way he's *not* getting something."

"I know! That's exactly it, Quincy. But it's not a discount. There's got to be something else."

"So you don't know who's going to be recommended from now on I suppose? Not... that I don't feel very sorry for the horrible death of my colleague."

"Oh I know what you mean, but no, I don't know who they're going to go with. Maybe you could try asking at his shop. I think the gal that was working for him is there trying to make sense of the orders they still have."

"Maybe I will. Thanks for the info. And don't worry; I won't say a word of this to anyone. I appreciate you helping me out." I stood and made my way to the office door. "Oh, Linda. Just curious, but is there a new mortician on staff?"

"No, not that I know of. Why?"

"I passed a Hummer on my way into the parking lot and I just wondered who it was. I didn't recognize the car and it seemed to be coming out of the employee parking lot." I may have fudged the actual timeline of who was where and when, but that was neither here nor there. "So I just thought that it must be a mortician because of the expensive car."

Linda turned red from the top of her forehead to the very lowest point of her plunging, very ample décolletage, which happened to be framed by a button-down shirt where the top button had been fastened into the second from the top buttonhole and likewise the entire way down.

"Um—oh, that was Doug. He's from another office," she stammered. Her hand went straight to her neck and pulled the collar of her shirt closed. He's just...one of our on-call people."

"Oh," I said, nodding my head nonchalantly.

"He's one of the guys on call in case they need to go pick up a body. He has to be ready night or day," she offered without my coaxing.

Yeah I'm sure he's ready night or day. He's on call all right. For a booty call, I thought to myself, trying not to giggle.

"That's probably a nice job for a young person," I said. "Like a college student or someone just married." Now I was just being mean.

"Oh, he's not married," she said far too quickly. "He's just out of college."

Wow Linda. She was middle-aged with at least two kids that age.

"I'd best be going. Thanks again, Linda. Oh, by the way, I noticed your shirt is buttoned wrong. I would want someone to say so if it were me, so I thought I would tell you. Bye." She turned almost purple; I turned on my heels and made it to the exit as quickly as possible, just making it into the car before the laughter bested me and exploded into the air.

CHAPTER SIX

A trip to Derrick's shop was next on my list. The half hour drive gave me time to reflect on things I had just learned at the mortuary. It didn't make sense for someone to undertake this drive every day unless they were really making a profit on the flowers. From what Linda said, I knew he hadn't been giving any piece of the profits to the mortuary, which was absolutely baffling, but might explain his willingness to make the drive.

I remembered visiting the mortuaries when I first took over the shop. Greg Schilling looked at me with his reptilian, half-opened-eyelid gaze. "Well we have to go to quite a bit of trouble in advertising your product for you." That's how the conversation started; eventually he got to the matter of the expected discount. Not to mention the holidays, anniversaries, and birthdays when, about three days before hand, I'd get a call from him not specifically asking, but with the intent of me offering to give free flowers. Like clockwork, every time.

I felt kind of wrong going to Derrick's shop after they had just found his corpse in a coffin—before he was supposed to be dead, and in a coffin. But the window of opportunity had just been opened a crack, and I wanted to slip through before it was slammed shut by another of my competitors

Upon first visiting downtown Ogden one is confronted

by a spectrum of businesses and houses as colorful as the city's past. The location of Derrick's shop was no doubt one of the many speak-easies dotting the whole of downtown during prohibition. It was probably a drop-off site for the transport of bootleg spirits through the network of tunnels rumored to have connected a seedy, thriving underground scene. Now it was just a shabby hole in the wall next to a vacant furniture store and a dilapidated biker bar. Not exactly the cozy atmosphere one would think necessary for a nice flower shop.

I parked at the meter in front of the shop, although I could have parked around the corner for free, but I didn't dare risk getting mugged or worse. As I entered Derrick's shop, I could see the sales counter about ten feet back from the front of the store, with a three-door reach-in cooler off to my right. The place was dark and gloomy, with nothing but yellow florescent bulbs casting a sickly pallor over the space.

Posters of flower bouquets hung as loners on the walls, providing most of the color in the room. Two or three planter baskets with tropical houseplants sat on laminate-covered cubes, dotting the showroom floor.

I walked up to an abandoned counter. The unlocked front door served as the only proof that someone might be there. I walked noisily, with a heavy step to the back room, hoping not to frighten someone who may have been working and didn't notice the doorbell.

"Hello?" I called out. I peered into the back workroom and found a woman sitting with her feet propped on the design table, reading a paperback. With the immediacy of drying paint, she glanced up without moving anything but her eyes. Her face had obviously been through some hard living, and the look on it signaled her annoyance at having to stop reading her book. She said nothing but continued to glare at me, her eyes saying, "What the hell do you want?"

"Hi, my name is Quincy McKay. I'm from Rosie's

Posies in Hillside."

Her probably late forty-ish body, which looked more late sixty-ish, started to heave and rock, presumably in order to get her legs moving off of the table. I couldn't imagine how she got them up there in the first place. She sighed heavily as she snapped her paperback shut and used her now free hand to grab the table after some major coaxing of her stomach muscles to lean forward. It wasn't exactly that her body was that much overweight, at least not to the point of being morbidly obese, it just seemed to be quite underused. She exhaled loudly and I couldn't tell if it was more a communication to me of her annoyance or a forcing of air out of her lungs as she rocked forward once and again in order to build up the inertia to sit up.

"I'm sorry, I don't mean to bother you," I stammered.

"Djuh need a funeral arrangement or somethin'?" She asked, out of breath.

"I um… No, I'm from another flower shop in Hillside and I thought I would come to offer my condolences."

"Oh. Yeah, okay." She looked as if she were going to try and sit back down and kick up her legs, and while I would've loved to see how she could possibly accomplish that gravity-defying feat, I couldn't ignore my mission.

"So, do you work here all the time?"

"Eight days a week," she deadpanned with her ten-Camels-a-day voice.

"I bet it's been hard for you with all that's been going on around here."

"Phew, you're telling me. People have been calling almost non-stop. Yesterday I had to take the phone off the hook."

She squinted and cocked her head to the side as if trying to retrieve a thought. A long pause ensued.

"Oh my good hell!" She shouted, followed by a phlegmy, wheezy, cackle. "I guess I forgot to turn that damned thing back on!" She ambled over to the phone, where the handset sat on the counter next to the base. She hesitated, opting not to replace it, and instead walked back to the high-legged chair and gahlumped down again. "Yeah, it's been quite a zoo around here. Except that I haven't had a single order since then. Been able to catch up on some stories." She picked up the paperback. "You ever read these romance novels? I quite like 'em."

"Well actually, the reason I'm here, if I can be honest with you," I changed my tone as if offering something in confidence, "I was wondering, do you know who the mortuary is going to call for flowers now that, well you know, Derrick and all?"

"Oh hell honey, I have no idea. Absolutely none. To tell you the truth, I don't even know why I showed up today. I just wanted to see if my paycheck would get here. I've been waitin' for it for four days now. It's late for the second month in a row. I've quit countin' on Derrick to show up with it."

Especially now, I thought to myself. "Oh, did Derrick use a payroll service?" Unless he had, I didn't see how she would be getting her check after her boss had been found in a box. Maybe she expected his ghost to bring it by.

"He used one until about three months ago. Then they started calling everyday asking if he was here, which he never was of course. They finally said if he didn't pay his bill, they weren't going to send us any paychecks."

"It seems like you guys were pretty busy all the time from all the arrangements I've seen at the mortuaries. Are there other employees that aren't getting their checks?"

"It's just me and sometimes my daughter. Like I said, he was hardly ever around, so I did all the designs and once in a while my daughter would help."

"Wow, that seems like a lot of work for just one or two people. Didn't you guys have like a whole funeral a day?"

"Oh, honey! We had three and four funerals every day. Mostly just blankets, but every day I was doing three or four 'em." She incorrectly called the casket sprays blankets, but who was I to correct this over-flowing font of information? "He charged a pretty penny for those things too. My sister's husband died and he let me have the employee discount, but there's no way we would have paid full price. I mean go look at them picture books; they have the prices in 'em. They start at six hundred dollars. For a half-casket size!"

Six hundred dollars was extremely expensive for the minimum priced half-coach casket spray in our area. Mine started at two hundred dollars on the low end.

"Them flowers cost that much and he's late with my paychecks? Too many damn toys if you ask me. Have you seen that car he zipped around in? A Porsche for hell's sakes. Fire engine red. He's got a truck and a big yellow Hummer too. You tell me where he got the money for all that."

A yellow hummer? Like the one Linda's boyfriend drove away in? Was he involved with the Vulture? I put it on my mental checklist to find out more about lover boy.

"It doesn't make sense to me," I said. "So how are you going to get a paycheck if the guy that gives it to you is dead?"

"Well I was gonna see if it was laying on his desk in there or wait for the mailman to come. He didn't write them out himself, someone named L.D. Stanwyck always signed them."

"Who's L.D. Stanwyck?"

"Hell if I know, but they didn't bounce.

"So you don't know what's going to happen now that Derrick's gone?"

"No but I got the idea he was getting ready to split. I was thinkin' of quittin' soon. I did overhear him talking to an old man that's been coming around here a lot lately. I think they were maybe talkin' about him buying the business."

My ears perked up at that; exactly the news I did not

want to hear.

"You say he's an older guy?"

"Yeah, about seventy or so."

"Is he a florist?"

"Well I think he owns a shop with his wife over in Plainville."

"Oh, you mean Irwin and LaDonna."

"Yeah, that's him, Irwin. He's a nice old man, but I don't know what he'd be doing talking to Derrick. I wouldn't trust him as far as I could throw him. Now I've always gotten a paycheck—eventually, but I wouldn't ever trust Derrick in a business deal, not for a million bucks. Hey, didn't you say you're from a shop?"

"Yes, I own a shop in Hillside."

"You know I should give you my number in case you're ever hiring." She reached for a piece of paper on the table and tore off the corner then pulled a pen from behind her ear and began writing. "I've got design experience."

"Thanks," I replied as I took the paper from her hand. Unfortunately for her I had witnessed first hand her customer service skills and her design capabilities.

"Speaking of phone numbers, you wouldn't happen to have Irwin's number around handy would you?" I asked.

"Hell it's probably on his desk in there somewhere. I'm gonna go out for a smoke. You can go in his office and look for it. If you see my paycheck sittin' around come and get me, will ya?" She cackled herself into a coughing fit.

"Sure thing. Oh, before you go outside, I was wondering if you might have an extra can of leaf shine that I could buy from you." We had run out and were getting a new shipment of plants that needed to go to the hospital gift shop. They looked like they were coated in a gray film when they arrived at our shop because of the water spots from the sprinklers at the nursery. The leaf shine adds what we call perceived value to the plants. People think they're a lot more valuable when they're shiny and unnatural looking.

If they have natural healthy leaves that have just been sprayed with needed water, people think they look like they are unhealthy and dying. The American culture's screwed up perceptions of health and beauty are not limited just to people.

"We've got a whole case of 'em in the plant room. You don't have to pay for it. Hell, who am I going to tattle to?" The cackle continued with phlegm-induced interruptions caused by a lifetime of smokes. "Just find what you need. I'll be outside."

I smiled and watched as she turned to go outside, her waist long, brown-streaked-with-gray braid swaying as she rolled from right foot to left. I had a pretty good idea this would be a long smoke break, so I figured I could look at a few things in the office. I had permission to be there, so what if I just happened to accidentally run into some sales figures or something like that?

Derrick's office desk was cluttered with papers, yellow envelopes and everything else one might find at a work desk. Nothing jumped out at me and said, "Look this is why I was murdered." I didn't see anything that looked like a paycheck, but I did see a three-fold glossy pamphlet with the title "Switch Grass, Bio-fuel of the Future." I had heard of switch grass before, it was on the list of availability from one of my suppliers. I hadn't known of its use as a bio-fuel, so I picked up the pamphlet out of curiosity. A picture of a grassy looking plant with a man standing next to it covered the front fold. The grass stood at least a foot taller than the man. I folded the pamphlet in half and put it in my back pocket for later. I didn't think anyone would miss it. Nothing else on the desk stood out.

It occurred to me that the police had probably already been through things here, since the owner of the desk had been found mysteriously dead.

I walked over to a little room wedged between the design area and the bathroom. It was full of floor to ceiling shelves made of two by fours and plywood. Four and six inch potted houseplants dotted two of the shelves. Most of them were wilted for lack of water. One wall of shelves was completely full with wicker and split willow baskets in all different shapes and styles. A sink, probably never cleaned since the day it was installed, leaned on one wall and next to it, a small counter top where plants were arranged in the baskets. A plastic garbage can full of potting soil rested under the counter. The box next to it looked to be full of sphagnum moss.

I looked all over the crowded little room, not finding the metal cans of leaf shine anywhere. Then I remembered she had said a case of it, meaning there was probably a cardboard box full of them somewhere. I noticed a cardboard box underneath the p-trap of the sink and reached down to open it. Because of the dim lighting in the tiny room, I couldn't see the water damage to the box where it touched the sink pipe. I reached into a squishy, slimy, wet blob that smeared all over my fingers. Repulsed, my immediate reaction was to jerk my hand out. While gagging, I noticed my fingers were covered in dark green— almost black goo which was probably a product of decomposing plant and cardboard. I decided to be a little more cautious and reached again for the cardboard box. I pulled and slid it out from under the sink. As I did, something fell down and slapped the floor.

I blindly reached under the sink, toward the direction of the sound until my fingers made contact with something on the floor. I pulled out a black three-ring binder full of paper and tabbed dividers. I wondered why anyone would keep a binder full of paper under the sink with the drips and moisture all over the place.

Inside the binder I found a ledger labeled for February's sales figures. Everything was hand-written. Each day of the month had its own column, and under each column was written a number. It was not uncommon to see $3,000 to

$8,000 hand-written under each day.

I turned the page and found a similar chart with the same titles and numbers, only, it was all typed; nothing was handwritten.

I was looking at the official version of the February sales figures. To make sure it had the same date as the handwritten page, I compared the amounts in each column to the previous page. On the typed page, there were several days with no sales at all. In fact, on the days when sales should have said $4,000, it would say $500 or $250. Not a single column matched up between the two pages.

Derrick had been keeping two sets of books. I wondered if the L.D. Stanwyck who had signed the paychecks for Derrick's loquacious designer got to see the typed or the handwritten version of the business records.

What kind of idiot keeps two different sets of financial books in the same binder? I wondered. *The same idiot who found himself resting in a coffin in the mortuary.* Maybe Derrick's not-so-fancy bookkeeping had ended up getting him killed somehow.

I turned to a page with the title "Extra Receivables***" written across the top. Three columns were titled April, May and June. Under each month was written $10,000. *What kind of ten thousand dollar jobs is he getting?*

Another question popped into my mind. It hadn't been too difficult to find this little black book. You'd think with a murder investigation, the police would have searched the place. Maybe that's why the desk had been so messy. Perhaps the cops had already been there and found something they were looking for.

The front door bell sounded, startling me. I looked out of the little room to see if the designer had come back in yet. She wasn't there. I moved over to the office, so I could look through the one-way glass that made it so you could watch the front of the store without leaving the office or being seen. A tall man with a mustache walked in. He wore dress slacks and a shirt and tie, and a badge with black leather backing hung from his belt. I decided it probably would not bode well for me to be found by the police in a dead man's office. Especially a dead man I had been arguing with at the scene of his forthcoming murder, of which I might be a suspect.

I tucked the ledger into the back waistband of my pants and said an internal thank you for the one-way glass. Then I made my way as quietly as I could to the back door which had been left open by Derrick's employee. I hadn't ever asked her name, and now was not the time for pleasantries. I started to jog once I hit the pavement outside and when I reached the woman smoking around the back corner I gave her a heads up.

"Thanks for your help, I have one more question. Haven't the police been here?"

She snorted and shook her head. "Hell, some asshole detective called and said he would be here, but he never showed."

So I wasn't the only one to experience the pleasure of talking with the asshole detective. I didn't want to have to repeat the experience if that's who had just walked in.

"Thanks again, I've got to get going now, but I thought I'd tell you there is a customer in the store. Oh, and maybe you'll forget that I was ever here." I pulled a twenty out of my pocket and put it in her hand. She could buy at least a couple more packs of Camels with it.

"Give me a call," she croaked then looked down at her palm. "Now how did this get here?" She looked at me and winked before she snuffed her cigarette out with her foot.

I peeked around the front corner of Derrick's shop, and after making sure the guy from the police was otherwise engaged, I got into the car and got the heck out of there.

CHAPTER SEVEN

The blacktop in the parking lot of Rosie's Posies tugged at my shoes with every step. The chatter of traffic came out muffled under the oppressive rays of the afternoon sun and my face felt like it was close to sliding off. I noticed my van wasn't in the back parking space. I walked in to find Allie alone in the shop, tying extra bows to put in planters or vases in the future. Like me, she had been taught by Aunt Rosie that idle hands are the tools of the devil, and that slow times in the shop were the times to be productive, not to take a break.

"Hey, where's Cindy?" I said.

"She left about an hour ago."

"Wow. Good thing you remember how to do everything."

"Well, enough to get by," she laughed. "I would've called you if I ran into any trouble."

"I'm so glad you're here. Cindy does pretty well, but the minute she doesn't have an arrangement to make, her behind finds the nearest seat. After a while I get sick of telling her to stand up."

"It's just habit for me to stand and work. I guess that's what Aunt Rosie taught. Before Brad made me quit my job at the jewelry store, I would always hear my coworkers complain about having to be on their feet so much, but I never minded it."

"A designer on her feet is worth two on her seat," I repeated from memory.

"Where did you come up with that? I don't remember Aunt Rosie ever saying it."

"Actually, it was LaDonna Shaw. She owns a shop in Plainville; I've run into her a few times at the wholesaler's and at design shows. Her ears must be burning. It's the second time today her name has come up. Anyway, where's Nick?"

"Let's see. Cindy called to ask if he would bring her a drink on the way back, and he said it would be a while because he was in Roy, so she left."

"Roy! What's he doing in Roy? The delivery slip on the board says the hospital in Ogden. He's thirty miles west of where he should be." My anger boiled up so easily lately. Was it completely due to Nick? Or were there contributing factors such as Cindy, the mortuary, Derrick or maybe the poo arsonist? Unfortunately for Nick, he was the Chairman of the Board in the Piss Quincy Off conglomerate. I'd had it with him.

I stomped over to the phone and punched in the number to his cell phone. It felt as if my hand might crush the handset.

"HELLO," he shouted over the blaring music in the background.

"Nick! This is your boss! Where are you?"

I heard a curse then the background music stopped.

"Well?"

"What?" He replied as if my angry tone was uncalled for.

"Where are you right now in my van?"

"I'm about ten minutes away."

"You make sure and get here without a new scratch on my car. Do you understand me?" I think my eyes were glowing red.

I wanted to slam the receiver down but couldn't afford

a new phone, so I just mimed the behavior several times before I could hang it up softly.

"Um, Quincy?" Allie said, "I'm sorry to add to your stress but there's something I think I should to tell you before I forget. Cindy asked me an interesting question today."

"Oh yeah, what was that?"

"I don't know how to go about this so I'll just blurt it out. Cindy asked me if you're gay."

"Wh...hat?"

"Yeah. Just a little bit of a surprise. I didn't know what to tell her."

"Why not? It's a simple answer, yes or no. What *did* you tell her?"

"I said no. I asked her where she got that idea. She said that her older brother went to school with Randall, and they still keep in touch. He said you were a lesbian, and that you had lied to him about it the whole time you were married."

"Wow." I wish I could have said he'd sunk to a new low, but this was pretty run of the mill for my ex-husband. "Of course, the only explanation for a woman leaving Randall would be because she's gay. I'm sure it's never occurred to him that his suggestion means that being with *him* made *me* prefer women."

Allie giggled but covered her mouth as if she shouldn't have allowed herself to laugh.

"'Hey everyone,'" I mocked my ex-husbands voice, "'I drove my ex-wife to lesbianism, but I'm too stupid to realize I'm makin' fun of myself.' Randall is a moron. I don't have time to waste on worrying what he says about me. Anyone who hears him should consider the validity of the source."

"Quincy, this isn't funny. Randall knows a lot of people. If he's telling this stuff to old high school buddies, I can't imagine all the rest of the people he's blabbing to.

Maybe you should make it a little more obvious that you're not—you know."

"How did you want me to go about making it more obvious? 'Hi, I'm Quincy; I'm not gay, nice to meet you.' Is that it? Maybe I could get the title heterosexual printed on my business cards. Allie, I've got nothing to prove. The people who are important to me know who I am."

"I know, I know, you don't have anything to prove. But since you do happen to not be gay, it wouldn't hurt for people to know that."

This argument was going down a familiar path. I hadn't decided if it was the influence of church or mother or both, but appearances and the impressions of others meant a lot more than they should to people in my town, especially people like my family.

"Well anyway," Allie said, "it doesn't matter, but since you're straight, single and pretty, it wouldn't be a bad idea for you to open your eyes and notice the very handsome, also not gay police officer who seems to be so interested in you." She batted her eyes.

"Thanks for the compliments but I've got plenty of other things to worry about right now, including needing to find a new delivery driver."

"Don't change the subject! All you do is work and then when you go home you think about work some more. It would be good for you to get out a little. I'm not saying you have to get married again. I'm just saying you could stand to socialize a little more. And since you just happen to have one of the most gorgeous guys on the planet interested in you, I'm thinking you should probably snatch him up before you drive him off."

I knew Allie just wanted me to be happy, but I couldn't afford to invest in a relationship. Not now. Maybe not ever.

"Allie, I don't have time for a boyfriend. Besides, getting back to reality, what am I going to do about Nick?"

"First of all, lame excuse. You have time; you just

don't want to think you have time." She peered at me, hands stuck on her hips. "Secondly, you don't have to have a boyfriend. Go hang out a few times. And about Nick, before you attack when he walks in the door, get his story first. It doesn't look to me like you've got a spare driver hanging around anywhere."

Good point. The back door opened and Nick walked in.

"Quincy, I swear I didn't do anything wrong," were the first words that came out of his mouth.

"Where was your delivery to?"

"Ogden, but..."

"And where were you when Cindy called?"

"Roy, but..."

"But what? Don't you find it to be an amazing coincidence that your girlfriend works in Roy, at least thirty miles from where you were supposed to be?"

"I didn't go see my girlfriend. I—didn't want you to find out." He bent his head and looked at the floor. "I don't drive on the freeway, I almost got in a wreck once, and it freaked me out, so I took the old road."

I stood, silent for a beat, not knowing what to say to this pathetic attempt at deception.

"Oh,   give   me   a   break! You...are...a...delivery...driver," I paused to contain myself, "and you don't drive on the *freeway?*"

"I know, I know, it sounds lame, but I'm telling the truth, Quincy."

I stared at him for a good twenty seconds. Allie stood off to the side and her words about not having an extra driver sat in the back of my head.

"Nick, I want you to leave right now. Don't say another word. I'll see you tomorrow. Don't be late, don't screw up, and by hell take the freeway if you get a delivery to Ogden. Don't speak. Just shake your head. Do you understand?"

"Ye..." I glared at him with the look of death. He

shook his head in the affirmative.

Turning off the open sign felt better than it should at the end of the day. My plan at the start of it had been to seek more business.   As the workday came to its close, I questioned whether I had the will to stay with a business where I had to put up with constant problems and very little pay to show for doing so.

I drove straight to the drive through on the way home. There's not much a good Coke can't fix.

As I turned the corner, I noticed a familiar old SUV parked in front of my house. Alex Cooper stood on my front porch. Instinctively I leaned over to the rear view mirror to take a look. Yep, I confirmed the ragged state of my hair and the dark circles under my eyes. There was no amount of first aid that could change this mess in time to exit the van and reach the porch without raising suspicion.

"Hi." I asked, more than stated. "Were we supposed to meet today?" It was unlikely, but with the stress of the last two days, I could have forgotten anything.

"No, no meeting. I told you I would drive by and check on things." He wore a friendly smile on his face and a tight gray t-shirt on his muscular body, with a sweat-darkened area trailing down his chest.

"Geez, I'm sorry. What I meant to say was thank you for checking up on things. Wow, not just a drive by, but also a house call. To what do I owe the honor? I hope you haven't been chasing my sister's ex-boyfriend away," I said as I glanced again at the "V" pattern of sweat that accentuated the perfect pecs filling out his t-shirt.

"No, nothing like that. Last night after I left I was thinking the smoke from your burning porch pile probably damaged the ceiling. Since I had today off, I thought I would come and take a look."

"Alex, thank you, but you didn't have to do that."

"It was my pleasure. I brought some stuff to clean the smoke damage, and I hope you don't mind, but I found the spigot in the back yard and filled up these buckets. It doesn't look like you'll need to repair or replace any of the wood."

"I'm speechless. I...."

He reached down to pick up the buckets and I caught myself gawking at the well-defined muscles in his back and arms, which were hardly concealed under his t-shirt.

"It was no big deal," he said.

"Well, I owe you," I said, then thought of all kinds of ways I could repay him.

"I've already thought of a way you can pay me back."

"Oh." I squeaked in surprise. I covered my mouth with my hand in reflex—startled by the thought that he had read my mind, which was much like reading a dirty book at that moment. Page fifteen was especially embarrassing. "Um..."

C'mon, steady, focus! I took my time and swallowed. I tried to appear nonchalant as I slid my hand to the back of my neck and scratched an imaginary itch. "Really?" I said feebly.

Alex smiled. His eyes twinkled in what I could only surmise to be amusement—or sympathy. "How would you like to go get something to eat?"

"I—um, okay. Yeah, I could eat something."

"I meant with me," he said.

"Well then yes, for sure."

"Cool, let me just change my shirt." My heart fluttered up in my chest as I caught him swallowing another grin. He grabbed the tools he had been using and took them to his truck.

"Do I have time to go in and check my messages?" I said.

"Sure."

I went inside and did a quick clothes change into a less

crafty-gardener looking shirt, and my eternally-hopeful-of-slimming jeans. I did a quick hair-fluff and teeth check in the mirror. Yeah, okay it is something my mother would do, but I really didn't need to find out after the whole night that I had a piece of black pepper decorating one of my front incisors.

I went into the kitchen to check the voicemail on my home phone and Alex came in. He had a new shirt in hand.

"Do you mind if I change here?"

What a silly question.

"No, go ahead. The bathroom is right around the cor—" Before I could finish he peeled his shirt off and exposed a ripped six-pack and sculpted pecs.

"I'll be right back." He was obviously putting on a show, and I didn't mind having a front row seat.

After some near-hyperventilating I listened to my voicemail. The final message began in the middle of a conversation between two male voices. The voices stopped abruptly and then I just heard a faint breathing sound. It lasted for about ten seconds. It could've been a wrong number, yet I had a squiggly feeling in my "gills," as Aunt Rosie liked to say. I couldn't tell why, but there was just something creepy about the mouth breather on the phone.

"Should we go?" Alex's voice sounded from behind me.

I let out a little shriek and jumped.

"Not the reaction I was hoping for. Is anything wrong?"

He stood there in a black t-shirt with a slight v-neck. The fit was snug but not too tight. I hadn't noticed before that he wore a darker pair of jeans which seemed to wear better on him than the first pair I saw him in, which I would have deemed impossible, were he not standing there in front of me in all his cute-ass glory.

"Nothing, absolutely nothing." I said dreamily. I glanced up and saw Alex looking amused or pleased or a little of both. It didn't matter which; I thought I would incinerate from embarrassment. I had to say something. "Where should we go?"

He grinned for another beat while looking at me with those addictive brown eyes. The pause was killing me but it was a pleasant pain.

"Are you in the mood for fancy shmancy, healthy, or good?"

"I'm definitely in the mood for good" I said.

"I know the perfect place. It's just downtown. My buddies at work all told me about it when I first moved here. It's called Skinny's."

"Skinny's is great. I've been going to Skinny's since he really was skinny. It'll be perfect." Actually, Skinny never had been skinny, but that little tidbit would've ruined my punch line.

We pulled up to Skinny's and found a little wedge in the corner of the oddly shaped parking lot. Alex had to drive his car up and over a small pile of dirt on the end to fit. I think it's a requirement when you drive an old box on wheels to find parking lots that are blocked with piles of debris you can conquer.

"Pretty impressive car. What's it called? I yelled over the engine before he turned it off.

"It, as you so callously call her, is an old International, a Scout. She's been with me through everything, she's a classic."

"Yeah, but is she as indestructible as the Astro Van?"

"Ha, not even a close comparison," he teased.

"We'll just see about that. The Astro is nicknamed 'Zombie Sue.'"

"Why?"

"Because she should be dead by now, yet she still runs strong. She's undead. You can knock her around but she keeps on going."

"Undead huh? Maybe we should get inside. Sounds

like you're getting delusional from hunger."

All the booths around the perimeter of the room were occupied, as were three of the eight counter stools which held up precariously under the weight of their occupants, all of whom were wearing some variation of denim either in the form of coveralls or jackets. The men hovered over their food, arms encircling their plates like dogs protecting their bowls, their forks positioned in hand with thumbs pointed down as one would hold a shovel to one's mouth.

Skinny's was one of the best-kept local secrets—a great place with inexpensive prices. Housed in an unassuming plain tan brick building, it's what the misinformed might call a dive. Neither the three hundred fifty pound Skinny nor his daughter, Elma were too concerned with updating the style of decor. The sentiment appeared to be the same when it came to scrubbing the walls. The cowboy print wallpaper and the mini jukeboxes at every table represented bygone days that Skinny didn't want to forget.

It certainly wasn't Elma's sweet disposition that kept people coming back. More likely than anything it was the giant fry-bread the size of a dinner platter and as thick as a steak, with homemade honey-butter slopped on top. The prices were from the same era as the wallpaper. People could go to Skinny's and get fed to full for about eight dollars including the sales tax and the tip for frowny Elma.

We found a seat in the alcove to the side of the main room. No one seats you at Skinny's. You just look around for an open table. If there isn't one, you stand there and look forlorn until someone stands up to leave. It doesn't work to give people dirty looks if they sit there and gab after their meal is finished. They'll just drink some water and ask for a refill of their glass for spite.

Luckily, a group had just vacated their table. No need to wait for a busser to clean it, there wasn't one. Just Elma when she got around to it. While we waited for Elma to arrive, I grabbed some paper napkins out of the table dispenser and wiped up the ketchup mess left by the last diners. Elma walked over, eyeballing Alex with a rarely seen pleasant expression on her rouged, hound dog-jowled face.

"Hey, handsome. I don't usually see you out of uniform. I like what I'm seein'." She put her hand on her ample hip and stood there, salivating. Alex smiled and nodded, not even blushing a little. Elma had been the hostess there for about thirty years, since she was a young teenager. She's what you'd politely call heavyset for her five foot five frame. Her almost beehive hairdo hadn't changed since she'd landed the job and even then she was wearing a style too old for her age.

Good thing I wasn't interested in Alex or I might have felt just a little jealous. Of course, even if I wanted to tell Elma I didn't like it, I wouldn't have. No one ever tempts making Elma angry after the Great Showdown of 1997. Elma banned Bobby Kremp after he told her his burger was cooked to medium-rare instead of medium-well. She reminded him that every burger at Skinny's was cooked to Skinny's version of done as she escorted him out with her press-on nails digging into his left ear. It was Bobby's stupid fault, he knew better than to challenge Skinny's cooking.

"Hey, gorgeous, good to see you too." Alex's eyes sparkled when he said it. He sure knew how to throw on the charm. "My friend Quincy and I thought we'd grab a little dinner." He looked over at me and winked. Elma looked over at me and scowled with her shocking blue-painted eyelids. The black liquid eyeliner drawn out to her temples accentuated the crows feet that deepened with her scowl.

"Hello, Quincy. How's your mother?" She asked out of obligation, not actual interest. Elma grew up in the same neighborhood as my mom.

"Oh she's fine. She goes to DUP as usual."

"Good. Good to hear it. Tell her hello for me."

"I will, she'll be glad to hear from you."

"What's DUP?" Alex interjected.

"Daughters of the Utah Pioneers," I said.

"Oh."

"Waddaya want to drink?" Elma asked, annoyed.

"I'll just have water." No need to run to the bathroom all night from caffeine overload.

"How about you, handsome?" Elma's carnelian red-painted lips curled into a wicked smile and she gazed at him with come hither eyes.

"I'll have a beer."

A tidal wave of silence washed over the inside of the restaurant. The sound of a lone fork dropping onto a plate echoed throughout the cafe. An elderly couple sitting at the table next to us posed frozen in mid-bite, staring in our direction; the woman looked like she had just seen a naked man run by. A young family sat on our other side. The mother covered her child's ears with her hands, like earmuffs. She looked horrified, and the father sneered.

Aside from the trendy restaurants or good old fashioned bars, there was nowhere in town where a person could order a beer without eliciting the same reaction as someone who punched an old lady right in the face in front of a crowd. Even then people would say, "I'm sure he had good reason to punch the widow Smith in the mouth," rather than accept someone ordering a beer out in the open on a weeknight. Being the levelheaded non-judgmental Jack Mormon that I thought I was, I tried not to look uncomfortable or surprised at the order. I don't think I did very well.

"What?" Alex asked.

"Ooh, he's a rebel too," Elma said. "I love a man with a wild side." She fanned herself with her order pad and exited toward the kitchen.

"What's she talking about? What did I do?"

"Nothing. You did nothing wrong." I said.

"Then why did you just have that look on your face?"

"Okay, this might sound weird, but people don't usually consume a lot of beer in this town, especially not in restaurants or really in public, at all."

"That's not true. Plenty of people at the Ranch Hand Bar were drinking beer in public the other night."

"Keep your voice down, do you want to attract an angry mob?" I said.

"Quincy, what in the hell are you talking about?" Great, now he was cursing and drinking in front of people.

"I guess it must be pretty confusing. People just aren't accustomed to seeing someone *not* in a bar drinking alcoholic beverages."

"What's wrong with drinking a beer?"

"Nothing. There is nothing wrong with drinking a beer. Just not around the Mormons."

"Oh. I didn't realize…is it considered a sin or something?"

"Well, technically no, it's not a sin, it's just…we'll just say it's frowned upon."

"Huh. It's a little confusing to figure this culture out. Last month a bunch of us from the station went out to celebrate a guy getting married and I know that some of those guys are Mormon. They drank beer."

"I know. It's confusing." Oh please, couldn't something get me out of this conversation? He had gone out with a bunch of hypocrites but it wasn't my place to say. Besides, I was feeling confused about the whole religion and culture thing myself. It made my insides squirm just thinking about the subject or anything related to it.

"Here we are. One water and one Budweiser." Blessed Elma. She put the drinks on the table then beamed as she took Alex's food order then switched to her normal scowl as she took mine.

After she left, we conversed as we waited for our food to arrive. Alex tried to steer the conversation toward getting-to-know-you-type topics, which I wanted to avoid.

No matter how tempting it was to get to know Alex, it would probably require reciprocity. And that would eventually lead to dredging up my past, and then probably talking about the future. Neither of the two topics were anything I wanted to contemplate on an empty stomach. Or a full stomach. Or any stomach.

My focus in life at the moment had to be keeping the flower shop going. I failed in competition after my short stint as a beauty pageant queen was derailed due to getting married. The marriage helped me to fail at getting a degree too, since my duty was to husband and home only. I wasn't even close to succeeding at being a good Mormon, especially in my mother's eyes. The only thing I had going for me was the business that my aunt started, and currently it was struggling, too. I couldn't let her down, and all of my attention needed to be directed at the shop, where I had a glimmering little hope of finally doing something right. Alex was not going to become an entry on my list of non-achievements.

But he looked so fantastic. His body was an embarrassment of masculinity packaged within perfect skin. While I pondered that skin, and the scruff that had developed on the face end of it, I thought back to his moment of undress in my house. Unfortunately, the replay of that scene led me to think about the voice mail hang-up I'd heard just before Alex had come in from the other room.

The message still nagged in the back of my mind. I had no reason to believe it was anything, except for the fact I had been feeling nervous and creeped out a lot lately. It wasn't normal for me to feel that way, at least since I got over the fear of the Housewarming Gifts.

I wanted to tell Alex about the phone call, but I didn't want him to feel like I was asking for anything else from him. If I shared my fears, he would react as the protective cop, or worse yet, he would feel like I needed a man to lean on. Although, thinking of leaning on him in the literal sense made for a great visual.

"Quincy, everything okay?"

"Everything's great. Why?"

"You seem distracted."

"I'm sorry. I started thinking about work. It's hard to leave the shop behind." A good all-purpose excuse for everything.

"I'm having a hard time getting a read on you."

"What do you mean?"

"Well, you're this tall, beautiful woman. You seem intelligent and confident. I just wonder why you're not with someone. You told me you've been married before, how long ago was that?"

"Not long enough to want to do it again."

"That good, huh?"

"Let's talk about something else. I'd like to forget that era in my life. What about you? Have you ever been married?"

"For about two seconds. I was young and dumb and it didn't help that I was in Europe, married to an Italian girl. It's probably best we don't talk about that either. There's some complicated legal stuff."

"Did you break some immigration laws?" I asked

"The only thing that got broken was my heart."

"Oh, please."

"What? I'm wounded here and you're making fun of me?"

"Would you do it again?"

"If I met the right woman, I'd do it in a heartbeat." He gazed at me in a sweet but serious way. I swallowed involuntarily; the weight of everything in the atmosphere felt like it had just increased. An uncomfortable silence sat between us, right in the middle of the table with the ketchup and the saltshaker.

Alex finally broke the silence. "How well did you know that florist that just died?"

"Not well, but what I knew, I didn't like very much."

"What didn't you like about him?"

"Just that he was an underhanded, backstabbing moron."

"Oh, is that all?"

"Yeah, just that. I heard he was found in a coffin." I didn't need to tell Alex from whom I had heard it. "It's been all over the news, but they haven't really given any details. Do they know how he actually died?"

"The coroner hasn't released a report yet."

"I guess it doesn't matter, except for the fact that he was murdered. I'm just itching to know who put the flowers on the casket and who made them."

"How did you know about that?" Alex asked.

Oh crap. "Oh, you know, just the regular gossip circles."

"There shouldn't be any gossip circles. That information wasn't released, Quincy. Where did you hear about the flowers?"

"I'll only tell you if you promise me I won't have to talk to that jerk detective who called yesterday morning. I thought he was the one who would come about the hit-and-run. I was so glad to see you instead of him."

"I would love to fully appreciate the flattery, if only it wasn't such a weak attempt at changing the subject. It's not my case. I can ask Detective Arroyo what the status is, but you need to be honest with me. How do you know any details about the Gibbons murder?"

Something wasn't right here. What was Alex keeping from me and why was he asking about it now? He told me not to worry about it last night.

"How did you know that I knew Derrick?"

"It was just an educated guess," he said. "Your turn."

"Okay, I'll give you a little hint that might help you with investigations in the future."

"Oh yeah, what might that be?"

"There are two places where you can find all the gossip you need to know in a town. If one doesn't know, the other one will. Either the hair stylist or the florist is the first to find out anything." He wasn't going to tell me why he knew what he knew, so I wasn't going to reciprocate. "Of course there's no guarantee they'll share that information." I said.

"How would one get them to share this privileged information?" He asked with a mischievous lilt of the eyebrows and glint in his eye.

"I'm sure there are ways one could be persuaded."

"Really?" He asked.

"I'll have to think of some persuasions," I said.

"I'll look forward to a report." His eyes were doing that melty thing again. "Seriously though, Quincy, what did Arroyo tell you?"

"Why do you care, it's not your case?"

"Call it maintaining professional integrity."

"I call it being nosy."

"Are you two finished?" Elma interrupted indelicately as she approached our table.

"We are. Delicious as usual." Alex said.

She thumped the check down on the table. "You pay up front." She winked at Alex then looked at me and flared her nostrils then walked to the front counter.

"I'll be right back." Alex went up to the counter to pay Elma. After he paid, I watched as he turned back toward me, and walked away from Elma. Suddenly, his eyes bulged open and he jumped about six inches into the air. I looked past him to Elma, who giggled like a schoolgirl. This time she winked at me then puckered her ample lips and blew a kiss to Alex.

"What just happened?" I asked when he returned to the table.

"She goosed me!"

"Elma's got good taste." I said.

###

As we drove home I divulged the conversation I'd had with Detective Arroyo on the phone. I felt sorry for Alex and his brush with Elma's deadly grip of desperate spinsterhood. "I don't know why he wants to talk to me; I didn't know Derrick that well. And why did he tell me not to go anywhere? The jerk just decided not to show up after he scared me half to death."

"Arroyo likes to think he's intimidating. I wouldn't worry too much about him."

"You said that before."

"You really keyed that Derrick guy's car?"

"Yeah, I did. But it was an accident. Kind of."

I described to him my last visit to the mortuary before they found Derrick's corpse. I had seen Derrick the night before. I found that he had blocked the entrance to the flower door with his convertible Porsche. I fumed as I pulled up and noticed his blond tipped-dark brown spiked hair going through the door. I thought to myself, *what kind of florist can afford a car like that*? I cracked my shin on the rear bumper as I tried to squeeze between his car and the back wall of the building. *A stupid car to drive in Utah, anyway. Just wait 'till the first snowfall.* I'm sure the look on my face was murderous as I inwardly cursed from the pain in my shin.

In the back of my mind I knew about the security camera pointed at my scowling face, as I ripped open the rear entrance flower door. It led to a small room with a tile floor; plant stands stacked along the sidewall, and a set of cabinets with a sink. Sometimes, in years past, before the mortuary expanded, it wasn't uncommon to find a stretcher with an occupied black body bag sharing space with the flowers. Much like the one I had encountered earlier, containing Mr. Clark.

The security cameras had been installed to capture the

goings on in the flower room, which is clear at the back of the building, and heaven forbid Gaylen Smith the two-ton mortician should have to walk anywhere outside the perimeter of his office during the day. Besides, after closing time, the flower room had to be left open for floral deliveries being left for evening viewings on the night preceding the funeral service the next day. I always thought the real reason for the cameras was to scare off florists from rearranging the work of their competitors when no one else watched, a crime of which I had been the victim a few times.

When I got into the glorified closet labeled "flower room," I noticed two other small planters on the stands lining the long narrow space. I looked at the labels on the enclosure envelopes to determine which planter came from which shop. One came from JoAnne's Flower Basket, and one came from Countryside Floral, the shop in Plainville owned by Irwin and LaDonna Shaw. On the left, was the garage door; the one where I met my one-minute stand in a plastic bag. Past the garage door was a set of cabinets with a small stainless steel sink and two small drawers left open, the sloppy contents left on the counter. Make-up brushes, small round tins of disturbed rouge and plastic hair combs remained to tempt or scare the imagination.

The entrance to the main part of the mortuary rested at the end of the standard issue public school linoleum squares and yellow fluorescent lighting. The door and frame were fashioned of beautiful cherry wood. On the other side of that door, thick pile carpet colored in rose, cream and peach muffled the sounds that might have bounced off the cherry wood paneling matching all of the door frames in the funeral home. A sign posted on the wall above the employee time clock next to the door read, "No florists past this point."

Knowing Derrick couldn't have delivered a casket spray, let alone any matching pieces in his tiny car, I assumed his driver must have delivered everything earlier and he was just here to schmooze. I recognized the voice of Gaylen Smith coming from around the corner.

"Did you guys get that plot set-up finished?" He shouted to unseen persons.

A dull quiet voice answered "Yeah. We'll put the chairs out tomorrow morning."

"Wuhl yeah," Gaylen's belligerent voice replied, "you don't want to put 'em out tonight. People'll steal 'em if you put 'em out tonight." Somebody liked being in charge. "Be here tomorrow at seven," he ordered, "the viewing's here at nine."

"Okay." The answer was monotone, not reflecting any reaction to the condescension in his superior's tone.

"Hey, Derrick what can I do ya for?" The boss was in a better mood all of a sudden.

"Just seeing if we're still on for our two o'clock tee time tomorrow."

Gaylen told Derrick he was still "a go" for golf.

"Great I'll just put it in my iPhone."

"Wow that's quite a phone," Gaylen said. "Is that gold plated or something?"

"Not the whole phone. Just the skin. I had it made special by a guy I know." I rolled my eyes to the very tops of my eyelids, quietly placed my puny planter and tried to slink out of the second class quarters before the non-combative gravediggers came in to punch out on the time-clock.

I carefully opened the back door, so as not to bump into Derrick's car, then just as carefully slid out of the opening and inched my way around his back bumper.

"Hey. Watch the paint job." A nasty male voice yelled behind me.

"Oh. Hi, Derrick, how are you?" I asked politely.

"Who the hell are you?" He replied.

"I'm Quincy McKay. We met at the last designer's

showcase, remember?"

"I wouldn't remember something like that. Just watch yourself, you probably scratched my paint."

"No actually, I didn't scratch your paint. I was very careful to avoid your car, even though you parked it as if you wanted someone to have to touch it. You must have emotional issues that make you try to force people to get close to you vicariously through your car. Or you have issues with the size of a certain thing, which causes you to buy stupid, expensive cars that you can only use for four months of the year, that make you feel validated or— something. Whichever."

"So," I said to Alex, "it wasn't like I went there just for the purpose of finding his car and scratching the paint with my keys. He shoved me and my keys were in my hand as I reached out to catch myself. The keys hit his car and I didn't end up catching myself. I hit my head really hard on the pavement. He drove off before he knew if I was okay or not. I guess I just wanted to finish my artwork as he left, since he had been so thoughtful," I said innocently. "He didn't even look to see if I was under one of the tires. By the way, I'm telling you this in confidence. You won't get me in trouble, will you?"

"No worries, Quincy. Besides, there's not a lot of complaining he can do about it *now,* is there?"

I laughed. "I guess not."

"But I'd be a little more careful with what I said to a guy like that. You don't know how a person will react. It doesn't matter how rude they are, you gotta let it slide off your back."

He was right. I could get "lippy" sometimes, as my mom would say, and usually it wasn't for my own good.

"Do you think that's why Arroyo wanted to talk to me?"

"No one else saw you?"

"No one else was there in the parking lot, but it could

have been on the security camera."

"I'll look into it. Meanwhile, could you try not to mouth off to any more tough guys?"

"I'll try to contain myself."

"Hey, I want to ask you something, since I'm so clueless when it comes to the habits of the natives around here."

"What is it?"

"I heard that Mormons don't have sex before they're married. Is that true?"

"Yeah, that's true."

"Wow, that's pretty amazing. But not everyone has that kind of willpower right? I mean, I'm sure there are exceptions. It's not possible that every adult, single Mormon isn't having sex."

"I guess it's just like the alcohol and tobacco thing. People have the ability to choose."

"So, having sex isn't a sin before marriage either, its kind of a loose guideline more or less."

"It's a little different in the case of sex before marriage, but that's a long conversation that someone like me is definitely not qualified to talk about."

"So, I guess I should have asked before, are you Mormon?"

He had just showed his hand; that's what this whole conversation had been about.

"You can stop with the whole innocent outsider act, Alex. That's what all of this has been about hasn't it? You've known me for what, a day and a half, maybe the equivalent of two days?"

"I guess so, what's wrong? Did I say something offensive?"

I mimicked back, "'Hey, Quincy, I heard Mormon girls don't have sex. You aren't Mormon are you?' Why didn't you just come out and ask if we could go back to your place and get to it?"

"That's not what I meant! I asked if you were Mormon because I didn't want to say or do anything else to offend you. I heard some things about the religion and I wanted to know if they were true or not. I was asking you because I thought we were friends and that we could be honest with each other."

"Oh." I said, sickened with embarrassment.

Alex pulled over to the side of the road. I had done it again. I have this inability to shut my mouth in time to stop my thoughts from spilling out as verbal incarnations. We were about three blocks away from my house. It felt like three miles. He was probably going to tell me to get out and walk home. I deserved it.

"Quincy, I already regret what I'm going to say right now."

Here it comes, I thought. I reached for the door handle in anticipation of getting the boot.

"What are you doing?" He asked.

"I'm getting out of the car; you don't have to say anything. For what it's worth, I'm really sorry. I have an overactive imagination and sometimes I don't have a very good censor when it comes to sharing things that I'm thinking."

"Sometimes? You mean there's more in there that you haven't said out loud? You're nuts, do you know that? Don't get out of the car, that's not why I pulled over."

"Why did you pull over?"

"I must be nuts too. There's something I want to tell you and I pulled over so that I wouldn't wreck the car. Quincy, for some strange reason, for which I'm sure I will realize later and want to strangle myself, I am very attracted to you, despite the fact that I think you might be a crazy person."

"I..." Again, rendered speechless by Alex.

"I've been laying it on pretty thick since I met you. I mean, I'm not all that bad am I? Elma thinks I'm O.K., that should count for something shouldn't it?"

"You're so much more than not that bad. It's just that I don't know if I'll ever be ready to be serious with anyone again." Tears were welling up in the corners of my eyes.

"Quincy, lighten up. I'm just looking for some friendship. It's not like I asked you to marry me. I just don't understand all the resistance you're putting up. You seem interested in me; I know you're interested in looking. Don't think I haven't noticed you noticing me." He smiled at me wickedly.

I'd been caught with my hand in the cookie jar as the warm, melty, sinfully decadent double chocolate chip cookie smirked at me from the driver's seat. I sat there with my mouth hanging open.

"Okay, I'm gonna be honest with you. There was a time not long ago, when a guy who said nice things about me would have had me mesmerized. If he told me I was pretty, I would have dropped everything else and followed him around like an obedient dog as if there was no other point to my existence. I did that for a long time. It was very important for me to be the pretty one. Nobody seemed to disagree with me either.

" I wasted precious years of my life trying to be the perfect pretty daughter, and then girlfriend and then wife. I entered beauty pageants as a teenager, and I won some of them. I had no ambition other than to be pretty so that the prince who came and swept me off of my feet could feel proud to have such a trophy at his side. I almost lost my life because I couldn't see through the lie of that fairy tale. The handsome prince turned out to be the evil monster. I still don't know how I managed to escape, but I did, and I will never, ever go back there again."

Alex seemed to look at me with understanding. "Why don't we get you home and we can finish talking there?"

"Good idea. Blegh, I didn't mean for things to turn into a Lifetime channel movie. You're right, I need to lighten up. Let's change the subject again. When's your next date with Elma?"

He laughed. "I don't know. I think she might be too much woman for me. My butt still hurts where she pinched me."

As we turned the corner to land on my street, a little red pick up truck sped past.

"Oh shit!" Alex exclaimed.

I turned to look at what had caused him to curse, and gasped. My chest felt like someone was stomping on it and squeezing all of my air out. Orange flames about two feet high licked upward near my front porch. The fire burned from a hydrangea bush I had helped my Grandma to plant. Alex slammed the truck to a stop, jumped out and ran over to the hose. He grabbed it and aimed the sprayer full blast at the burning bush. Sirens in the distance grew louder by the second. I found out later my neighbor called the fire department after noticing the fire when she went outside to dump the garbage.

Alex had nearly put the fire out by the time the fire truck stopped in front of the house. He conferred with the men from the fire department, as my neighbor Sarah came over and sat with me. She told me how sorry she was about the hydrangea bush. I had previously asked for her advice on how to care for it and keep it growing. She knew what it had meant to me. Alex came over to where Sarah and I were standing.

"They say it was definitely arson. Whoever did it wasn't too smart about it either. They left matches all over the ground. At least they didn't burn the house down." He put his hand on my shoulder. "I'm so sorry, Quincy. I'm sorry I didn't take the last fire more seriously. Obviously something's going on. I'll make sure we look into your sister's boyfriend. Is there anyone else who has a grudge against you, maybe a disgruntled customer, or something like that?"

"You mean besides my psycho ex-family? I haven't seen them in a while but I saw a red pick up truck passing us when we came around the corner. I didn't see inside of it, though."

The fire captain came over and told us his crew was ready to leave. Both Alex and I thanked them. Sarah gave me a hug and went home.

"Lets go inside, we need to talk." Alex's tone wasn't nearly as fun as it had been in the truck.

We went in and sat down on the couch.

"Quincy, I feel responsible for this."

"For what?"

"For all of this. If I had listened to you after the first fire, this wouldn't have happened. I could've been here to prevent it."

"We were out together. You wouldn't have been here without me. You shouldn't feel any kind of responsibility. You just happened to stumble into the situation with the hit-and-run."

"No. What if you had been here? What if he plans on coming back later to see if you're here? I know you don't want some guy telling you what to do, but I let this happen. Let me stay here on your couch tonight and keep watch just to be safe."

My overactive imagination thought this would be a great idea, and I was thoroughly tempted for a few seconds, but then I remembered my big speech about not needing a man for anything. But how bad would being a hypocrite be? It's not like I could be put in jail for that right? I didn't need the man, but wanting was a different story. After a little carnal daydreaming I came to my senses.

"Alex, I appreciate the thought behind your offer, but you're right. I don't want some guy telling me what to do. I'll be perfectly fine on my own. I've managed to make it this far by myself, and it's important to me to keep doing so."

"That's the stupidest thing I've ever heard. Just let me stay here. I'm a cop for hell's sake. It's not like I'm trying to hit you over the head and drag you to my cave. I protect people for a living. Quit being stubborn and do what's good for you. You can't be in charge all of the time."

"Well it's my house we're talking about here, so I think that I can be in charge. Whether I'm stubborn or not, you're not staying here tonight. Thank you for dinner and for extinguishing the fire. I'll be sure to lock up after you leave."

Alex stood and glared at me, his mouth open with no words coming out. His fists were knotted at his sides.

"You're too hard-headed for your own good."

I didn't speak another word. I just watched him leave before triple checking every door and window lock in the house.

CHAPTER EIGHT

After a night spent imagining what I should've said to Alex, I realized I wasn't going to be sleeping any time soon. At six a.m. I pulled on some running clothes and laced up my hardly worn shoes. As I left the house I imagined Brad Wilkinson watching me with his undeservedly handsome face, but realized he would more likely be stalking at my mother's house, since Allie had stayed there the last night.

I decided the feeling of being watched was due to the lack of sleep and I began to jog. The sunlight had just peeked from behind the mountains, and people were already out working in their yards to avoid the skin-crackling high desert sun of the afternoon. I jogged for about ten minutes, painfully realizing it had been too long since the last time.

I walked the rest of the way. While I strolled, my mind ran through all of the events of the previous days. A colleague had been murdered, my driver and van had been through a hit-and-run, my sister had been beat up by her boyfriend who then set a bag of poop on fire on my porch, and then did the same to my prized hydrangea bush. I'd met a handsome police officer, found out my dead colleague had been cooking the books, I'd accidentally eavesdropped on a love affair, and I had groped a corpse. Pretty impressive for forty-eight hours.

But I still hadn't uncovered the secret for winning back the funeral business referrals and until I did, the future of my business was in jeopardy. I needed to think of any leads that could direct me to the right person to talk to. Derrick's designer had mentioned an older guy, probably Irwin Shaw. As soon as I could, I would pay a visit to the shop he ran with his wife.

It was still early when I made it to work, so I took advantage of the time to get some bookkeeping done. If only I got up this early every morning to do paperwork, I would be caught up. The time flew by and before I knew it, Cindy let herself in.

I was in the back design room when I heard the doorbell. I leaned over and peeked around the door to make sure it was her. It was her all right. Her hair was teased and sprayed in an apparent homage to Dolly Parton and the singer's wigs. Her breasts were displayed in a way that might also have made Dolly proud, in a sheer yellow peasant blouse with a generously cut neckline. The black lace bra, which was obviously filled to capacity and then some, added that touch of style that can only be found at truck pulls and state fair breezeways. She completed the ensemble with a denim mini-skirt and brown cowboy boots.

"Morning, Cindy."

"Morning, Quincy." Her voice rang out nearly in song. She sounded giddy.

"New outfit?"

"Yeah, do you like it?"

I paused to think of what kind of day we had ahead, and whether it was worth answering truthfully or not. She interrupted before I had to make the decision.

"I went shopping yesterday. I read in one of my magazines that this job is good for at least one thing."

"Oh yeah, what's that? An income?"

"Ha ha, Quincy. No, working in a flower shop is one of the top ten places to work for meeting guys."

"Really?"

"Yeah, so I decided to take advantage of something I

was already doing, which is working for you, and all I have to do is look like I normally would while I'm out meeting guys. And you get to benefit, because I'm all dressed up for work now."

She certainly was. I wasn't going to point out most of our male customers were married or sending flowers to girlfriends.

"I'm glad that you're being proactive, Cindy."

She beamed at the compliment, and while it pained me to keep my mouth shut about her outfit, I was proud of her for taking action to reach a goal.

The phone rang and I answered a call from a man who wanted to pick up an expensive bouquet in twenty minutes. Hooray! I could use what was left of my fresh inventory, and buy some new when the bucket truck came around in the afternoon. The order was unusually large for a summer day; it couldn't have been better timing for my bank account.

I went into the cooler and started gathering flowers. With an order that size and a customer who says, "Just make it pretty," it feels like an all you can eat buffet for a floral designer. You can pick whatever flowers you want to use and you can actually design the best possible arrangement with the prettiest flowers, rather than being stuck within the strict confines of a pre-determined recipe trying to duplicate a picture of an out-of-season bouquet.

I faced the back wall of the cooler as I pulled oriental lilies, dendrobium orchids, flax, dogwood branches, gerberas and bells of Ireland out of buckets. The fan droned on near my ear.

"QUINCY," Cindy yelled. I shrieked and squeezed the flowers to my chest, breaking the petals of a ten-dollar lily. I looked behind me to find Cindy standing less than two feet away.

"What?"

"Your mom is on the phone."

Fantastic, only fifteen minutes left now to make this expensive bouquet for a great customer, and my mother wanted to talk. Perfect timing as usual.

"Did you tell her I was here?"

"Yeah."

Damn. "Okay," I sighed. "Will you prep that cool green vase with the swirls while I talk to her, and take these out of my hands, and replace the lilies that I just broke?"

"I guess so." Such enthusiasm.

Following Cindy, I ducked out of the cooler doorway, which was custom built with a higher step, for someone who barely broke five-feet-tall.   I then braced myself against the wall next to the phone in preparation for the forthcoming conversation. "Hello, Mom."

"Quinella Adams McKay." Not only had she used my full name, it came out of her mouth like a machine gun in short angry spurts.

"What did I do?"

"Lorraine Elliot informs me that she saw you at Skinny's last night."

"Mom, I don't even know who Lorraine Elliot is. If I did I would have said hello, I swear it." My mother's legion of spies encompassed a network of ward members, old schoolmates and the multitude of relatives that come with having a polygamist great-great grandfather.

"Well I don't expect you to remember everyone, my dear…"

Lie.

"I'm calling to ask what you were doing having dinner with a young man who ordered a beer?"

"Oh for hell sakes, Mother…"

"Now you're swearing too? I don't know where I went wrong with you, Quincy. I just don't know what else I could have done to raise you. I'm going to call Bishop Denning and make an appointment for us to talk to him."

"Mom, you are not calling the Bishop. Besides, why

haven't you mentioned the fire at my house last night? I thought for sure your spies would have followed protocol and contacted you immediately with the presence of a fire truck in the neighborhood."

"A fire! What fire? Why doesn't anyone tell me anything anymore?"

What was I thinking? The last thing I needed was for my Mom to have something else to worry—no, make that nag about. She would add this to her list of grievances about her rebel daughter Quincy, whom she would ask her Relief Society sisters to help her pray for.

"Mom, it was nothing, just a neighborhood prank that got a little out of control. A tiny plant in the yard was damaged a little, not a big deal." She didn't need to know that maybe Allie's crazy ex-boyfriend had targeted my house not just once but twice in two days.

"I'm glad no one was hurt. It's a good thing Allie was here with Brad. At least I know where she was and who she was with."

"She was with *Brad*?" I couldn't believe the sound of his name as it came off of my lips. What was Allie doing? I wanted to ask my mother what they talked about since I'm sure she had an ear to the door.

"Yes, she was with her returned missionary, not someone who drinks beer."

"Mother, I don't have time to argue the virtues or lack thereof of the son of a bitch my sister has gotten herself involved with. And beer drinking is not a sin."

"Oh, Quincy. What am I going to do with you?"

"Think of the Word of Wisdom as more of a guideline. And besides, even though I am an adult, I hope it will offer you just a little consolation to know that I didn't order a beer myself. But you never know. Your spies can't be everywhere all of the time. Maybe there's a six-pack of cold ones sitting in my fridge right now. In fact, go ahead and make that appointment with the Bishop, I'll bring some refreshments along."

"You're teasing me now aren't you? You're terrible."

"I've got to go, Mom; I've got an important customer arriving any minute. Goodbye."

"But Quinc…" I hung up before she could continue. The man would be here any minute and I needed to get that arrangement finished before then.

I was relieved to find that Cindy had prepped things like I had asked and I went to work, slicing furiously. My body was on autopilot, I didn't notice each individual cut made to the stems of salal and trachelium. I formed the base of the arrangement with greenery, which was my usual habit. I often found myself using designing time for deep thinking.

I couldn't stop dwelling on the fact that my mother had always favored Allie over Sandy or me. A rose snapped when I shoved it into the vase and realized I wasn't heeding the advice of my Aunt Rosie who told me never to project my negativity into the flowers as I arranged them. Still, I couldn't stop thinking about my sister.

What are you doing Allie? My heart ached to hear of my sister being so foolish. After what she'd been through already with him, and after what we had talked about, how could she stay with Brad?

"Ow!" I felt a familiar hot burning in the fleshy part of my left thumb. I dropped the knife and saw blood running from the tip of the thumb down to the first knuckle. Just as I had thought of that creep's name I had sliced a digit instead of a flower stem with the serrated edge of the knife. I had cut myself many times before; it's just a regular part of the job. But the blood pumped out of the gash where the skin had been filleted open. The pain throbbed with my pulse. This was gonna leave a mark.

Cindy came over when she heard my exclamation. "Lemme see." She grabbed my hand and examined the damage. "Eww gross. That looks bad. You're gonna need stitches."

"Stitches? I don't have time for stitches. If you're going to be a florist, Cindy, you've got to get used to this happening once in a while." I showed her a little florist's first aid by cleaning the wound at the sink, and then slapping some wadded toilet paper on it and wrapping it up with pot tape. Adhesive bandages don't stay on a cut like that while you're trying to work. Pot tape is made to secure wet floral foam to a container, so it's water proof and very sticky. It worked perfectly.

The bouquet looked spectacular when I finished. I did a double check to make sure the blood from my cut didn't leak onto any of the flowers, stems or leaves. The customer who had ordered it arrived just minutes later. He loved it and complimented ebulliently. I'll never get tired of that type of customer.

I needed a few things from the bucket truck that comes to my shop every afternoon. Keith Tanner, the owner of Daily Fresh Floral Delivery and driver of the truck had been coming to the shop every day since before I took over. Every shop owner in northern Utah knows that if you want to get any information about the industry, you ask Keith.

If anyone knew anything about the goings on in the funeral flower business and Derrick Gibbons, it would be Keith. He pulled up in his heavy-duty cargo van at the usual time. I walked outside to meet him as he got out of the van. I didn't want Cindy to overhear my inquiries on the subject of Derrick.

Keith should be the pin-up model for the all-around good guy. When times are slow, he extends a little credit with the promise of payment later and he doesn't hold it against you when it's just plain slow and you don't want to buy any flowers that day.

I approached the driver's side as he stepped out, then

we enDerrickd in the strict parliamentary procedure, which must be followed when a transaction of industry gossip is being proposed.

"Hi, how's it going today?" I asked. Pleasantries are the first step in the unwritten rules of decorum.

"Oh it's kind of slow but things seem to picking up a little bit."

"I don't have any special orders today, but I do need a few every-day things." Now, according to the dance, he would open the back doors and pull out the tray he had custom built to hold buckets of flowers.

"So I'm sure you heard about Derrick." Keith said.

"Yeah, I heard. It's awful. I feel so bad for his family." That much was true. "Did you ever do much business with him?" I asked, innocently.

"I did a fair amount of sales with him. I talked to his designer this morning. Until further notice, she's gonna keep the shop going. She asked me to come up there today."

"Really? I'm surprised. But, I suppose the Hansen mortuaries in the other cities still have services to take care of. That's the only reason I can think of that they would need flowers. Derrick couldn't have had very much walk-in traffic in that hole-in-the-wall shop."

"I've never seen them sell a vased arrangement out of there." Keith said. "In fact, all I've ever seen there are funeral flowers; mostly casket sprays."

"What I don't understand is why everyone is buying from them. The arrangements are ugly and overpriced." I said.

"Well you didn't hear this from me," this is an obligatory phrase in the gossip exchange, "but Derrick used to talk about his business partner a lot. He never said his last name just Doug." Keith informed. "I wonder if the partner was the marketing guy for the business."

BOOM!

A blast that seemed to suck the air out of the atmosphere rippled through my body. I reached out and wrapped my fingers around Keith's forearm in a death grip, while he ducked down like a foot soldier in a foxhole.

We looked up at each other, eyes big as dinner plates.

"Holy shit, what was that?" I said.

"It sounded like a shotgun." Keith said.

We paused; remaining crouched for a few seconds, and then looked around.

"Maybe it was a car back-firing," said Keith, as we rose slowly. There is a busy street on the North side of the building, but I wondered if a car could have produced the percussion I felt ripple through me from that far away.

I laughed, "Wow, that was intense. I'm glad it doesn't happen every time you come around. We might have to change our business arrangement."

BOOM!

A shriek escaped me; Keith exclaimed some kind of oath. I don't remember what he said; the feeling of my heart bursting from the sudden shock served as a bit of a distraction.

"Let's get outta here!" he yelled.

We both tried to run while crouching down and covering our heads with our hands. We were two chickens flapping our wings up around our beaks as we ran toward the building.

We ran all the way to the design room in the middle of the store before we stopped. We both breathed as if we'd run the 100-meter dash.

"Someone was shooting at us!" I exclaimed. "There is no way that two cars back-fired in a row out there! Who would be shooting—why would anyone shoot at us?" I looked at Keith in disbelief.

"Okay—" he breathed for a few beats "lets—just—listen for—a few minutes," he said between breaths.

We paused in silence. Nothing happened. Not a sound.

"Should I call the police?" I asked.

"Yes!"

The thought of having to call the police again caused a new, different type of anxiety. Despite, and in addition to, all the mental and physical discomfort caused by the knowledge that someone had been shooting at me, I felt something in my chest drop and travel down my esophagus into my stomach.

I called 911 this time. Being shot at seemed like enough of an emergency to use the service. I used the portable phone and stayed on line with the operator while Keith and I made our way to the rear door. We stood on either side of the clear glass in the top third of the door, taking turns peeking outside to see if anything was happening out there. I peeked and could just make out the nose of a navy and white cruiser as it pulled up.

"It looks like the police are here," I said to the operator and then hung up with her permission.

Alex had arrived within minutes. Of course it had to be Alex Cooper. Didn't they have any other cops in this city?

"What's going on?"

I nearly jumped out of my skin. Cindy stood a foot behind me. I don't know where she was during the melee. I felt a little guilty for not searching her out when we ran in. Keith regarded Cindy with a murderous glare.

"I'll explain later Cindy. Go to the front of the store, lock the door and wait up there in a safe place until I tell you to come out."

She looked at me like I was deranged then shrugged her shoulders and returned to the front of the store.

I returned to my post with Keith. We watched as Alex approached the back door nonchalantly. I opened the door for him. "Now someone is shooting at us!" I said as he passed the threshold.

"Hello, Miss McKay." His appellation was delivered with frost.

He turned to Keith and asked him to recount what had happened.

After Keith finished his version, Alex turned to me and said, "There's something you need to see outside." The corner of his mouth turned up and betrayed the serious cop exterior he was trying to maintain.

"I don't want to go back out there."

"Well I know you don't want a big, overbearing man to tell you what to do, but as the only member of the police force in the room, I'm going to have to require you to come outside."

I glared at Alex and extended my palm indicating he could lead the way. I looked over at Keith.

"I guess you two know each other." Keith said.

"Unfortunately we've met a few too many times lately." The tone in my voice must have told Keith he didn't want to ask any more.

We followed Alex as he practically skipped over to Keith's van.

"So you were both standing here behind the van like this, right?" He mimicked looking over the flowers and pointed to a particular bunch of celosia and mimed being overwhelmed by its beauty. He placed one hand over his heart and looked skyward.

"Cute." I said.

"Now if you'll just follow me I will show both of you the perpetrator of this horrific crime."

Alex walked around the opened doors of Keith's van and led us to my van, which Nick had parked earlier before he left for the day.

"Oh man," Keith muttered as we approached.

The van looked funny. Not funny comical, funny odd. After a long perusal, I realized the passenger side of the van rested lower than the other side. My van was lopsided because both of the tires on the passenger side were completely flat.

"Here's your sniper," Alex said as he tried and failed to suppress the gleeful "I told you so," that I'm sure rested on the tip of his tongue.

"Oh geez," Keith said. "I don't believe this. I almost had a coronary because of a blown-out tire?"

"Two blown out tires," Alex reminded as he held up two fingers like a peace sign.

"What are the chances of two tires blowing out within a minute of each other?" Keith wondered out loud.

"I've never heard of it happening before," Alex said. "Who was the last person to drive the van, Quincy? It wouldn't have been—Nick would it?"

"Nick!" I yelled. "That little jerk! What did he do to my van?"

"Well, I'm not going to be any help here, and I'm way behind on the route. Do you mind if I go, Quincy?" Keith asked.

"I'm so sorry, Keith. This is embarrassing."

"Don't worry about it. How could you ever know that both of your tires would explode? Why don't you grab the bunches you need, and just write them down, I'll catch up with you tomorrow to write up the ticket."

"You're the best." I hustled over to his van and grabbed some sunflowers, solidago, purple monte, Kermit poms and the beautiful celosia by which Alex had pretended to be so smitten.

Alex offered to help me with the flowers as Keith drove away.

"No thank you, Officer. I'd hate to keep you from your appointed rounds."

"I think that's the postman you're talking about."

"Whatever. The flowers aren't heavy. I do this every day."

I turned to go back into the shop; Alex walked ahead of me and opened the door.

"Thank you, Officer Cooper, but I could have opened

the door even without a man's help."

"Oh give it a rest, Quincy." He furrowed his brow and waived me past, into the back workroom.

I turned to face him. "Thank you for coming here and doing your job by responding to a call. I appreciate it. I wish you could appreciate how embarrassing this is, and stop prolonging the moment by being here."

He took the bunch of flowers from my arms. "I like being here. You've got nothing to be embarrassed about. How could you know that both of your tires had exploded? That never happens to—anyone. Well, anyone besides you that is."

"Exactly." I don't know what's going on lately, but right now it feels like I'm a magnet for strange disasters. I had nothing to do with Derrick's murder, and yet ever since they found him, bizarre things have been happening to me. I groped a corpse the other day for crying out loud."

Alex looked at me and cringed. "I don't even want to ask—but, aren't there any living bodies you would rather be groping? I believe corpse groping is an actual, serious medical disorder. I think they've got a name for it."

"It was a brief encounter. And it wasn't intentional, but that's not the point. It's just that I was barely starting to feel like I was in charge of my life when all of this weird stuff started happening."

"It's really important for you to feel in charge isn't it?"

I tilted my head and clutched my hands together dramatically, "Is that a crime officer?" I batted my eyelashes.

"No, but it sure is a way of repelling people from your life."

Epic fail on the cutesy routine.

"Maybe I don't need people in my life."

"Oh really? Well Miss Independent, just a quick question. Isn't that van out there your sole source of transportation these days?"

Damn it, he was right.

"Yes." I answered quietly.

"Do you happen to have two spare tires for that van?"

"No."

"So it looks to me as if you might need help from a big stupid man right now."

"Alex…"

"I can call a tow truck for you."

"Are you serious? I'm going to have to buy two new tires; I can't afford a tow too."

"I don't think my spare will fit on your van. I don't know how we're going to get it over there without a tow."

"I know—I'll call Danny. He'll let me borrow the spare from his delivery van. I'll just have to wait for his driver to come down when he's finished with their deliveries. Ergh, I can't believe this is happening."

Alex put his hands on his hips. "I'll give you a ride to Danny's. In fact, I might even help you put the spares on if you're nice to me." He winked and smiled a melt-your-heart smile. Why did he have to be such a cute, big stupid man?

"I'll go tell Cindy what's going on." I felt as deflated as the tires, but he was right about my needing help with them.

I called Danny and he graciously offered to help even more, but I thanked him and told him that Alex and I would be up soon. As we drove out of the parking lot I slowly ducked down in my seat, remembering my mother's spies on every corner.

"Are you feeling okay?" Alex asked.

"I'm great. Nothing wrong here."

"You're slumping, are you sure you feel okay?"

I was too embarrassed to tell him about my mother and her network, so I lied.

"I just feel kind of funny being in a cop car. It's like I've been arrested."

"The criminals don't usually ride shotgun, Quince."

"Oh yeah, I guess not." I sat up a little straighter to appease him, and just made sure I kept my head turned toward him. I covered the side of my face with my right hand and rested my elbow on the window frame—trying to look casual.

"By the way, they've released some information about your friend Derrick."

"He wasn't my friend."

"He wasn't someone else's friend too. But they still don't know why. His body was embalmed, and there were no obvious wounds on the body."

"Is it okay for you to tell me that?"

"No, but since you are the source of all information, I thought you should know."

"Thanks."

We pulled into Danny's back parking lot and after Alex turned off the car we entered through the delivery door. Danny buzzed around giving directions to his staff. His short quick steps stood out in direct contrast to the elongated point on his high fashion loafers. They made a clicking sound with every heel strike as he approached.

"Well hello, dear," Danny said. He turned his attention to Alex and gave him an obvious once over, "Gee, Officer Krupke, I don't believe we've met."

"Danny, this is Alex Cooper."

"It's a pleasure to meet you. Quincy dear, I'm so sorry for your car trouble. I've had Paul go out and pull the spare tire." Paul was his delivery driver. "He put it inside the back doors of the van."

"Thanks Danny I'm really racking up the favors."

"Don't you worry about it."

"We'll bring the spare back as soon as we're done." Alex said.

Alex had already turned to go outside as I said goodbye to Danny. Seizing his opportunity, Danny placed his hands on his hips over the pristine green and white striped apron covering his Armani long-sleeved shirt. He mouthed the words "he's cute" when Alex wasn't looking. I gave Danny an exasperated look. He shrugged and said, "What? It's true."

It was true and I was in absolutely uncharted waters.

CHAPTER NINE

When we finally got both spare tires on the van, Alex followed me in his police cruiser to the tire store. I pulled into the front lot while he found an open spot around the corner. I went in and explained what had happened and asked for two of the least expensive tires I could get by on. I had used this garage before, but it was under new management since the last time I'd been in. The guy behind the desk proceeded to tell me the new tires would cost three times as much as the tires I knew I needed.

Just as I had finished mentally constructing the chewing-out of the century, so I could deliver it to this Neanderthal without wavering, I heard the door open and saw the tire guy's expression change.

"Hello," he said, all smiles and cheerfulness.

"Hey how's it goin'?" the new customer said behind my shoulder. "Everything going okay in here, Quince?" I had been too focused on delivering my speech to notice Alex had come through the door.

"Oh—ha, are you two together?" The tire guy said.

"Yeah, don't mind me." Alex replied.

I opened my mouth to deliver the knock-out punch of a verbal assault when the tire guy interrupted.

"You know, I just realized I probably looked at the wrong price on the list. I misquoted you on that tire. It can get confusing sometimes, heh." His face bloomed into a fuchsia color and beads of sweat appeared at his receding hairline. He glanced quickly at Alex before pointing to the tires on the wall. The cheaper price was posted on the tire in question on a giant yellow price tag.

"That's okay." I said. "I won't be buying any tires here today. I'll take my key back please. Let's go, Alex."

"Wh…how come? Don't they have what you need?"

"No, they definitely don't."

I explained what had happened when we got outside.

"So why did you leave? He probably would have sold you tires at cost after I got there. I knew he looked guilty about something when I walked in."

"I'm not buying tires from a guy who tried to take advantage of me because I'm a woman! I wouldn't take them if he gave them to me and put them on for free. I can't believe you expect me to just accept that kind of garbage. Just because you came in wearing your uniform, looking like some superhero dressed like a cop to save the young maiden, doesn't mean I'm going to support his chauvinistic attitude."

"Hey, don't be mad at me because you needed me! Besides, you caught a break, why not take advantage of it?"

"I didn't need you! I was just about to rip the guy apart because I knew what he was up to. I didn't need a rescue."

"You know, I didn't have to come along. I could have just responded to the call and been on my way."

"You're right about that. I'm sorry to have been such trouble to you. It won't happen again."

"Quincy…"

Alex's cell phone rang before he could finish. He looked at the number that came up on the screen. "Great," he said sarcastically. "I have to get this." He answered the phone. "He's where? You've gotta be kidding. I can't believe he'd be that stupid. Okay, I'll be there in five." He hung up and told me he had to leave.

"Alex, wait. I don't want you to think I don't

appreciate your help with the tires. Thank you, really."

"We'll talk later. Will you be all right on your own—I mean with the van and the tires?"

"I'll be fine." I was a big girl, but I didn't need to overdo it with the "do-it-myself" stuff. I was grateful to Alex, a little annoyed—maybe—at the knight in shining armor behavior, but that was probably due to my perceptions and not reality. He was quite chivalrous. Why should I complain about that? Was I crazy? I decided not to answer that question.

I was furious however, at the scam artist salesman, and heaven help the guy at the next tire shop.

Nick was fired the next morning. Now I would be without a driver, but the summer was always a slow season anyway, so I could probably make do for a week until I could find a replacement. I dreaded the thought of putting out a want ad. Doing so was akin to announcing free admission to the demolition derby. The freak-fest starts before you can say, "Start your engines."

Personal recommendations aren't that great either. Nick came highly recommended by one of my customers. Turns out it was his aunt. He had been staying in her rental duplex and she was sick of getting stiffed on the rent money.

For the time being, I would use Allie's help at the shop. I would delay thinking about a driver until I absolutely had to.

With only two orders for the day, I decided my time would be well spent getting back on the trail of the elusive funeral work cash cow. I decided to pay a visit to the man Derrick's employee told me about. She said he had spoken frequently about a big account. What could be bigger than all of the funeral work in two counties?

Irwin and LaDonna Shaw owned a shop in a small town

called Plainville on the outskirts of Ogden. The majority of
residents there worked full-time at the Air Force Base or
were farmers who kept horses and other animals on land
first tilled by their ancestors. Plainville was in the
beginning stages of the suburban take over that many other
small, agriculturally based towns in Utah were facing.

Farmers died or retired, their land came available, and
was bought up to make subdivisions. Along with the
houses came the clash of people moving outside the big
town, wanting the suburban lifestyle in a rural community.
New houses were popping up next to century old farms
where the new residents would then complain to the city
about the smell of cow manure.

Derrick's manager told me the older man visited the
shop frequently, and she had implied he was the one taking
over the mortuary account. The pamphlet I "borrowed"
from Derrick's place had a sticky note on the inside that had
the name Irwin written on it with a phone number. I had
met Irwin and LaDonna Shaw previously on a visit to a
wholesale house, and Irwin Shaw fit the description given
by Derrick's employee.

I arrived at a very old brick building with windows
fronting the entire shop. The front display consisted of
some white wood shelves topped with silk arrangements in
colors and flowers that had been popular about fifteen years
before. Once inside, it was apparent the silk arrangements
had been on those shelves for close to those fifteen years,
since they were several shades lighter on the exposed side.

A flower cooler to the right of the entrance held a small
assortment of arrangements; a dozen roses and some mixed
bouquets in varied containers. The mixed arrangements
looked very similar to the Western triangle style I had been
taught by my Aunt Rosie, and lent an immediate feeling of
familiarity to the small shop.

I walked to the counter and knocked on the Formica.

"Hello, anybody home?"

"Oh, hello!" someone called.

I recognized LaDonna Shaw peeking around the frame of a door to the design room.

"I know you, don't I?" she asked warmly.

"I believe we've met before. My name is Quincy McKay."

"Come on back here, Quincy. I'm just messing with this computer. We've had it for two weeks and I still can't figure out how to turn it on. It's so good to see you again." Her voice had a quality reminiscent of days spent with my grandma and of warm banana bread just out of the oven. "The last time I saw you was that day at Sunrise Wholesale. It was the first time we had been in a wholesaler's. We had just bought this shop from our son. I remember you were so friendly and helpful to us then. That isn't such a common thing you know. We've gotten the cold shoulder from a lot of other florists."

"Really? I'm so sad to hear that." The floral industry in Utah was a small circle. Many older shops made it a practice to shun any newcomers and other shops bad mouthed their competitors.

"Do you know anything about computers?" LaDonna asked.

"I don't know a lot, but I might be able to help. What are you having trouble with?"

"I don't even know how to turn the darn thing on."

She showed me into the office where a nice new giant monitor and computer sat along with a new printer and scanner and every accessory you can think of. The newest name brand software packages sat unopened on top of the desk. On another table sat a brand new point-of-sale system still in the box.

"Wow, this is a nice computer! And this point-of-sale system is top of the line. I know because I've been looking into getting one myself."

"Oh good. Maybe you can help me to get it running.

The salesman said it should be ready to use, and we need it to get all of our on-line orders from the wire service. But I can't even turn it on. Oh, wouldn't it be wonderful if you could help us, Quincy?"

How could I say no to a grandma? As I looked over everything, I realized they had spent at least $20,000 on all of the new equipment.

"LaDonna, who did you say you bought this from?" A system this nice should have been accompanied by some coaching on how to use it.

"I got it from the wire service. They said that if we bought the fancy computerized cash registers, we would get a twenty- percent discount on the rest of the computer and all the other equipment. They said they would show us how to use it but..." she chuckled, "well like I said; where do you turn it on?"

The Shaws had obviously been had by a slick salesman from a third-rate company. I spent the next hour getting their system in order and then demonstrating to LaDonna the basics of how to use her computer, and how to find the user guide if she had any questions. The point-of-sale system would have to wait until another time.

While crawling on the floor and squeezing myself between the desk and the wall hooking up cords, I chatted with LaDonna and learned a little bit about her. She was a talkative woman.

I listened while waiting for software to load, and then the ringing of the telephone interrupted us. I overheard LaDonna during her phone conversation. She spoke loudly and repeated herself often.

"How did the meeting go? Any luck? Oh." LaDonna's face darkened, the wrinkles around her mouth deepened. "Well we weren't expecting much anyway. Drive carefully. Okay. Bye." Her head remained down-turned after she replaced the receiver. Her trembling chin betrayed her before she looked up with moist eyes. She awkwardly tried to coax a handkerchief from her pants pocket. She wiped her nose then looked up, remembering I sat in the office with her.

"Oh, I'm sorry. I don't mean to blubber. That was my husband on the phone. We've had some bad news in our family, and we're trying to get it sorted out. Oh listen to me; here I am rambling on, sweetie. You've been so nice to help us; I'm probably scaring you from ever coming back."

"Not at all. I'm sorry for your troubles."

She drew a chair next to me and sat down. She began to tremble; her petite frame looked as if it were a dam holding back a swelling river. "You never stop worrying about your kids no matter how old they get. He was my baby. Irwin always said I coddled him, but he was special. He was always more sensitive than my other boys." I wanted to divert the conversation. I didn't think her frail grandma heart could withstand what it would take for her to reveal everything welling behind her eyes.

"How many children do you have?"

Her face lightened a little, the corners of her mouth curved upwardly just slightly. "Seven. Three boys and four girls. Two of the girls are twins. By the time Bobby came I had my hands full with the twins, and I always felt like he didn't get enough attention."

"Is Bobby the son you bought the store from?"

"Yes..." Her face reverted back to pain. "We bought it because he...well, there are different reasons, but one of them is that Bobby was in poor health."

"Oh," I said. I could see that her heart ached for her son.

She took in a deep breath. "He had HIV. He found out about two years ago."

I made assumptions based on the way she kept referring to her son in the past tense that she had lost him to the horrible disease. I could see the very edge of LaDonna's garments peeking out the collar of her shirt, so I knew she was Mormon. I was impressed that a little old lady like her could talk so openly and lovingly about her gay son.

"LaDonna, I'm so sorry."

"He'd been following his treatments, and doing real well. He didn't ever have full-blown AIDS. He was working full-time running the shop. Things were going real good. He bought the store from a friend just after he'd found out his diagnosis, so that he would always have a place to work." Her face twisted with emotion again, and her eyes blinked out more tears. "Yep he was doing real well…" her voice broke off and her body racked in her chair while she attempted to stifle her sobs. "We bought the store from him later so he wouldn't have to worry about bills and things like that, and he could just concentrate on being healthy." She sniffled and wiped her eyes. I patted her hand. "My Bobby…my Bobby… took his life about a month ago."

Her face was ashen now, almost lifeless. "We thought he was doing so well, but I guess he just couldn't handle the pressure of everything—that—man—and then he got pneumonia from the stress of it all. We didn't know he was that depressed."

We sat in silence for a minute. I didn't know what to say. This wasn't a flower consultation. We had no business to talk about to distract us from talking about the death of her son.

"I don't know what to say, LaDonna. That's just awful. I am truly sorry." I knew I sounded like an idiot, but couldn't help it. What does one say in this situation? Sorry your son killed himself? Sorry your son had HIV? Sorry you bought a flower shop and didn't know you would be running it a few months later without a clue of how to do it?

LaDonna was gracious despite my awkwardness.

"Listen to me going on. I bet you wish you hadn't come in here today."

"Not at all!" I objected. "It's been wonderful to visit

with you."

"I guess it's been a while since I've had another female to talk to besides my daughters."

"I understand completely. You're welcome to call me and talk any time."

"You are a treasure. You'll, never mention any of this in front of Irwin—will you, dear? He doesn't like to talk about Bobby. He never understood Bobby and his— lifestyle. And now he just can't talk about him at all."

"I won't say a word."

I heard the back door open. LaDonna and I turned and watched Irwin walk in. He looked like a typical grandpa. He had a little bit of a limp. He wore a plaid shirt, slacks with suspenders, and he had a shock of thick silver hair combed back just so. "Irwin dear, this is Quincy. You remember her from when we met at the wholesaler's last year?" LaDonna asked.

"Oh, I don't remember those kinds of things, Mother. Quincy, did you say?"

"Yes, hi," I stood and offered my hand, "I'm Quincy, from Rosie's Posies. It's nice to meet you. Your wife has told me all about you."

"I'm sure there's not that much to tell about me. But Mother here, she's the interesting one."

"Now that's not true." LaDonna insisted. "Quincy is an angel, she's been here showing me how to work the computer and she set it all up for us. Isn't that wonderful?"

"Gosh, that's great. Are you sure you can use it though, Mother?"

"Yes, I'm sure." Her voice reflected annoyance at his lack of confidence. "How about you? I can show you how to use it now." She was proud of her newly found skills. "Guess what else we found out? Quincy's Aunt Rosie and I worked together at the same shop in Idaho Falls all those years ago."

"Isn't that something?" Irwin said. "Well, thanks a

million for helping with the computer, Quincy. Maybe I should hire you on to do the rest of the office work." He chuckled out loud.

"I'm happy to help." I wanted to jump right in and ask about the funeral account, but I didn't want to be too blatant about it. We had just become reacquainted. But it's not like I went there to get cozy with the wife so they would tell me everything about their business. Was it? I needed to handle things delicately, but I also needed to act quickly to see if there was any way to get a piece of the action.

I thought maybe I could just bring up the common news of Derrick's murder. Then I could segue into talking about his funeral work, hoping Irwin would volunteer that he was taking over the account. I was finally ready to put my plan into action when the phone rang and Irwin went to get it. I waited for a few minutes, while LaDonna practiced logging on and off of the Internet. The phone call seemed to drag on, and I realized I needed to get back to the shop.

"LaDonna, I wonder if I can come back later and set up your cash register system."

"Oh you don't have to do that. You are such a sweetheart to offer, but I don't want to cause you any more trouble. You've spent so much of your time already."

"It's no trouble. And besides, I want to get the name of your sales rep and see if he's the same guy as I have. If he is, I've got a few things to ask him regarding your computer system." I didn't tell her I was going to call and chew him out for taking complete advantage of an elderly couple.

"Well, if you really want to, it would sure be nice."

"Okay, I'll call you later when I can look at my calendar. Do you have the phone number for the sales rep?"

"It's over on Irwin's desk." She was getting sucked in by the computer. "It's on a business card, go ahead and take it," she said, without looking up.

I went over to a massive, ancient roll top desk, scattered with papers that resembled what once could have been different stacks. Envelopes were scattered among the mess, many of them from utility companies, banks, and credit card companies stamped in red ink saying "payment past due." A glossy pamphlet protruded from a still-intact pile. It was the same pamphlet I found on Derrick's desk about bio-fuels of the future. Maybe all the florists were receiving the same junk mail.

I found the business card nearby, said goodbye to LaDonna and waved to Irwin as I left.

The drive to the Shaw's shop could definitely be classified as off the beaten path. The narrow, small town road did not allow for any passing. As the road left the enclave of the Mayberry-like Main Street merchants, it merged into the old highway with many twists and turns. A ditch on one side and a canal on the other flanked the roadway. The yellow goldenrod and ancient equisetum growing along the ditch banks reminded me of what was right with my profession. If only I could sit and enjoy the creek beds just once during the summer. I considered stopping at the next turnoff, to get a closer look at the native wildflowers and grasses thriving in the marshy conditions next to the waterway. But as always, the shop beckoned me back. I had spent too much time away from my business while helping someone else with theirs.

My mind returned to the Shaw's and their predicament. They were stuck trying to run a flower shop after the tragic loss of their son. They got sold on an expensive computer and point of sale system that they would never learn to master in their wildest dreams, and they were in their seventies as far as I could tell. They should have been doing what retired people do. LaDonna should've been joining the quilting group in her ward, and Irwin should have been doing whatever it is Irwin wished he could be doing.

As much as I felt sorry for him, I got kind of a bad vibe from Irwin. He had been guarded. Not that he should share his life story upon first meeting me, but I caught him glancing at me suspiciously throughout the time he was there.

Maybe I was misreading him. I didn't know either of them very well, yet we had bonded quickly and I was concerned for their welfare. LaDonna reminded me too much of my grandma.

I needed to play a CD so I could sing along and stop thinking about the Shaws and their travails for the moment. I had my own concerns. I took my eyes off the road for a quick second to look at the CD on the passenger seat, then returned my gaze to the highway. I glanced at the rear view mirror where I saw a little red pick up truck driving way too close to my bumper.

I was driving about five under the speed limit, so I sped up realizing I was probably being a Sunday driver while my mind wandered. The truck stayed right on my tail. I sped up a little more and gripped the wheel tightly. The highway curved frequently and I didn't want to nose-dive the van into the five-foot deep portion of the canal on the side of the road. I glanced in my mirror. The truck couldn't get any closer to my bumper without slamming the van. I slowed way down. The jerk could pass me if he were in such a hurry. Finally the truck started to swerve around the driver's side. I felt relieved. I could ignore the hand signal I was sure would be coming up along side.

I looked over my left shoulder to see when I could return the gesture. The truck had caught up as far as the van's rear tire. The headlights of the truck flashed on and off. I heard the horn blast several times. Suddenly the truck slowed down and violently swerved back behind the van.

There were ten miles left before I would reach the interstate. It felt like mice were running around in my stomach; my hands were glued to the steering wheel with a white-knuckled, steel grip. I sped up. The truck mimicked. My mind raced faster than the van. I didn't know what I had done to cause this road rage, but I was feeling some rage of my own.

I could see two bearded men in the vehicle. I was going seventy on a fifty-five. Where was the highway patrol officer who liked to write tickets for going three miles over the speed limit when I needed him?

I sped on. The V-6 in the Zombie Van was powerful. I could've out run these guys if the road didn't wind so wickedly. I didn't see the yellow sign showing the extreme curve in the road until I had almost passed it. I slammed the break pedal, hoping not to roll the van. My head jerked forward as the red truck hit my back bumper. I continued to slow down, but I didn't want to stop. I was too scared to be angry at this point. I just wanted to get out of there. After the sharp turn I floored the accelerator. I looked in the rear view. The truck was slowing down. Their front bumper hung down on the passenger side. That's the last time I looked back. Zombie Sue rides again.

I found the freeway exit and called Alex as soon as I remembered I had my cell phone. My heart pounded and it seemed I had a grapefruit lodged in the back of my throat. My hand shook as I attempted to push the tiny numbers on the cell phone while I watched the road. I knew I had no credibility since the fake sniper attack. I took a long slow breath through my nose and blew the air out of my mouth, hoping for a steady voice.

The phone seemed to ring twenty times. Maybe Alex was screening his calls, or at least any calls coming from me after the way we'd left each other the day before.

"Cooper here."

"Alex, I just had someone in a red truck tailgate me and then slam the van." I panted between words. I wondered if I was having a panic attack.

"Whoa! Quincy? Slow down. You were hit?"

"Yes!"

"Where are you now?"

"I'm on the freeway."

"You're driving?"

"Yes. I don't think they're still following me. I didn't know what else to do. I know you probably don't believe me, or want to hear from me but I didn't know who else to call."

"Quincy, it's okay. Of course I believe you. Are you okay? Are you hurt?"

"I'm fine. I'll probably have a sore neck for a while, but I'm okay. Other than I think I might have wet my pants."

Alex laughed then sighed, sounding relieved. "Are you going home?"

"Are you kidding? I have to get back to the shop. I've got to get back so Cindy can leave."

"Okay, I'll meet you at your shop in a few minutes."

"Alex, it isn't necessary. I just wanted to tell you I was involved in a hit-and-run by the same jerks that Nick described. I don't know who the hell they are, and why the hell they're hitting my van, but it really happened. Okay, I just freaked myself out a little bit."

"I'll see you in a few, Quincy."

Having someone to call, that I could truly rely on, was a relief and a comfort. The sound of Alex's voice made it seem like it was okay to feel like things were going to get better.

Alex jumped out of his police cruiser the moment I pulled into the parking lot behind my shop. The reality of what had just happened flooded in. I sat gripping the steering wheel, my seatbelt still fastened. I didn't remember the depth of fear I felt during the chase, but now that all was quiet and I felt safe in my parking lot, the heaviness of it sank in completely. My body shook. I just needed to cry to release all of the stress and fear, but I couldn't.

Alex opened my van door.

"Quincy? Are you okay?"

I looked up at his face. The muscles around those brown eyes crinkled with concern.

"I'm—yeah—I'm okay." I tried to convince myself it was true.

"Are you hurt? You said they hit you."

"They rammed the back bumper. Do I even have a bumper left?" I pushed the latch on the seat belt to get out of the van to go look, but, Alex put his hands on my thigh and my shoulder.

"Quincy. Slow down. Are you hurt?"

I gently removed his hand from my thigh and looked up at him. "I'm okay, Alex. I'm just—pissed off." I slid out of my seat, but he stood inside the van door and didn't step out to make room. I found myself standing very close to him and looking up into his eyes. I could get lost in those warm pools of chocolate. I snapped back to reality. "Oh, my poor van! Things cannot be looking good back there. They only stopped because their front bumper was hanging off."

Finally, he gave me some space.

I walked back to inspect the damage to the rear bumper and Alex followed. To my surprise there was not even a little scratch.

"I don't believe it. I thought the whole thing would be hanging by a thread as hard as they hit me."

"Wow. The legend of Zombie Sue is true. She's impressive." Alex said. "With as little damage as it had when they hit Nick, I thought for sure he must have been lying."

I looked at Alex, surprised at what he had just said.

"What?" He asked.

"You just admitted that someone hit Nick, not the other way around."

"Yes I did. And I'm thinking these same guys probably set the fire at your house, and hit you today."

"So I just want to make sure I'm hearing right. You

actually believe me and you are admitting to it?"

"Of course I believe you. Now I need you to tell me everything you can about what happened. Don't leave anything out."

Alex's concern for me was genuine and he believed what I had told him. This did nothing to help me keep him at arms length emotionally. It only made him sexier and more irresistible.

As soon as Cindy saw us walking in the shop, she darted to the counter and snatched her purse.

"You're finally here! I have to go." She looked over at Alex and then me. Her gaze returned to Alex and lingered until I spoke.

"What do you mean *finally*? I'm five minutes early."

"Well, I have a date, with this new guy Tim, and I have to get ready."

"Great. Have a good time." As I said this, she returned her stare to Alex and practically drooled.

"Manners—where are my manners?" I said. I was hoping Cindy took the less than subtle hint about her staring. "Cindy, this is my friend, Officer Cooper."

"Are you in trouble with the cops?" Cindy asked.

I could hear Alex snicker under his breath.

"No, I'm not in trouble with the cops. Alex is a friend of mine."

"Hi Cindy, nice to meet you." Alex even sounded good looking. It wasn't helping.

"Oh, um hi." Cindy took one last look at Alex for the road, and then she looked over at me with a confused expression. "Well, see ya." At that, she put her giant sunglasses on, turned and left.

"What was that look she gave you?" Alex asked.

"Cindy asked Allie if I was gay. I guess she just couldn't wrap her mind around what someone like you might be doing with me."

"I—what the…" He couldn't finish.

"Yeah, it's best if you don't try to talk right now. I understand. So, I was driving on the highway coming out of Plainville…"

I recounted everything I could about the chase. After I thought I had told him everything, he got up to go.

"I'll take all of this back with me and add it to your file," Alex said.

"I have a file?"

"I—mean the file from the first incident with Nick." He said quickly. "I've got to go check in at the station and then I'm done for the day. Do you want to come with me?"

"No thanks, I'll be fine. Besides, the shop is open for another hour. I can't leave and turn away any walk-in business. People will be coming in to buy flowers on their way home from work."

"I don't like leaving you alone."

I couldn't help letting out a laugh. "Alex I'm here alone at closing time almost every day. I've been fine up until now."

"How about I go get changed and I'll come pick you up. I want to show you something that will take your mind off of everything that happened today."

I hesitated, thinking about how it ended up the last time we went out together, but those chocolate eyes were mighty persuasive. "Okay. I could use a nice distraction." As if Alex wasn't distraction enough just standing there.

As he left I admitted to myself it was cute the way he worried about me. The truth was, I was a little worried. This was the third encounter with those guys in the red truck. What I couldn't figure out was why they were targeting me.

Or was it just me?

Maybe they were going after my business. Maybe that's why they hit the van when Nick was driving. Who knows if they really knew it was me driving today? Maybe they had seen my van parked at my house when Alex and I were out to dinner. I didn't remember offending anyone personally lately. Maybe someone just wanted *me* out of business—the way Derrick was now out of business.

CHAPTER TEN

In a flower shop there's a never-ending supply of things needing to be cleaned, organized and re-filled. At closing time I began the mundane but physical tasks of washing buckets and sweeping and mopping the floors. The simple routine helped me to calm down after the car chase and provided an outlet for the energy that had caused my heart to pound. My legs had stopped shaking, but my heart hammered in my chest again when I looked out the front window and saw Alex's car at the intersection.

So much for wanting him at arm's length.

I didn't want my relationship with a man to define me ever again, but if I was honest with myself, I wanted—make that needed—companionship, and Alex might make an ideal candidate from what I had experienced so far.

He parked his Scout in front of the shop just as I finished counting the money in the till. He wore cargo pants, hiking boots and a Pendleton button-down shirt. He looked amazing in his uniform, but his casual clothes won the prize. The persimmon color of his shirt brought out the tan in his skin and the blond highlights in his hair. The top two buttons were undone showing off little hints of the golden hair on his chest. He carried a colorful bouquet of flowers. I inhaled sharply as soon as I caught sight of him. Until then I thought a man only took a woman's breath away in movies or romance novels.

"Looks like you're on the way to pick up a date." I said. "Who's the lucky girl?"

"You need to ask?"

"Yes, I do. Because I don't know anyone who would walk into my flower shop holding a bouquet from somewhere else."

"Unless, it's a bouquet designed especially for you by the famous Danny Barnes." Alex said as he presented the flowers.

"I thought you didn't know him before we went to his shop."

"I didn't."

"Then how did you know about him—I mean, how did you know he was a famous floral designer?"

"Research—I called your sister while you were in the tire shop."

Great. Could I be any more horrible? I had been mad at him for being an insensitive member of the Good Old Boys Club just after he had so thoughtfully asked my sister how to do something especially nice for me.

The bouquet featured a euro-influenced design of gloriosa lilies in an armature of Kiwi vine and flex grass.

"You had to have paid a fortune for these. I *know* how much they cost."

"Don't worry about that. Danny wanted you to have something nice that he said only you could appreciate. So did I."

"Wow, thank you, this was so thoughtful. I suppose I can let you off of the hook for bringing in contraband."

I couldn't help gazing a little too long at Alex as he came around the front counter.

"You look kind of dressed-up casual, I look a little dressed-down bag-lady."

"You look incredible," he said.

"Thanks." I felt my cheeks burning. "But I have a feeling I'm underdressed—where are we going?"

"It's a special place where you dine al fresco. I can't tell you anymore than that."

"Oh, it's a secret?"

"More like a surprise. Ready to go?"

"Yeah, just gotta grab my stuff and shut out the lights."

When we got to Alex's truck, he opened the passenger door for me. I always thought the act of opening the door for a woman was an archaic tradition, a way for a man to let a woman know her place, to show that he was in charge. Until Alex held the door for me. It felt chivalrous and romantic.

We climbed into the Scout and drove up to Highway 89, then turned south.

"Quince, are you sure you're okay after everything that happened today?"

"I'm fine. I was thinking about it after you left. Each time those guys and that truck have shown up, my van has been there. I don't know why they've picked poor Sue, but she's offended them somehow. Maybe Nick did something to them while driving for me and it made them mad enough to make a vendetta against the van."

"I suppose it's possible, but no matter what the reason, it's getting dangerous. I worry about you being alone."

I waved away his concern. "There's no need to worry. I held my own against them. They left our little meeting today with the worst of it. There's a reason zombies are hard to destroy in the movies."

He didn't look convinced. "It might not go the way you expect if something happens again."

Nothing in my life was going as I expected it to. This man was so deliciously tempting, but I could not return to any semblance of the life I'd left behind with my ex-husband. No matter the absence of any similarities between Alex and Brad. I couldn't risk returning to the nightmare.

For now, I would practice being friends with a man so that I didn't fall into the trap of being a dependent, mindless zombie like I had been. I'd leave that up to Sue, she was doing a bang up job all on her own, and she didn't need any helpers.

"I appreciate your concern for me. But I'll have to admit, I think I overreacted when I got back to the store today. It wasn't as scary as I made it sound when I called you."

"Uh-huh." I don't think I persuaded him not to worry.

As we talked, he turned toward a bucolic farm town between Hillside and Salt Lake at the base of a canyon. We continued east as the truck wound around a narrow mountain road. The canyon walls plunged from their high ridges on either side of us. Granite jutted out from craggy walls with a few brave bushes growing out of fissures in the rock every hundred feet. Further into the canyon, pine trees towered above the rest of the trees like the royal family of the forest. We bounced around in the Scout all the way up to a little parking area at the base of a trail that seemed to disappear into the trees. Ours was the only car parked in the lot.

"I've never heard of a restaurant up here." I said sarcastically.

Alex had a wry smile on his face. "No more questions, you'll have to wait and see." He walked to the back of the Scout and opened the door. He pulled out a giant backpack that looked stuffed to capacity.

"I hope you don't mind a little hike," he said. "The place we're going isn't too far."

"I don't mind. It'll be good for me."

Alex led the way up the trail. After the first four feet we didn't get sucked into an alternate universe, as it had appeared we would, but the parking lot quickly disappeared from sight.

Scrub oak, pine and quaking aspen flanked the path. Wild roses, raspberries and golden aster lined the trail. We continued on a steep climb for about two hundred feet, then the trail leveled out and we continued on for thirty more yards. Birds sang and spoke to each other continuously as we walked. They had the safety of the high trees. The warm spicy scent of Russian olive trees wafted on the air.

"Perfect timing. Our table is ready." Alex announced as he stopped.

He motioned for me to continue in front of him. Off to the right, the trail opened into a small clearing that dropped slightly in front of a campsite next to a gently flowing stream.

I turned to Alex. "This is unbelievable! It's so beautiful."

"I hope you worked up an appetite. We've got to eat this dinner so I don't have to carry it back out."

We walked down to the streambed. In a flat area with sparse grass, Alex unclipped a blanket, which had been rolled up under the backpack. He then proceeded to remove an entire dinner that had been pre-packed in different storage containers. By the time he set everything out, a gourmet feast awaited us on the blanket.

"How did you get all of this done in the hour after you left the shop?" I swept my arm out like a game-show model.

"I might have been working on some plans when you called."

I rested my hands on my hips, "How did you know I would be available?" I said playfully.

"Don't take this the wrong way, but you're pretty...predictable." He cringed and ducked his head, holding his hands out like shields. "Like you said, you're always at the shop or your house. I hoped you would be tonight."

Yep, I led the life of a rock-star.

"You've gone to way too much trouble—the food, the flowers—what's next?" I asked.

"You'll have to wait and see what's next. And it wasn't

too much trouble. You're worth it."

A girl could get used to this. At least, eventually I could, but for now I wasn't used to that kind of flattery. I didn't know how to react, so I busied myself looking down at the plates as I made them up, for fear my face would betray my internal squirming.

We ate dinner and talked over the forest music in the background. He told me about growing up in Oregon and California with his parents and a brother and sister. He was shocked that I had ten aunts and uncles, and that I didn't think it was a lot compared to some of my friends from school. He was so proud of his four-year-old nephew and two-year-old niece that he kept a picture of his sister's little family in his wallet. His face glowed when he talked about them.

"If your family is still on the West Coast, what brought you here? I asked.

"The job. I was working in NoCal and I hated it. I saw a posting for a job in Salt Lake and I jumped at the chance. I love kayaking and rock climbing so I knew this was the place for me." Of course he liked kayaking and rock climbing. His physique liked it too, and I loved his physique for liking it.

I felt at ease with Alex unlike anything I had experienced with another person. The awkwardness that usually accompanies a one-on-one conversation with someone you're attracted to wasn't there. It felt comfortable, as if we were friends from school getting reacquainted.

After eating we walked down to the stream to cross it on stones that had been placed there for that purpose. He took my hand as if to help me across but then paused and said, "After you." I crossed first, but kept hold of his hand. We took the path on the other side of the stream and explored the surrounding area. Alex quizzed me on the names of the flowers we passed along the way. Most of them were wildflowers I didn't recognize, but I did know about the stinging nettle that looks like mint. I carefully demonstrated the way you feel the stem to see if it's square for mint or round for the nettle.

"Don't touch the leaves, this is nettle for sure." I explained. "Ooh, but there is something worth touching," I said as I pointed to my left. I walked to the other side of the path to a huge wild raspberry bush. "These are the best raspberries you'll ever taste," I said. As I pulled, trying to coax a berry from the stem, I heard a raspy clattering sound at my feet. I pulled my hand back at the startling noise. About two feet in front of me was a rattlesnake, camouflaged in the dappled sun that reached through the trees on to the dirt trail. It was now highly alarmed and coiled.

Icy blood ran through my legs, which felt cemented to the ground.

"Quincy," Alex's voice came quietly and calmly from behind my right shoulder, "don't move, I'm right behind you." I felt his breath on the side of my face and his arm slipped slowly around my waist.

I didn't dare swallow for fear the snake would strike. The chattering of the birds now seemed like a roar above my head. I was afraid one of the birds would fly too close and threaten the deadly viper more than it was willing to ignore. After a few seconds, which seemed more like minutes, the snake lowered its head and made its way across the path in front of me.

We stood together, frozen until the tail of the snake had long since disappeared. I made no move but exhaled heavily in relief. I felt the aftertaste of adrenaline rush on my tongue.

"That was too close." I whispered. The words were raspy as they left my dry throat. "I didn't see it at all." My fear had caused me to forget Alex's arm wrapped around me. Just as I began to delight in my favorable position,

Alex gently tugged and I followed his lead to turn around. We stood face to face.

"You really seem to attract trouble you know? Good thing I'm an adrenaline junkie."

My heart continued to thunder in my chest, but for an entirely different reason. "I don't know. You might want to keep your distance."

"Oh no. I like this distance just fine."

He gathered me even closer. With the hand that wasn't holding the small of my back, he cradled my chin and gently coaxed it upward. The pad of his thumb brushed my mouth.

I watched his perfect Cupid's bow lips coming closer until they softly touched mine. The thrill of a first kiss with someone new, that can only be experienced once, rushed through my every cell starting at the tip of my toes and ended at my lips.

I lost myself in the perfect moment, the perfect kiss.

Too soon, it ended. Alex lifted his head then looked down into my eyes. Both of his arms embraced me and my arms encircled his neck. There were no sounds, no sights, just us.

"Wow," was my articulate reply.

CHAPTER ELEVEN

The high from my date night with Alex wasn't even close to wearing off the next morning. I woke up just before the alarm sounded, snuck in a few sit-ups (maybe a few would be an exaggeration; a couple—well one full sit-up really, but it was a good one) before leaving home, and still I arrived for work a whole fifteen minutes early.

The lock gave no resistance for a change and I balanced an iced-tea in my other hand. After setting everything down, turning on the lights and the computer, and putting the money in the cash register, I was ready to begin the day's business.

Cindy walked in just after nine and actually started to apologize for being late. Something new was definitely in the air.

We needed to do some summer cleaning in the dreaded basement. I gave her the task of organizing everything downstairs so we could throw away the worthless stuff which had accumulated year after year. It was unlikely we'd be able to use the broken handled ceramic mug with "Happy 1999" printed on it.

I went to the phone and retrieved a message on the voicemail from the hospital reminding me they needed a refill. They asked for baby boy arrangements, no girls, ten single rose vases and six mixed bouquets—a good-sized order for the morning. I turned the radio on and got to work.

After setting out all the vases and containers I would need, then filled them with water, flower food and arranging foam. I retrieved bunches of leather leaf, salal, myrtle and Oregonia. I began each arrangement using memorized recipes, which made for assembly-line style speed.

I stepped into the walk-in. In an attempt at efficiency, I piled my arms high with flowers instead of making multiple trips in and out of the cooler. I moved to the furthest end near the fan. Of course I thought I heard the sound of the phone. I paused, but heard nothing. The cold, heavy air began to feel eerie. Having a severe fear of being locked in the cooler accidentally, I hurried to the door and popped my head out in order to take a deep, anxiety-quelling breath of dry, non-humidified air. Instead I screamed.

Only three inches separated my face from that of a stone-faced large man. I jerked back to see him better. He stood about six foot three, with a stout chest and muscular build. His hair was short cropped, like a military cut. His brown eyes were deeply set, framed with heavy but neatly kept, angled brows. He sported a dark, well-trimmed mustache that covered the slight upturn in the middle of his upper lip indicating he may have had a cleft palate at birth.

"Can I help you with something?" My voice still shook after being startled. The door to the walk-in cooler was well behind the customer counter dividing the store. He had no business being back there.

"I'm looking for Quinella Swanson."

No "I'm sorry" or "excuse me," he just started right into using my former and never since used names. He was either from the church or the government; they're the only ones that know my real first name besides my family.

"Excuse me." I said as I exited the walk-in. He didn't move an inch until I turned to shut the door and knocked him in the face with all of the flowers in my arms. I used my foot to slam the door shut. I walked over to the design table and carefully unloaded my cargo, but it was difficult to coax my arms to move. They had been frozen in place when this well-dressed stranger startled me. Although, I wasn't sure he was a complete stranger. In fact I was fairly certain I'd seen him before.

His dark slacks and pinstriped button-down shirt coordinated well with his olive green tie. A policeman's badge hung from his leather belt. He wore large gold cuff links, and a watch that said Rolex in huge lettering; I guess it was supposed to be obvious it was expensive.

"How do you know that name? Who are you?" I assumed we weren't going to be exchanging pleasantries.

"I'm Detective Arroyo from Hillside City Police. I assume you *are* Quinella Swanson?"

"I'm Quincy McKay. Swanson was the name my ex-husband gave me when we got married. I gave it back."

Then it hit me. This was the cop I had fled after visiting Derrick's shop.

He strode slowly toward me.

"Mrs. McKay?" He asked as he approached the design table.

"Yes, that's me." I didn't bother correcting him about the Mrs. and I didn't think he would have listened anyway.

"I need to talk to you about a couple of things."

This was the detective who ordered me to stay at the shop the morning Derrick was found dead. He had finally caught up with me. I got sick to my stomach and I could feel a ball of anxiety rising up in my throat.

"Would you like to sit down at the table?" I indicated the consultation table at the front of the store with an open palmed hand like a model at the auto expo.

"We can sit if you'd like," he said with no emotion, his face stern.

Both of us made our way to the little table.

My behind barely made contact with the chair before I blurted out, "You know I'd really like to get something off of my chest." The words were loud, fast and breathy as I could hardly get any air to pass into my lungs. I felt my cheeks stoking.

He arched a neatly waxed eyebrow. "Oh?"

"I just, well…first of all…" I sighed heavily. The words weren't coming as fast as the thoughts. I'd had a couple of days of distraction in which I had forgotten Danny's brother was probably in jeopardy of losing his job because of me. I'm sure my speechlessness sounded like a stereotypical air-headed woman to him, which made my blood boil all the more. The words come out even slower.

"Mrs. McKay," the detective said sharply.

"You can call me Quincy. And it's Miss not Mrs.," I corrected.

"Ms. McKay." He paused to make sure I heard his generous correction. What a guy. "Let me help you get started," he said. Wow he was helpful too. "You've been a difficult person to catch up with."

"Really? That's surprising. I'm here most of the time. Did you leave any messages? Maybe they weren't delivered to me."

"I'm sure I did." Liar. He said it dismissively, staring at his manicure. With all of Cindy's less desirable qualities came a few good ones, including taking phone messages. I think it stemmed from nosiness. If a police detective came in or called for me, I'm sure Cindy would have been salivating at the chance to know why. And if it weren't Cindy it would have been Allie, who of course would have given me the messages. And then there was my voice mail. I was the only one who checked it. He hadn't left a message there.

I ignored his attitude and forged on. "I'm glad I've finally got a chance to talk to you about Derrick. Well, what I mean is how I know about him. And I just wanted to let you know *how* I knew about his death before most everyone else. The person I heard it from is really a good person, and would never have shared this information with anyone else, I think he just wanted to know something about Derrick, and since I'm in the floral business, he thought I might know him, and…"

He interrupted sharply, "Ms. McKay, I don't know what you're going on about right now. You do know Derrick Gibbons?"

What a jerk. I just finished telling him I knew who Derrick was. He didn't listen to a word I had just said.

"Well, I know who he is, I mean, was," I said. "I met him at a floral conference, and he was a competitor. I didn't really know him though. There are probably several other florists or anyone else who knew him better than me."

"Where were you the day before Mr. Gibbons was found at the mortuary, Ms. McKay?"

"I can't even remember where I was yesterday let alone back then." Okay that was a bit of an exaggeration, since I did remember being with Alex last night really well, but he didn't need to know that.

I paused to give his question some more thought, while simultaneously wondering why the heck he was asking me.

"Danny didn't call me until the morning I talked to you on the phone." I tried to help the detective out with his timeline. "I don't know how you guys even know that he told me, but I swear I didn't tell anyone, and he only called me because we both know who he is—Derrick, I mean."

Detective Arroyo's gaze became fierce, he could have split an atom with the pupils that aimed at mine when he said, "Ms. McKay, again, I don't know who you're talking about, and I find it to be very strange that you can't answer a simple question. I asked you where you were the day before they found Derrick Gibbons' body at the mortuary."

My face must have looked as astonished as I felt at that moment, which is the same moment Cindy came to the front of the store. She didn't notice the detective and me sitting there as she yelled out my name and started talking.

"Quincy what do you want me to do with this cat's pee?" She shouted out. Cindy referred to a flower, which starts to develop a nasty, distinctive odor as it ages and dries out while it's still in water. Its common name is Caspia. Cat's pee is a great pneumonic device for remembering the name of the flower. She continued walking up to the front of the store when I didn't answer her.

"What's going on? Why is there a cop car out front?" Just then she looked over, saw us and brought her hand to her mouth and shrugged in embarrassment. "Oh, sorry," she said, "I'll just put it in a bucket."

Good thing she wore another of her impressive man-finding outfits that day. He didn't seem to mind too much, not surprisingly. The small interruption broke some of the tension in the air, but it also caused me to lose my train of thought. I started thinking about how ridiculous Cindy looked and how embarrassing it was, and thinking how unprofessional Detective Arroyo was being as he gawked. His eyes were practically popping out of their sockets.

"I'm sorry, Detective where were we?"

He snapped back into the moment without missing a beat.

"Where were you, on that day?" He sighed heavily.

"Okay where was I on that day? Umm, I was here until I went on deliveries. Nick had already left because he claimed he had an appointment. It was about two o'clock I think. I remember now, a guy wanted roses delivered to his girlfriend before she got off of work at three." I remembered looking up at the clock that day at about one forty-five and thinking I'd better get the van loaded and get a move on.

"Did you have any deliveries at the Hansen funeral home?" He asked.

"No. Oh wait, yes, I delivered a planter there."

"Were there any funeral services that night?"

"No, just a viewing right before the funeral the next

day—the day they found Derrick. It was for the Jackson services," I answered.

"Why would you take the delivery the day before if there weren't any services? Don't the flowers die or something?"

"No, a planter is a container with living plants actually growing in the soil. I took it the day before for that reason. That way I could save myself some stress the next morning by not having to wake up early just to deliver a single item when it's perfectly all right sitting in the flower room over night."

The phone started ringing just as a customer came through the door. Cindy helped the customer in the store, while having to just let the phone ring. The middle-aged woman tried to pretend not to glance over at the tense conversation in the corner while Cindy readied an arrangement for her.

"You know, I really need to get back to work and help Cindy out. I don't know what's going on or why you are asking me these questions. I really don't see how it helps you to understand Derrick any better. I didn't even know him that well. Besides, what does that have to do with whether I had any deliveries or not?"

"Ms. McKay," the detective looked at me with a cold stone face, "you were the last person other than the staff to be seen at the mortuary in the late afternoon the day before they found Mr. Gibbons."

"And…?"

"And," he said in a loud voice, "it has been said that you didn't like Mr. Gibbons. In fact, it has been reported that you had an altercation with him at the mortuary."

Oh that. It shouldn't be too hard to explain. To a normal person who didn't have it out for me.

The detective stood. "You know, I've had enough of your playing dumb. You've said to more than one person that you didn't like what Mr. Gibbons was doing, and it's been reported that you even admitted to wanting to kill him. You've complained to the mortuary staff about the decrease in business caused by them using the services of Mr. Gibbons. That sure sounds like a motive to me."

"A motive for what?" I yelled. Had this guy just accused me of murder? I stood up and pointed at him. The only trouble was, as I had been nervously sitting there, I had put my hands in the pockets of my apron to keep from wringing them in front of him. One of my Victorionox florist's knives had been stowed in the pocket as usual. The florist's knife is a part of my hand. There are very few instances when I put it down while at work. Of course I held the knife in my hand, slicing through the air as I pointed toward him. I always talk with my hands. The knife was more of a third index finger than a tool.

"Now you listen to me," I shouted as I pointed. "How dare you come into..."

"Put your weapon down," Detective Arroyo yelled.

"My weapon?" I looked down at my knife. "Oh, I'm sorry," I laughed, "I'm so used to holding one of these; I didn't even realize it was in my hand."

"Put the weapon down!" He yelled even louder this time, and then he drew his gun on me!

I slammed the knife down on the table.

"Mrs. McKay, I am placing you under arrest."

"It's not Mrs., and you've got to be kidding me!" I shouted.

"I am not kidding. I'm placing you under arrest!"

"Under arrest for what?"

"For attempted assault on an officer with a deadly weapon. And resisting arrest."

"What?" Before I knew it Arroyo had put the gun away, pulled out the handcuffs, grabbed my wrist and whirled me around. With my hands held behind my back he tightened the cuffs around my wrists until they squeezed tight.

CHAPTER TWELVE

My arrival and subsequent booking at the police station constituted a ridiculous circus act, which I made sure to tell the detective at every possible moment. Arroyo obviously had a reason to dislike me before we met. I had no idea why, and any attempts to ask him about it in the five-minute ride to the station were completely ignored. He definitely liked getting attention whether it was from people noticing his spiffy appearance or my customers and his co-workers seeing him arrest the most unlikely armed and dangerous criminal there ever was.

He delivered his hardened criminal amongst stares of confusion from dispatchers and fellow officers. The Hillside police department building is small, so pretty much everyone on shift at the time was there to watch the show. He led me to a plastic bucket seat chair with metal legs next to a desk. I looked over at one of the faces looking at me in bewilderment.

"Hey, Kathy." I said in a shaky voice. There was no possibility of keeping my dignity intact then, because there was no dignity to be had, but it would have been rude not to say something. Kathy and I were in the same graduating class in high school. I could feel the scarring that was likely occurring on the skin of my cheeks due to the bonfire going on just under their surface.

I asked to speak with Officer Cooper but was told he

wasn't available. Luckily, inspiration struck at the right time with the name of a customer who also happened to be a lawyer. Kathy looked up his number for me, probably at the risk of getting in trouble, and I made the call, balancing the phone between cuffed hands.

After sitting in another room in another plastic chair for two hours, I was given notice I could leave. There was no questioning, no talking, nothing during the entire two hours. Once Arroyo led me to the chair, I never saw him again. Kathy came and unlocked my handcuffs. Since I had been given a "ride" to the police station, I needed to find someone to give me a lift back to the shop. I tried Allie's cell phone, she didn't answer. I didn't call the shop; Cindy would have to leave in order to come and pick me up. I tried Alex's phone three times, each time the voicemail answered on the first ring. He obviously didn't want to be reached. So I called someone I knew I could count on and that person was Danny Barnes.

There was no need for anyone to tell me when Danny arrived. I heard. Along with the rest of the building and the court complex next door.

"Where is she?" A high-pitched voice demanded. "You people don't know who you're dealing with. My uncle is the Mayor and I am so calling him as soon as we get out of here."

Kathy opened the door to the room where I sat, and rolled her eyes. "Quincy, you can go now. Hurry up and get Danny out of here."

I got up and nodded at her, downtrodden and embarrassed.

"Quincy! Are you all right, my dear?" Danny's arms flailed into the air as he rushed toward me. His usually perfectly aligned dark hair fell down on his forehead, but he did remember to put on his suit jacket. Although he had forgotten to remove his apron.

"I'm fine. Thank you so much for coming."

"Oh, Roxie," he started to get red in the face and fanned his hand in front of it. "Oh," he bit his lip and appeared to fight back tears. "You don't have to thank me. Just tell me all about it when we get in the MAV." Danny was referring to his Chevy Suburban with the acronym for Mormon Assault Vehicle. When the mammoth vehicles were first introduced, it became the in-thing for every large Mormon family to get rid of the tired old station wagon and buy one of these Jurassic-sized transport vehicles.

I recounted the farce that was my arrest to Danny. As he pulled up to my store I asked him not to tell anyone, especially not anyone in my family about what had happened. My mother's spy network was vast and always on the look out. Danny promised, and then argued against just leaving me at my store. I assured him I would close early, that I just needed to pick up my van. He dropped me off, and then headed back to his shop.

I opened the door as quietly as I could. I felt so humiliated; I just wanted to blend into the walls. If I didn't have to make sure Cindy had a replacement when her shift was over, I wouldn't have set foot anywhere near the place where I had been arrested. Of course as I opened the door, the chimes sounded out as loud and clear as they had ever done.

I cringed and looked toward the front counter. Surprisingly Allie stood there instead of Cindy.

"Hi. What are you doing here?"

Allie looked sympathetic or embarrassed; I couldn't tell which. "Cindy called and told me what happened. She said she had a date tonight." We both rolled our eyes, since Cindy had a date every night, "She needed to leave early, so I came in for her."

"Thanks Allie." Exhausted, I barely eked out the words.

"Quincy," Allie's tone told me what she was going to say next. "I just wanted to say I know you're mad at me about Brad and..."

"Let's not talk about that now, Allie." I was too drained to think about another jerk. I'd had my fill in that category for the day. "I'm so glad you could come in for Cindy. What did she tell you about what happened?"

"When she called at first, she said you had just been hauled off to jail. Then of course I freaked out and asked her for an explanation. She said she heard the cop say you pulled a weapon on him. What the heck, Quincy?"

"Yeah, I tried to jump a cop in my own store with a floral knife." My voice left no room for doubt that I was being sarcastic. "He was asking me some questions about Derrick, and I was talking with my hands like usual," I looked down and noticed my hands moving as I talked, "and my knife happened to be in my hand."

"What?" Allie's mouth hung open.

Arms folded, I turned my head to the side and mumbled out the words, "Assault with a deadly weapon and resisting arrest."

"How did you get out of it—I mean, why aren't you in jail?"

"I called…"

"Alex?" Allie interrupted, her hands clasped hopefully in front of her.

"No, not Alex. Well yes, actually. I tried to get a hold of Alex, but he couldn't be bothered with my little hassle of a problem. I called Cal Denny. He's one of my customers and a defense attorney. He's good too. I didn't even have to see him; he just got me out of jail over the phone.

"I am so sorry, Quincy. You need to go home."

"I agree. You don't mind staying?"

"Nope, I don't have any plans until seven. Then Mom wants me to go to a ward barbeque with her. She doesn't want to go alone."

Suddenly the fiery churning was back in my stomach. Worse than when I was being arrested. "Allie!" I reached out and grabbed her by the shoulders. "Does Mother know what happened today?"

She looked back at me; eyes wide open. "Are you crazy? I'd rather be drenched in soda pop and tied up to an anthill than to tell Mother any news like that. I was in the living room when Cindy called my cell. Mom was down in the laundry room. I don't think she heard anything."

"But you're not sure? You don't sound too confident."

"Quincy, I'm sure. She didn't hear."

"Okay, good. I'll live another day."

Allie took over the reigns and I took off. I shut off my cell phone and got in the van. I sat in the seat and stopped just short before I put the keys in the ignition. It was so perfectly quiet and warm in the car. I could shut my brain off for just a moment, forget all of the stress and humiliation from the day, and the frustration of not being able to talk to Alex.

But the trouble was, I couldn't shut off the feelings about Alex. Why wasn't he available? He didn't tell me he would be out of town. He said nothing about being unreachable by his cell phone. I thought he would at least check his messages at some point during the day. But there was nothing from him. Not a peep. I began to worry. What if he thought I was calling him too soon after a date? Did he regret kissing me? That was it. My desperate calls from the police station had been taken as a sign of aggression after a first date. How could I be so stupid? Here I had been telling him how I didn't want to get serious, how I didn't need a man in my life, and the day after our first kiss, I go to his workplace and hound him on the phone—or so it would seem to him. Great. Just great.

It dawned on me that the gala for the county fundraiser was coming soon and that many important people with a lot of connections would be in attendance. I would be doing the flowers for the gala and I needed the people who would be there to see my work and call me for their own flower needs. They would avoid me like the plague if they knew I had been arrested and what I had been arrested for. I turned the key in the ignition and switched on the radio. Since I couldn't turn my brain off, I would tune it out with some AC/DC.

When I got home, I pulled as far down the driveway as I could and headed straight for the back door. No stopping for mail or chatting with neighbors. I didn't want anyone to see me. I couldn't bear one moment of human interaction. And heaven help the bad guy or ex-relative who might just be lying in wait with a welcoming gift. I wasn't in the mood to do my usual security check. If I ran into one of them I would have a real reason for going to jail when we were finished.

I entered the kitchen and walked directly to the phone that sat on a little table. Out of habit I picked it up and heard the beeping sound that meant I had voicemail. I hung up the phone. I could listen to the messages later. *Although*, I picked the phone back up; what if Alex had left a message?

No. I put the phone down with emphasis. Alex could wait. He'd made me wait all day hadn't he? Instead of listening to voicemail, I decided to take a shower to get the over-zealous detective stink off of me, along with a number of other things that had probably hitched a ride after my visit to jail. Okay, so it wasn't really jail, it was a holding cell, a room really, but it was the same difference to me. I didn't want to imagine all of what I could have picked up. The possibilities were just too frightening.

I stood under the water in the shower until the hot water completely ran out. I took my time drying and styling my hair. I didn't feel much like eating dinner, but I thought I should probably have a little something. Comfort food was in order. I opened the cupboards and stared inside waiting for something to shout at me to pick it up and prepare it. Nothing took the bait. I perused a second, then a third time and finally the boxed macaroni and cheese got the nod. I set the water to boil and thought perhaps I should go ahead and listen to the phone message so as not to watch the pot into not boiling.

I regretted my decision to pick up the phone after I heard the automated voice repeat which number had called. It was the home phone number for my mother. Shit. Shit. Double shit.

"Quincy McKay! This is your Mother! Why do I have to hear from Barbara Colgate that my daughter was arrested today? How am I going to be able to show my face at the ward party tonight? Just tell me. First you're dating some...some...beer drinker, and then you've got the fire brigade at your house after you go out with this...this...man, and now you're in jail. People in jail have tattoos, Quincy. Oh no, did someone make you get a tattoo while you were in jail?" After more gossip enhanced crazy rants, the graces of heaven fell upon me as the voicemail time limit for my mother's message had been reached. It wasn't a difficult decision to erase that message and move on.

The next message was either a hang-up or the heavy breather was back. The automated voice said that the phone number was unavailable. I was too tired to be scared or worried, and frankly I was too pissed off at comrade Barbara Colgate to care.

Unfortunately, I knew I couldn't blame the spy network for getting me in this mess. I didn't know whom I could assign that responsibility to. If anything, I had kept my mouth shut about Derrick and the funeral flower business far too much. Danny was the only floral person to whom I had expressed my true feelings about the Hansen mortuary and Derrick. I had keyed Derrick's car, but I couldn't have been the only person to clash with him.

Whatever the reason, I was a suspect in Derrick's murder and I didn't know what to do about it. I wanted so badly to call Alex. But there was no way I would. My emotions were all balled up. I was embarrassed for many reasons, including what Alex probably assumed was my stalking him. But then I was angry with him for not trusting me enough to assume I would have called him from the station with legitimate intentions. Maybe he was in trouble for going out with me since he was involved in the hit-and-run case. Still, he could tell me so on the phone. I decided maybe I was getting the cold shoulder and that I was done with Mr. Cooper for a while.

"Never rely on a man for anything, Quincy. The only person in this world you can always count on is you. Never forget it." That's what Aunt Rosie had told me when I was ten. I didn't believe her then, but it turned out she had been right hadn't it?

CHAPTER THIRTEEN

Saturdays at the shop were usually quiet. With extra time on my hands, I could think of numerous things to do. Acting on those things was the hard part. I sat down at my desk and the computer with the intent of doing some bookkeeping. I drifted into doing *little* bookkeeping and a *lot* of Internet surfing. A few things nagged at me. Derrick's employee had said someone named L.D. Stanwyck signed her checks. I needed to find out who he was. I thought maybe if he signed the paychecks, he would know Derrick and possibly he would know something about Derrick's shop or his contacts.

I tried typing in the name of Derrick's shop, but just came up with Derrick's name. Then I remembered what had happened when I "Googled" myself. A lot more information appeared on the screen than I ever knew about me. So, I typed in L.D. Stanwyck and eventually found the name of a corporation, L & G Enterprises. A quick search for that name showed a link to a website with business names where Lawson and Sons Mortuary was highlighted. I had never heard of it. I typed in Lawson and Sons and found it was a discount mortuary in Ogden. It was too much of a coincidence that L&G Enterprises was linked to a mortuary.

I found the website for the State of Utah's Division of Corporations, and a page where I could input the name of a business and find the principle officers of the entity. I entered the names of L&G and Lawson's mortuary. A screen popped up telling me the system was down and it was unknown when the database would be accessible again. That trail had gone cold.

I thought of something else that had been taking up precious space in the back of my mind. I moved aside the piles on my desk and found the pamphlet I had borrowed from Derrick's desk. Another quick Google search netted an abundance of information about switch grass. Just like the pamphlet said, switch grass appeared to be a miracle bio-fuel. Inexpensive to grow and almost impossible to kill.

Not only would a switch grass farm provide the means for yielding five times the energy required to produce it, it would increase the carbon dioxide uptake from the air; just like the houseplants for sale in my shop. It sounded like a pretty good idea to me. Too bad I didn't have any money to invest in a switch grass farm. Although, if Derrick had had any connection to this particular farm in the pamphlet, I wouldn't want to touch it with the proverbial ten foot pole.

I didn't know what the connection was between Derrick and switch grass, and whether or not there was a connection between Irwin Shaw and switch grass, or whether it was just a coincidence his phone number ended up on a sticky note inside the pamphlet. But, I had little to go on, so I would have to investigate. And besides, I didn't believe in coincidences.

After prepping arrangements for our hospital account and watering all of the plants in the shop, I called it a day. As I walked across the parking lot it felt as if the bottoms of my shoes were becoming one with the asphalt. The van provided no refuge from the hot dry air.

I drove home with the windows down; the air conditioning wouldn't kick on until the end of the short drive. I decided to use the free afternoon to catch up on some yard work even though it would be during the hottest part of the day in the hottest month of the year.

With all the hectic activity during the past week I hadn't taken any time to take a look at the charred remains of the hydrangea bush. I found some ragged old gardening gloves and took the pruners and the shovel around to the side of the house. Thankfully the bush was on the shaded part of the yard now that the afternoon sun hung in the western part of the sky.

I moved sluggishly, not out of conscious effort but in a conservation of the energy required just to exist. I stumped over to the landscaped berm next to the house prepared to dig out the carcass of my cherished blooming plant. In place of what I expected to be a black charred plant, was a new, billowy hydrangea bush. In July, there was no way a water-loving hydrangea could survive without being watered every day.

I knew immediately whom I should talk to about this new small miracle that appeared to be thriving in my yard.

It must have been my neighbor, Sarah Jones. She was with me the night it burned. She was such a thoughtful sweetheart.

A rumbling sound commenced in the distant sky. A breeze started up and within seconds it had become a gusting wind. It looked like a microburst was brewing.

I turned and jogged toward my house. By the time I reached the back gate the rain was pelting down. Summer microbursts are a common phenomenon in Utah. They're considered a relief from the heat, or a curse from the outdoor wedding gods depending upon the situation you're in. It's impossible to do anything outside during the wind gusts that can take down an entire tent full of wedding guests and send large floral centerpieces aloft within seconds.

I ran inside the house and put a bag of popcorn in the microwave. I chose one of my standby movies, "Cyrano de Bergerac," in French with subtitles. I always dreamed of going to France and speaking French, but for now the subtitles would have to suffice. I went for the tragic romance instead of the happily ever-after love story; since that was the category my romantic life sat in.

Sarah's gift deserved a thank you and I dreamed up a floral design I would make especially for her the next day. I pulled some thank you cards from a desk. The bouquet Alex had given me on our date sat on the desk in an antique Art Deco vase. The fiery red and yellow gloriosa lilies reminded me of Alex the night of the fire. Alex had been so pushy then. He knew I was perfectly capable of taking care of myself, not to mention that no amount of coaxing would ever convince me to let a man stay overnight in my house after knowing him for less than a week. I don't care if I wasn't even in the house at the time the man stayed over. My mother would know about the sleepover and my life would be miserable from then on.

It was pretty heroic though, the way he bolted from his Scout and put the fire out. I realized I had been just a tad bit harsh on the guy. Plus I really had a great time romping around the forest with him. And he was a great kisser.

I should at least call him and thank him for helping me out so much during the fire, right?

I picked up the phone and dialed his number. It answered after one ring. I took a deep breath, listened to the greeting, and then hung up. I just didn't know what to say. He did, after all, ignore any attempts to reach him during my most desperate hour. It didn't make sense for his phone to be off. I mean, don't cops have to be available even on their days off in case of mass hysteria or something? I turned my cell phone on. Maybe he had left a message while it was off.

Nope. Not a word.

When someone who you went out with mere hours before, leaves several voice messages in a row, from a phone at the jailhouse, don't you think a person should at least check to see what all the fuss is about? I thought he should have. And, since he didn't like to reply to phone messages, I wasn't going to leave him another.

CHAPTER FOURTEEN

Monday morning, as I drove to work just before nine o'clock, the flashing electronic sign on the bank displayed the temperature as eighty-two degrees. It set an ominous tone for the day. The chances for Cindy to impress with her attire were high and likely. She did not disappoint.

A heavy sigh followed the ringing of the front door bell, announcing Cindy's arrival. She wore a mini skirt, giant hoop earrings, thigh-high black vinyl boots and a tight, fuchsia tank shirt with the words "Hot Slut" written across the front.

"No, Cindy. No, no, nooo." I said calmly, trying to remain friendly. "Just go home and change, come back, and we'll both pretend this never happened. Okay? Please?" I forced my face into a sweet expression, hoping she didn't take personal offense this time.

"What? What's wrong with this?"

"Seriously?"

"Fine." She huffed and walked out.

After her departure, a FedEx carrier arrived with a special order of David Austen garden roses I had special ordered from a farm in California. After signing for the box, I removed the cool packs, newspaper and wooden blocking to reveal the most beautiful bunches of watermelon-pink roses I had ever seen. Then I went into the back room to fill buckets with water and floral food. The aroma of the garden roses—which has been lost in commonly used hybrid tea varieties—filled the entire shop all the way to the back room.

Perhaps it was due to the euphoria caused by the rose scent, but as I lifted the first bucket full of water out of the sink, I was inspired by what seemed—at the time— to be a brilliant idea. While waiting for more buckets to fill, I could get in some weight lifting reps without having to go to the gym, or even leave the store. Talk about multi-tasking.

I started with bicep curls, twelve reps on each side. *Not too difficult. Let's take this up a notch.* I needed to work on leg strength and balance, so I placed the palms of my hands on either side of the bottom of a bucket and pushed it above my head. I took a big step forward with my right leg, brought it back to the starting position, and then I lunged with the left leg. My upper body strength was surprising— not too shabby for a skinny girl, I thought.

The next step was to test my balance. While holding the bucket above my head, arms fully extended, I carefully lifted one leg and straightened it out to the side in the air. I was shaky, but I held on. I began to visualize a new business idea as I balanced—I would inspire a new fitness craze—dry land water aerobics. I would make exercise videos and sell empty buckets as equipment. I would become the next world famous fitness guru.

"Hello!" A male voice yelled from just outside the doorway.

I shrieked. Balance was lost and limbs flailed. Water flew everywhere, mostly on me, and the overturned bucket landed on my head.

I ripped it off and peered between chunks of wet, dripping bangs to see a couple in their sixties staring at me from the middle design room. They looked frightened.

"I'm so sorry," the man said. "We didn't know if anyone was here."

"Yes—I'm here," I replied feebly. I wasn't

embarrassed by my appearance so much as wondering how much of my routine they had seen.

"Are you okay?" The woman asked.

"Oh, I'm fine, just fine." I grabbed a work towel and ushered them up to the front counter. "What can I help you folks with?" I said in the lightest, happiest voice I could draw out. Pools of water collected on the counter top.

The woman said, "We didn't actually come in to order flowers; we just wanted to know if you'd heard anything from the police lately?"

Police? I got a lump in my throat and felt tears working their way to the ducts—far too easily. *Dear Lord, what now?*

The man took over the talking. "Oh, my. We've really caused a mess for you today."

"I'm okay, really…" My voice cracked and the tears came.

"What my wife meant to say is that we saw a hit-and-run the other day involving your delivery van. We saw it happen as we were driving past on our way to the airport. We would have stopped, but we were late for our flight as it was. So we called the police on the cell phone and told them about it. We just got back into town today, and my wife was just worried sick about it. We haven't even been home yet."

"You saw the hit-and-run?" Things were suddenly sunnier.

"My wife saw the lettering on the back doors of your van, and recognized the name of your shop and…."

The wife interrupted, "We were in line to turn left you know, and a little red pick-up truck came around our left side." After switching back and forth through the story, they came to describe the accident just as Nick had done, with the same details.

"Oh my goodness. You don't know how happy I am that you came in." This time the tears in my eyes were due to relief that there were witnesses, or quite possibly because something had swung in my favor.

He continued, "Well like I said, we couldn't stop then, but we called the police and talked to someone there at the station."

"Did you by chance get the name of the person you talked to?"

"I'm sorry, I didn't think to ask. At first a woman answered, and after we told her what we saw, she transferred us to an officer, a man. He said he would take down our information, and make sure the owner of the van knew about it."

"Well I am so glad you came in. I just can't tell you how much I appreciate it."

The wife said, "I wish we had more information for you. It all happened so fast. We couldn't see the license plate of the truck, just the color, really."

"You both deserve a reward for this. I'll be right back." My hair dripped a trail to the cooler and I ducked in and grabbed a large mixed flower arrangement off of the display shelf.

"I would like you to have this," I told them as I put it in a specially designed carryout box.

"Well isn't that sweet?" The wife said. I took down their contact information, and thanked them again.

As they left I wondered why Alex hadn't told me about this. According to the couple, he got their report right after the hit-and-run happened. Why would he omit such a crucial piece of information? And wasn't it his duty to report it to me? Maybe he hadn't made sure they were legitimate yet, since they had been out of town.

He said he believed me about the case, but still, these witnesses would have relieved my mind—at least regarding the hit-and-run. Worst of all, he knew. He knew the whole time.

I decided to call the police department and find out why

I wasn't in the loop and to distract myself from the pain in my heart.

The dispatcher at the police station told me I would have to speak to the officer who handled the case, but that he was unavailable. *Yeah, tell me about it.* I told her I didn't want to leave a message. I would for sure leave a message on Alex's cell phone this time.

Reluctantly, I pushed the numbers on the phone. I paused before I pushed that last seven. I rolled my eyes at my own silliness. We were just talking about a case. That's all. I pushed the blasted seven.

I heard one ring, then hung up. Chickened out. What was my problem? I was angry with him for *ignoring* me? No.

The problem—the real truth—was that in the short time we had known each other, I was already relying on him for my emotional well-being. And that was absolutely against my rules for the way I was going to live life, post-ex-husband. I realized I couldn't yet trust my own judgment when it came to men. I just didn't have enough experience and I was worried I was merely infatuated. The way I felt in seventh grade, after a ninth-grader, Jeremy Briggs picked up my dropped notebook. Besides daydreaming about our wedding day on an hourly basis from then on, I also wrote "Mrs. Quincy Briggs" in that same notebook about a thousand times before realizing Jeremy wasn't that cute. In fact, he was stinky and weird and still is to this day.

I really did need to talk to Alex. I would come clean about my feelings. We could be friends, I could find other people to date, play the field. Or not. Maybe I would become a spinster like my aunt and once I saved enough money, I would travel the globe like she did and live a romantic, single, celibate life eating baguettes and wearing a beret at various outdoor cafés in Europe.

Yes. I would call Alex and face the music. Time to put the big girl panties on.

I punched in the number as fast as I could and took a deep breath. After the first ring, the voicemail picked up. I almost disconnected, but decided if I didn't do it now, I never would.

"Alex, this is Quincy..."

Before I could finish my message, Alex walked in the front door.

"Hi—I was just leaving you a message."

He slowly sauntered toward the front counter where I stood. "Well now you can tell me in person. How are you, Beautiful?"

He flashed a sexy grin and leaned his hip against the counter in a casual pose. I steadied my resolve and I told myself to batten down the hatches. I would not ignore what needed to be said or done just because of those long, jeans-clad legs and that strong handsome jaw and...oh my, I was starting to take on water.

"I came in person to tell you that my phone is totally ruined and I haven't had time to get a new one. Of course that's not the main reason for the visit. I wanted to see you."

"Oh." This could change my feelings about celibacy and the single life, just a tad. "So, you haven't heard any of the messages I left?"

"Not since Friday. Why? What's up?"

"What's up? Don't you work for the police?" I felt the heat rising along my neck and in my cheeks. A joke was a joke, but this was just cruel. "You know what's up. You're kidding around...right?"

"Quincy, what are talking about?"

"Friday. Friday is what I'm talking about. I mean I get that your phone was broken, but you couldn't find another phone? Don't you have to be reachable for work? And speaking of your workplace, I'm sure you all had a real good laugh at my expense on Friday."

"The only thing that I recall about Friday, Quincy, is

that I was late going to work because I was apparently wasting my time learning what a hydrangea is, where to find one—which was not easy by the way—and how to plant it."

"Wait, what?"

"Not only that, but I went all the way into Ogden to some special boutique that I was told is the only place to buy the expensive stationary I used to write your card. That's the only thing I know about Friday. I thought you would appreciate the flowers. I guess I was wrong."

"You did that?" I said, confused.

"Yeah, I did that. Wasn't it obvious?"

"No, I didn't see any card. You wrote me a note? On stationary?"

"Yes, I wrote you a note on some fancy damn stationary. And if I might say so, it was a great big pain in the ass." His hands were planted at his hips, his elbows bent out sharply.

"Alex—I had no idea. Honestly, I didn't see any kind of card."

"No card? I put it right on top of the plant. It had your name written on the front."

"We had a microburst on Saturday; maybe we had one Friday too, during the day when I was still at the station."

"Station? What station?"

"Alex, that isn't funny. I'm embarrassed enough. You know what I'm talking about."

"In the note that I left you, I said that I wouldn't be available for a couple of days because of work. Something came up last minute. I would have called to tell you, but I dropped my phone in the bucket of water I used to plant your hydrangea. I was running late, and I had already gone and bought the stationary and written the note, so I just scribbled a message on the back. I haven't had time to get a new phone yet. So, if I missed something from one of your messages I'm sorry."

"Oh." Did it just get ten degrees hotter in the shop?

"You know, you didn't miss much. Really, I'm probably making too big a deal out of it anyway. In fact, when you do get a new phone, you don't need to listen to any of the messages from me. Just delete away." A lame, withering chuckle escaped my mouth.

"You sounded pretty upset a second ago. What happened on Friday, Quincy?"

"I don't want to talk about it here. Let's go in the back," I said.

"Quincy, why is it all wet back here? And why are you?"

"I had a run in with a crazed water balloon bomber. Alex, do you swear to me you don't know about Friday?"

"I swear, Scout's honor." He lifted one hand like he was taking an oath then made an "X" across his chest with the other. "What happened?"

"I was arrested."

"What?" He laughed—way too heartily for my liking. "No, seriously…"

"It's not funny! Detective Arroyo came in here to ask me questions about Derrick Gibbons. He said I was the last person to be seen with Derrick alive."

Alex wasn't laughing any more. "So he arrested you?" The words sizzled with anger as they left his mouth. "What was the charge?"

"Assault with a deadly weapon."

"Quincy, this isn't funny. What really happened?"

I explained the whole knife thing and even showed him the deadly floral weapon.

"Are you okay?" He came over and put his arms around me.

I am now. I rested my cheek on his shoulder. His arms felt so strong around my shoulders. His masculine aroma, complete with a hint of the perfect aftershave made me feel like I could melt into him. So maybe an infatuated fool wasn't such an awful thing to be.

Okay, get a hold of yourself.   Remember the rules.
"I'm fine." I said. "It wasn't that bad." I leaned back, not willing—make that able to completely break physical contact with him. He was sort of like my caffeine addiction; I could cut back on the good stuff, but couldn't quit it completely.

"I'm so sorry I wasn't here. This wouldn't have happened if…"

"Arroyo has it out for me. I don't know why, but I don't think you could have prevented it. I tried to call you from the station but with your phone being dead you couldn't have known. But I thought at least Kathy or someone from the station would have mentioned that I asked for you."

"I'm so sorry, Quince. They don't know where I was."

I stepped back out of his arms, it was easier this time. "I thought you said you were late for work?"

"I was. It was for…training. I'm doing some tactical training for gang units in another city and we don't like to talk about it too much." He winked. "We don't want the gangsters to find out about it," he whispered sarcastically.

"Oh." There was something funny about the way he told me about the training. But I supposed he shouldn't be talking to me about anti-gang tactics at all.

"So, assault with a deadly weapon?" He said. "Should I be afraid right now, alone with you in this little room?"

"You should watch yourself, I can be dangerous."

"I have no doubt about that. But seriously, Quincy, please be careful. I'll make sure Arroyo doesn't bother you anymore but I worry about you. You won't let me help you."

"I don't need any more help. You've already done enough for me. I assumed the worst when I couldn't reach you on Friday. I'm really sorry. You must still think I'm crazy."

"Would now be a bad time to ask about your new

hairdo?"

I had totally forgotten about my new drowned rat look.

"Well, it's a funny coincidence. The couple that came in and scared me into this hairdo said they saw the hit-and-run. They said it happened like Nick described. Now we have witnesses. They told me they called the police station after it happened and that they spoke to the officer handling the case. That would be you, Officer Cooper. Why didn't you tell me they called?"

"No one called me. This is the first I've heard of it."

I put my hands on my hips and didn't prevent the suspicious expression from showing on my face.

"I swear, Quincy. I never got a call from anyone."

"I took their information down. I'll give it to you, but you have to promise you'll call them."

"Of course I will. I'll clear everything up. Listen, the other thing I wanted to tell you in person was that I had a great time the other night but..."

Here we go. Better to have a good offense rather than have to play defense. That whole willingness to play the fool thing was a passing fancy. I was *not* going to get dumped. A mutual agreement to be done with each other would be fine. But I wasn't going to be kicked to the curb.

I folded my arms and put more space between us. "You don't have to explain anything, Alex. I get it. It just isn't going to work out. I dragged you into my crazy life with the whole Allie's boyfriend thing and that was just the tip of the iceberg, wasn't it? Really, I would run the other way if I were you."

"Hold on there." He gently tugged on my tightly folded arms. "I was going to say I had a great time the other night but I'm afraid we won't be able to start where we left off until I get back in town."

"Oh." I cringed. How is it I keep doing that foot-in-the-mouth-thing?

"Do you think things aren't working out?"

Ugh. He did not need to know about the psychotic roller coaster of emotions I had been on regarding our relationship. Especially not the ride I took just minutes before he arrived. I needed to relax and let things go where they would, and stop wrestling for control of every small bit of—everything.

"No, I think things—you, especially—are great. My life is nuts, but that isn't your fault. I just feel guilty for dragging you into Allie's mess, not to mention my recent criminal past, and my exploding tires."

"You didn't drag me into anything; I had to find some way to get closer to you." He pulled me toward him and looked down into my eyes. He touched my wet hair and chuckled. "You are crazy, but I'm having fun."

I stuck my tongue out and crossed my eyes. He laughed and put his arms around me again.

"I'll miss you while I'm gone," he said.

I leaned away from him, "Why are you leaving again?"

"I told you about the Metro force training out in Tooele, didn't I?"

My shoulders slumped. "Oh, yeah. You did." I sighed. "You guys sure do a lot of training. Anyway, I guess I forgot. I've been a little distracted."

"It's understandable." He hugged me again despite my still-soggy state. "I'd feel better if someone were here to keep you company. By the way, how are things going with Allie?"

"She's back with Brad. She claims he's suddenly changed. He's been on best behavior lately, but that will end soon. She's out with him now. He took the day off to go shopping with her. She thinks it's a sign he really cares about her and that he's changed. I tried to tell her it's all part of his manipulation. He'll be back to his usual behavior, but it will be worse the next time it starts up again. He's allowing her to work here, just to show what a great guy he is. I told her that if he touches her, I *will* find a way to make him hurt just as much."

"Quincy, stay out of it. I don't want you to get hurt too." He brushed a wet strand of hair off of my cheek with his finger.

"Don't worry; I know what I'm doing."

"Uh-huh. Whatever you say, Quince."

"It's just so frustrating. I can't force her not to see him. He's so bad for her. But she won't listen to me even though I know first hand what could potentially happen. You just can't force someone you care about to do something just because it's good for them."

He sighed and then smiled at me. "Don't I know it?"

I jokingly punched his arm.

"You know, we could start where we left off the other night right now instead of waiting until I get back." He wrapped his arms around my waist.

"Are you saying I'm someone you care about that can't be forced to do what you want?"

"I am," he said in his masculine, stomach butterfly-inducing voice.

He dipped his head and slowly bent toward me.

"How long will you be gone?" I asked.

This time he drew back. "Only a couple of days. Why? You don't need me for anything do you?"

"Of course not. I just wanted to make plans, that's all."

"Ooh, a welcome home surprise. I love it!"

"I didn't mean..."

He pulled me into him. Electricity flowed through me as his chest pressed against my breasts. His lips touched mine so gently in contrast to the strength of his embrace. A zing shot through my core and I held him tighter. My pulse pounded, I wanted to keep kissing him all day. A happy moan came from low down in his throat. With my eyes closed, the only awareness I had was of his soft, perfect mouth and the way that it fit perfectly with mine.

The front door bell sounded a vicious assault to my

contentment.

He let go of me quicker than a teenage boy on prom night when the chaperone cuts in. We were obscured from view in the back room, but it didn't keep him from beaming red in the face and I felt the heat on my cheeks just the same.

I put one hand on each side of his face and gave him a quick peck on the lips. "I'll be right back," I whispered.

"Hang on a sec, Qui…"

I had already reached the doorway when he began talking. I turned and held up a finger and mouthed, "Just one minute," and smiled at him sweetly.

"I need to tell you…"

"I'll be right back." I took a deep breath to try and cool off while walking up to the front counter. Cindy stood, dramatically posed in the doorway at the front of the store. She had one hand on her hip and the other hand hovered above her shoulder with keys dangling from her fingers. She wore the same outfit as before and as she approached the front counter, she struggled to walk like a model in her spiked heels, while forcing her lips into a petulant "I've-been-wronged" pout.

"I'm done. Here's your keys." She slammed the keys down on the counter, and tried to flip her hair around in an indignant fling. Perhaps it would have been successful had she not teased, gelled and sprayed her hair until it was a shellacked mass of one single unit rather than individual strands able to fly around independently for effect.

I didn't say a word the entire time she was there. I just picked up the keys and looked at her blankly until she turned around and marched out to the parking lot where she plopped into the passenger side of a sports car, which burned rubber tearing out of the parking stall before she had a chance to shut her door.

I realized that my mouth hung open. I had no idea what I was going to do now, but I could worry later, and there was a nice broad shoulder I could cry on just a few yards away. Maybe leaning on someone wasn't so bad once in a while

"You won't believe what just happened!" I called out to Alex as I retreated to the back workroom. I crossed the threshold and took a breath to recount the story and saw that Alex wasn't in the room. He was gone.

"That's it," I exhaled more than spoke.

I was done. I had to get out. There was no plan, no forethought; the only thing I wanted or knew was to leave the moment and the place I was in. I trod slowly to the back door, but before I opened it I realized the hot glue pan was on, so I locked the back door and turned around, walking toward the design room. On the way to the counter where the glue pan sat, I passed the office and realized I would have to turn off the computer and the same went for the stereo. Just as the "off" button popped up on the monitor screen, the absurdity of the moment hit me.

I wasn't going to leave the store, I wasn't going to shut off my phone, or drive away where nobody would recognize me. My vehicle had the store name, logo and phone number slapped all over it in giant vinyl lettering. I wasn't going anywhere. I was tethered for so many reasons, not the least of which was the promise I made to my Aunt Rosie. I propped my elbows on the desk and sank my head into my hands. *Just breathe*, I told myself.

For a few moments I sat that way, the hum of the cooler helping me to meditate around the stressors. The meditation only lasted a few seconds, and then the negative thoughts came flooding in. How could I even pretend to make this shop a success? And how could I have let myself be fooled not once, but twice, by the same man? He had come in and sweet-talked me, gotten a little sugar and then quite literally run away from me. Damn his handsomeness and his charm, and the perfect way he kissed me too.

Oh my hell, I've turned into a country song.

I was stressed into submission. As if on autopilot, I found myself gathering things. I went to the cooler and pulled out the prettiest flowers I could see. I didn't care how much they cost, or what I would do with them after I was finished, I just had to direct my energy somewhere.

I used a five-inch milk-glass cube and created a texture-filled box with lush Irish green trachelium, chartreuse chrysanthemums, pistachio colored cymbidium orchids, Kermit button poms, English boxwood, and little pieces of equisetum, or snake grass. Everything was green. Green is the ultimate neutral. Green is both calming and nurturing. It's a spiritual healer. No wonder I was drawn to green flowers then. As I finished tucking in the last tufts of sculpted tree fern, I felt tears gathering in the corners of my eyes. It wasn't long before I let go and let myself cry. I held nothing back.

"Pull yourself together, Quincy," I said out loud after a few moments. What had I expected to happen? Fantasy men didn't just drop out of the sky without some kind of consequences attached to their chutes. Just as I slid a damp chunk of bangs out of my face, I looked up and saw Allie being dropped off in the parking lot. She walked in all sunshine and cheer. Once she reached the design room, she looked at me with a puzzled expression.

"What in the world…"

"Don't ask," I said wearily.

"Um, okay."

"I've just had the worst day ever. I'm still all wet, I don't have a boyfriend, I don't have any business today and I don't have a delivery driver or Cindy as an employee."

"Quincy, I'm not going to ask about any of those things right now, but I will remind you that we work next door to a salon that just might have a hair dryer you could borrow."

"Excellent idea. I need a break."

"Yes you do," she said. She looked at me as if I were some sort of bizarre sea mammal.

"I'm gonna go next door."

"Great, I'll take over here," Allie said. She stopped short of pushing me out of the front door.

I tried not to ponder the situation at the shop as I emotionally limped next door to the salon, but trying isn't the same as doing. For the time being, I could do the majority of the designing, especially when Allie inevitably left. But I needed to find a driver fast and I was just going to have to grin and bear the dreaded Freak Show Parade that would happen once I took out a want ad.

Upon opening the salon door I entered an alternate universe. It was as if I had walked into a beehive, the noise of women talking and hairdryers blowing created a symphonic buzz amongst the hair clippings and perm rods.

"Hey, Quincy, what's up?" asked Jenny, the salon owner.

"I wondered if you might have a spare hair dryer?"

"What happened to you?" Jenny asked while trying to stifle a laugh.

"Just another day on the job. A work hazard." No way would I tell her how my hair really got wet.

"I have a dryer you can use, in fact I've got a few minutes, would you like me to style your hair for you? On the house?"

"No that's okay. I…actually, that would be fantastic Jenny."

She led me to her station and fastened the cape around my neck then she washed my hair at the sink. She took extra care in massaging my scalp, which felt wonderful— just what I needed. After the blow dry she set about using the flat iron and after a short time she spun my chair around to face the mirror. "Well, what do you think?"

"I absolutely love it. Thank you so much, Jenny. I really needed this today."

I stood up and we both made our way to the front of the store.

"I need to pay you; you can't do this for free," I said.

"It was nothing. I'll never make up for all the beautiful arrangements you put on our front counter every week. You should let me pay you."

"Oh no, I wouldn't hear of it. I may come in for more pampering someday though."

"You're welcome any time," she said. "Hey, Quincy, I heard that you fired your delivery driver the other day."

"Yeah, I'm gonna need to find a new one quick, but I just can't bring myself to put up a want ad."

Jenny blurted out, "I would never do that! The last girl I hired from an ad like that turned Elsie Turner's hair orange, and didn't know how to fix it. She had all kinds of references, a nice looking resume, and everything else, but she didn't know how to color hair.

"Elsie went to her DUP meeting and her Relief Society homemaking night, and told every one of the ladies there how badly my salon had treated her. Quincy, I personally fixed her hair, and of course I didn't charge her. I offered her free wash and sets for the next six visits—which she took! But she still told everyone she knew not to come here. I can't tell you the damage that lying little hairdresser caused me."

I nodded my head in agreement. As I unwrapped a peppermint candy from the bowl on the counter, a woman who had been sitting on the couch in the waiting area approached Jenny and me.

"Excuse me," she said in a shockingly deep alto voice. "I couldn't help overhearing." I felt my face heat up from chin to forehead. She looked like she could be one of Elsie's cohorts. I knew we hadn't said anything bad about Elsie, but she hadn't been cast in the most complementary light and we had probably talked very loud in order to hear over the noise in the salon.

The woman looked to be between fifty and sixty. She stood about five foot five with chestnut colored hair except for her crown, which was completely gray. I imagined that's what she had come in for. She was a good-sized woman for her height. Her center of gravity seemed to be located in the upper half of her body due to the huge bosoms that rounded out near her waist. She had the chesterly endowments of many a great aunt from my youth—the kind who hugged you, smothering you with their "assets," leaving you with an oogie feeling for the remainder of the family reunion. She wore glasses on a gold chain that swayed from side to side as she made her way forward.

"I'm so sorry, I..."

"Hold it right there." The woman pointed at me.

I gulped and stood at attention.

"Don't you apologize for anything. A woman should never apologize for speaking her mind. My goodness, all you did was come in here for a style. Nothing wrong with that."

"Quincy, this is K.C., she has an appointment with Shannon," Jenny said.

"Karma Clackerton," the woman barked out. She grabbed my right hand and shook it with vigor. "Call me K.C. I come in every so often and replenish my youthful color. I had mousy brown hair as a young lass and I hated it. Now it ranges from chestnut brown to sexy red depending on my mood." She cupped her hands around her mouth. "I think my mood is auburn today Shannon," she yelled toward Shannon's station at the back of the salon. A seventyish year old woman sitting in the chair closest to us looked at K.C. with disdain.

"Well what's the matter Nedra?" She asked the old woman. "You should consider yourself lucky to have heard me at all."

Jenny covered her mouth to suppress a laugh. I couldn't hide my surprise at hearing her talk to the other woman that way.

"Oh don't worry; she didn't hear most of what I just said. She never wears her hearing aid, and she always has that look on her face. Like she just smelled a sour dishrag."

I bit my bottom lip to cut off my laugh after the visual K.C. had created.

"Well I need to get back to the shop, Jenny, and it was nice to meet you, K.C." I backed up a step to leave.

"Don't leave yet." K.C. gently, but firmly put her hand on my forearm. "I meant to say earlier, that I overheard you talking about needing a delivery driver."

"Do you know someone?" My interest was piqued but I prepared myself to hear about her darling granddaughter, who had just passed her driver's test two weeks ago, and would love a fun after school job. No thank you.

"Yer lookin' at 'er." She saluted and curtsied, all at the same time.

"Oh." I paused, not knowing how to respond.

"Well don't look so surprised. I may be old but I'm not useless!"

"I'm sorry, I didn't mean to be rude."

"There you go apologizing again. A woman never needs to apologize for speaking her mind."

Shannon walked to the front of the salon and said, "K.C., I'm ready for you now."

"Don't go anywhere," K.C. said. "I'll come over after I'm done. I'll be the one who looks like Elizabeth Taylor." She laughed with an astonishingly high-pitched giggle and tossed her head dramatically, flipping non-existent tresses into the non-existent wind as she walked back with Shannon.

I returned to my shop where Allie was busy arranging electric blue belladonna delphinium with red carnations and white Queen Anne's lace.

"Quincy, I'm alright here for the rest of the afternoon if you want to take off. That is after you tell me about your day."

I recounted the exercises, the drenching, the hit-and-run witnesses and Cindy leaving. I left out the part about Alex leaving. It was too embarrassing to share how gullible I'd been. "Tell you what," I said, "I'll take you up on your offer after I finish entering that stack of invoices into the computer."

I sat at the desk then noticed the little pocket notebook I had used to scribble some notes about Derrick, and a to-do list I had compiled of people I could talk to about Derrick's business with the mortuary. I had written the name of Irwin Shaw and next to it was a question mark with the word pamphlet written to next to it. Just what was the connection between Derrick and Irwin Shaw and the switch grass pamphlet? It wouldn't hurt for me to pay the Shaws a visit, since Allie would be covering the shop, and I had promised to help them finish setting up their computer system.

The door chimes sounded and I looked out from behind the desk to see K.C. She sported a warm auburn color, and lots of volume in her curly do. She fluffed her hair as she walked toward the front counter in a Marilyn Monroe fashion.

"What do you think?" she said in a deep voice, reminiscent of a 1940's movie star.

"It looks great! I love the color on you."

"Why thank you. Of course the way she styled it is way too big for me. But it's nice to have it done up fancy once in a while. Now, about that driving job..."

"I was thinking about that, and I decided we should have an interview." I said with my best attempt at authority.

"An interview! Pshaw. We don't need to waste time with an interview! Besides, we're doing an interview right now. I'll just tell you all about myself and you can see what you think. I've got thirty years of driving experience, commercially. I drove a school bus. And let me tell you, if I can drive a fourteen-ton bus full of forty screaming kids, without getting in any accidents in those entire 30 years, I think you can find me safe enough to deliver your flower arrangements. I never lost a child either."

"I don't know. Do you have any retail experience?"

"No, but I'm responsible, and I'm a good driver, and I'll work for fairly cheap. I expect to be paid, but I don't need a lot. I've got some money saved up for retirement. And I don't have a family at home to worry about. I can come in early and work late. Whatever you need. My kids are all grown, and my husband passed away last year. Basically I need a little bit of money coming in to cover the fun stuff, and I need something to do. C'mon kid. I need a job and you need a driver. Whaddya say?"

I paused for a moment to think about the problems that might arise from hiring an older woman. I'd experienced plenty of problems recently with my younger employees.

"She's hired!" Allie's voice sounded from the middle of the design room.

"K.C., let me introduce you to my sister, Allie."

"Hello, Allie," K.C. leaned over the counter and waved at Allie through the false window, "It's a pleasure to meet you. Well, Quincy?"

"Okay," I said, "lets give it a try."

"Yippee!" said K.C.

"Have you ever driven a mini-van before?"

"No, but if you can drive a bus you can drive anything."

"Do you think it will be a problem lifting things? Sometimes these buckets are kind of heavy."

"If I can't do it as is, I'll find a way to make it work. I think you'll be surprised, Miss McKay. This old mule has got a lotta kick left in her."

"I'm sure you do." I said with a laugh. I liked this lady. She appeared to be honest and trustworthy, but mostly, she said whatever was on her mind, and I guessed that she did whatever she pleased. I didn't know if I felt bullied by her or lucky to have met her. Maybe it was a little of both, but it was a perfectly timed change and it was exactly what I needed.

CHAPTER FIFTEEN

After finishing with K.C., I drove to the Shaw's flower shop. It was in a quaint, pretty, town, but a business in such a small, out-of-the-way place was unlikely to be providing a full income for the Shaw's. I hoped they had some money saved to live on.

I walked in the front door to find no one in sight, just as before. I knocked on the front counter. "Hello, LaDonna, are you here?" I called out.

"Hello?" A man answered, with a sharpness to his tone.

"Irwin, is that you? It's Quincy McKay."

Irwin came out of the office and peered up to the front of the store. "Oh, Quincy. LaDonna's not here I'm afraid. She's gone to the chiropractor."

"Oh, well I was just going to help finish putting the office together. I suppose I could do it without her."

"Uh, I don't know if that's such a good idea. You know Mother will be the one using the computer, and I, well this just isn't a good time. You'll have to come back later."

Irwin glanced at his watch then turned his body to look back into the office. He returned his attention to me and sighed, his mouth wrenched into a crooked line.

"Okay, no problem, I can come back," I said. I moved toward the front door. *No, no, no*, I didn't want to come back. I wanted information now. Since I had been connected to the unsolved murder of Derrick Gibbons I needed to gather the information that would clear me of any involvement. I wasn't sure Irwin would be of any help to me, but that switch grass pamphlet was too much of a coincidence. It could also be a clue. I wasn't sure about what, but it was something.

I turned back and said, "I'll have to call LaDonna before I come next time. I'm sorry to have interrupted. I'll see you later."

"Okay, yes goodbye." He walked toward me wearing a patronizing half smile and shaking his head. He held his arms out to the sides, shepherding me toward the door.

I watched him over my shoulder as I moved. Before he reached me to shoo me out, I spun around abruptly to face him. "Irwin, I just had one question; maybe you could answer."

"Oh, okay, what is it?" He took another glance back into the office then dropped his arms to his sides.

"Well the other day I was talking to JoAnne from JoAnne's Flower Box and…"

"Awful woman," he mumbled.

"Yes well," I continued, "she was talking to me about a business opportunity, and I wanted to get your advice about it."

"Oh?" His bushy eyebrows rose. I had piqued his interest.

"It's about farming a certain type of plant. It's a type of foliage that I've used in the shop before, but apparently it can be used as an alternate type of fuel. It's called switch grass."

I watched Irwin carefully for his response. It didn't take long for his nostrils to flare, his eyes to grow large, and his face and neck to turn as crimson as a red anemone.

"He told her, too! That son-of-a-gun told me it was exclusive. Only a select group was to be involved." Spittle collected in the corners of his mouth as he growled out his words. "How many others has he told? He gouged every one of us, making us think we were the only ones. I paid for the whole operation. He didn't tell me about other investors." He pointed a thick finger into his chest every time he mentioned himself.

Irwin looked down at his hands, "He sure got what was coming to him. Too bad I couldn't do it earlier." He still looked at his hands, which he balled into trembling fists.

A sickening swell of anxiety expanded from my stomach up my esophagus. I gulped down what I could and forced myself to speak. His demeanor told me I shouldn't ask what he should have done earlier.

"Irwin, are you all right?" It was the only thing I could think to say. He was shaking all over and any part of his skin that wasn't covered with clothing was red and sweaty.

"I…Quincy, you have to go. I'm sorry, LaDonna's not here you'll have to call her." He turned around and walked back to the office. He was surprisingly quick. His old man limp from my previous visit was not apparent.

"Okay, bye," I said to the space he used to occupy. I sprinted to my van. I didn't know exactly what had just happened but it scared me to death. He had to have been talking about Derrick. I didn't know if part of the rage was because it was JoAnne that I lied about talking to, or just that Derrick swindled him out of a lot of money. No matter why, he said he should have done it sooner. Whatever "it" was.

K.C. arrived the next morning bright and early. I found her sitting in her car in the parking lot when I arrived at five minutes to nine.

"Good morning, K.C."

"Mornin,' Kid. Not much of an early riser huh?"

"Not at all."

"Tell ya what. After I've worked here for a little while, if you see fit, you can give me a key and I'll come in and clean up to get things started in the mornings. But only after I've earned your trust." She winked at me and we made our way into the shop.

I showed K.C. around, acquainted her with the cash register, basic phone skills, the cooler, delivery slips and procedures, and the fine art of bucket washing.

Allie arrived soon after and she and K.C. exchanged pleasantries. I showed K.C. how we make arrangements and in what order things should be done.

"Are you ready to go on your first delivery?" I asked.

"Ready and reporting for duty, Boss." She clicked her heels and saluted.

We got into the van with K.C. in the driver's seat. She carefully buckled up, adjusted the rearview and side mirror on her side and asked me to adjust the side mirror on the passenger side to her liking. The trustworthy van started right up and K.C. slowly edged us out of the parking lot.

We drove to Flannery's restaurant on the east side of town. I had a regular arrangement—pardon the pun—with the restaurant. My shop would put flowers on their front counter once a week, in exchange for referrals for weddings and special events, and the occasional free meal. Flannery's was a lavish and high-end eatery. They specialized in seafood flown in every morning from the West Coast to ensure freshness. They bragged an extensive wine list, which took five years of applications before the Alcoholic Beverage Commission of the State of Utah approved a license. The commission consisted of a majority of Mormons, with a teetotaler Catholic thrown in just for show.

Anyone who was anyone ate at Flannery's. It was the one place in the city where I could use high style design techniques with products such as antheriums, Vanda orchids and twenty-dollar-a-stem peonies to my heart's content.

The manager, Mickey Tanner, was at the counter. I usually made sure my driver got there before the lunchtime rush. It was great to take the delivery myself because I could catch up with all of the news I'd missed in the past month. Mickey was full of stories. Restaurants, salons and flower shops form the trifecta of sources for gossip in small towns.

"Hey, Mickey I'd like you to meet K.C. She's our new delivery driver."

"I'm pleased to meet you." He shook her hand. "Gorgeous as usual, Quincy. And you too, K.C. The flowers aren't bad either." He laughed like he always did when he made that joke. Mickey is as gay as the day is long, and the joke was predictable, but flattering.

"Quincy," he lowered his voice and tipped his head indicating that K.C. and I should gather in closer, "did you hear about that awful Derrick from Artful Blooms?"

Had I heard? He had no idea how intimately I knew the situation, but I wasn't going to talk about my arrest in front of K.C.

"I heard."

"Who are you talking about, and what happened to him?" K.C. whispered.

I let Mickey tell the story. He didn't leave out any feelings he may have felt toward Derrick. I'm sure Derrick had found a way to wrong Mickey in some way, just like everyone else he came in contact with.

At the end of the recap, K.C. stood straight up and looked at me for a moment. There was a long pause, and I thought we had definitely offended her. Suddenly, she let loose with a gasping, chortling explosion of the heartiest laugh I had ever heard. She was slapping her knee and wiping away tears.

"In a casket...with flowers!" she shouted amidst her guffaws. "That's the funniest thing I've ever heard of."

I felt a new appreciation for my driver. She really understood things the way that she should.

Mickey said, "Unfortunately he deserved to die in an

unpleasant manner. He was a nasty little man. Well, not so little after the *steroids,*" he crossed the back of his hand in front of his face and placed it next to his mouth, as if he were sharing a secret. "I have it on good authority from Thomas that he's been juicing up for quite a while now." Thomas was Mickey's life partner. "They go to the same gym. Or at least they did," he said out of the corner of his mouth then winked at K.C. She giggled.

"Does this man have any family?" K.C. asked.

"He did," I said "but they've moved out of state and disowned him as far as I know."

"Was he married?" she asked.

Mickey spoke up. "No he wasn't married, but he had a nice young beau on his arm for a few months. They used to come here together. They would get liquored up to the point we'd have to call a cab. But his friend always paid the bill, no problem. Derrick used to blab when he got tipsy, and talk about how the younger man fell into a bunch of money."

"His poor friend!" K.C. said with concern. "I bet he must be beside himself."

"Oh I don't think so. I got the strong impression that they broke up. Rumor was, it was a bad one. At least it must have been for the friend. Derrick was in here not a full week after the last time I saw him with the boy toy, with Camille LeFay. They had their hands all over each other."

"Who is Camille LeFay?" K.C.'s eyes were wide open and she hung on every word.

"Well I wouldn't want to call anybody names. Let's seeeee, how can I describe her?" He stroked his chin and looked upward, appearing to be thinking very hard. "The only words that come to mind are gold digger. She's a pro...so to speak." He mock coughed for emphasis after the innuendo. "She appears to be quite talented too. She's been Landon Powell's girlfriend, or escort or whatever she is, for at least a couple of years."

"*The* Landon Powell?" I asked.

"The one and only," he said. "About a month ago she was here every night of the week with either Gibbons or Powell."

"Who is Landon Powell?" K.C. asked, sounding confused.

"Landon Powell is a state senator. He grew up here and his family owns a lot of land. He's also a real estate developer, and what his family didn't originally own of this town, he has acquired through many years of dealings. He is very powerful and very well connected."

Landon Powell had tried to strong-arm my maternal grandfather into selling his farmland, which would have given him enough area to get the city council to rezone it so he could build a shopping mega-destination. My grandfather wouldn't sell and the deal fell through. Powell had resented my mom's family ever since.

"So let me get this straight," K.C. said. "This man Derrick, whom I gather neither of you liked very much, ends up face planting it in the final flower bed. Before this happens he's cavorting about town, first with a boy toy, and then with the mistress of some hoity-toity, too-big-for-his-britches politician. Have I got it right so far?" Mickey and I nodded. "Well all I can say is that this Derrick character must have had a pretty massive set of cojones."

"Except that the steroids must have shrunk them down to the size of pecans." I quipped.

"I have just one more question," K.C. said. Was Derrick gay or not?"

"Derrick was about as gay as my little sister with eight kids and one on the way," Mickey said. "Honey, he tasted the wine but he wasn't a connoisseur. Trust me, I know, I own the vineyard."

Mickey smiled wickedly when he saw K.C. blush and put her hand up to her mouth.

"Mickey, as always you have been an informative and

entertaining host. Now we need to be getting on our way. Thank you," I said.

"Anytime love. The flowers are magnificent by the way."

Once back at the shop Allie handed me the phone whispering, "It's for you."

"This is Quincy," I answered.

"Hello, Quincy," a soft, familiar voice responded. "This is LaDonna. I've called to offer an apology. I'm terribly embarrassed, but I heard about your recent visit and my husband's awful behavior."

"Well, thank you LaDonna but you don't owe me any apologies. I'm sure Irwin was just having a bad day." Of course I was thinking to myself that Irwin, not his wife, owed the apology but I wouldn't say that to the poor woman.

"Bad day or not, Quincy he shouldn't have treated you like that. He's a mean old grouch and I'm just about tired of having to apologize to our friends about the way he treats them. He just gets upset so fast." Her voice trembled as she spoke.

"LaDonna, I'm kind of worried about you."

"Oh dear, I didn't mean to upset you. I'm just a silly old woman. I cry when I see greeting card commercials on TV. Don't worry about me."

"You don't need to apologize. While I've got you on the phone, when can we meet so I can finish setting up your office?"

We decided on a time later that evening. I hoped Irwin wouldn't be there at the same time. His quickness to anger was looking like a bigger character flaw than at first glance. He had been so angry at just the mention of Derrick. Could he possibly have been angry enough to kill him?

After I ended the call with LaDonna, I turned my attention to managing my shop. We had the big gala coming up at the convention center, and we didn't need any last minute surprises.

When the fresh product arrived in a few days, the shop would process, hydrate and compose beautiful designs with the flowers. We would become rich and famous from all the buzz generated by new customers who saw what we created for the gala and wanted the same thing for themselves. Or at least, that was the plan. Not too much to expect, right?

K.C. was a huge help inventorying all the hardgoods for the big show, and she learned a lot of new terminology as she tried to locate all of the products on our master list for the event. She turned out the lights as I locked up for the night, and as she chirped out "see you tomorrow, Boss," I thanked my lucky stars to have found such a gem at the hair salon, of all places. She had been truly reliable, and I had the gut feeling I could trust her from the start. Unfortunately I'd had the same feeling about Alex, and I was *oh* so wrong about him.

CHAPTER SIXTEEN

The owner of Artful Blooms was *not* Derrick Gibbons, according to LaDonna Shaw.

When I arrived at the Shaw's flower shop after work, I was greeted by a very penitent Irwin. He apologized for getting so upset and taking his anger with Derrick out on me. As I worked on finishing all of the connections between their computer, their credit card terminal, point-of-sale system and their printer, they conversed and talked with me about their lives before being florists.

"Mother and I used to cover a lot of territory in some of our old jobs," Irwin said.

"We never went on any fancy vacations when the kids were young, but we got to see a lot of country on pick-up and delivery trips."

"What did you deliver?" I asked.

LaDonna interjected, "It sounds so crude to say it that way. We lived out in the rural areas in Southern Idaho, and in Arizona at one time. We would help the mortuaries transport the deceased."

"You transported dead bodies?"

"It was a great service," Irwin said. "In those rural areas, there might not be a mortuary around for hundreds of miles. So we started out working as transport for the mortuaries."

"How did you manage to heft the bodies?" I asked in

amazement. "I mean, you both seem very strong, but a dead body is really heavy." They both looked at me with surprise. "Or so I've heard."

"We had a specially outfitted vehicle with a hoist hooked to a winch, and we had the gurney and other equipment. Plus, the mortuary taught us how," Irwin said.

"He even got his own mortician's license, didn't you dear?" LaDonna smiled with pride at her husband.

Irwin blushed and looked away. "Hey, Quincy," he said, "there's a plate of chocolate chip cookies over there. Why don't you bring them over and we'll eat a few?"

"Sure," I said.

"Don't you dare, Quincy," LaDonna said sternly. "Irwin Shaw, you know you can't eat those cookies with you sugar diabetes. They can't regulate your insulin shots as it is."

"Oh, spoil sport." Irwin frowned like a grouchy little kid.

I tried to cut the tension in the air by talking. "Do you still do that kind of work?"

"Oh, heavens no," Irwin said. "That was years ago. We wouldn't be able to do that kind of work now."

I had all but finished figuring out login methods and easily remembered passwords for the Shaws. I just needed to compile a list of things to teach them and they could handle the system on their own. It was getting late though; both of them had heavy eyelids and they yawned as if in competition with one another.

"I think I should be on my way soon. I'll come back one more time to train you both how to use this whole thing, and then you should be in business. How does that sound?"

"Quincy, we can't thank you enough." Irwin said. "And I'm so sorry again about the other day. It's just that Derrick Gibbons caused a lot of heartache for our family. He's one person that just got the better of me, and I have a hard time forgiving. Please excuse me."

Irwin cleared his throat, as he was obviously emotional. At that moment a question popped into my mind, and I thought to myself that any normal person would see that now was not the time to ask that certain question. But I was not a normal person. I was a person of interest in a murder investigation, and I was a person who needed more sales, so I decided to ask.

"Irwin, I know this is probably not the right time to ask…there probably is no right time, but do you know who owns Artful Blooms?"

"Well it's not Derrick!" LaDonna burst out.

"Mother, calm down. Derrick always acted like it was him that owned it, but when our son bought this store from him, we did some looking and found out Derrick wasn't the owner of that other place."

"You mean Artful Blooms?" I asked.

"Yes. I started talking to Derrick about what I thought was kind of fishy business, and then he distracted me with all of the talk about an investment opportunity. At first he was looking for investors to share equally in the profits of a switch grass farm. What with all of the green this and green that, recycling and bio-fuel I was hearing about in the news, I thought it wouldn't be a bad investment. Except that it was with him. One night, he came to me while my son was away. He told me Bobby owed him a lot of money for this shop, and that he would tell everyone we knew about Bobby's…condition."

"His condition?"

"Oh," he swiped at his face and looked at the floor, "his messin' around with those…friends."

"Oh, right," I said, wanting him to keep talking. LaDonna's face twisted up and I knew she didn't agree with Irwin's attitude about their son.

"Well I didn't want him spreading the word around about Bobby, and I didn't want him to tell Mother about it. She was already worried enough about our son and his health. So I made a deal with Gibbons. I agreed to be the primary investor in the new farm, if he would agree to sign a paper saying that Bobby wasn't responsible for the debt from this flower shop." Irwin held his hands out, palms up, and the more he talked, the lower his arms dropped, as if he were physically trying to hold up the weight of his responsibilities.

"My son always had his head in the clouds; he thought he could run a flower shop just because his friend has one in Boise. Derrick saw him coming from a mile away. Anyway, I ended up paying for the entire farm because Derrick couldn't find any other investors, or so he said at the time, and now he's gone and got himself killed before we could sign the papers for Derrick to take on the sole debt for this shop."

"You're still paying for the flower shop now?" I asked.

"Well, no, we haven't paid since Bobby died." Irwin's voice grew shaky and he stifled the show of emotion. "It's his fault that Bobby is gone. And now he's gone too. That puts an end to things in my book."

"I see what you mean," I said, even though I didn't really understand.

I said goodnight to the Shaws and on the drive home I considered the new information I had about them and their previous work. Hauling dead bodies around? It certainly would come in handy if you were going to murder someone and then place the body in a mortuary. But Irwin was old and sometimes appeared to be feeble. I couldn't see him being able to handle the physical nature of that kind of job.

What was I thinking, anyway? These were sweet people who'd just had their lives blasted into pieces. Their son killed himself because of a scumbag, whom they then had to contend with because he had swindled their son in business. And to top it all off, they still owed him money, even though, by dying he wasn't around to collect the payments any more.

I would have to check Irwin Shaw off of my list of potential murderer's of Derrick Gibbons.   Unfortunately that kept my name on the short list, if I didn't find out who the real killer was.

Since Derrick was such a swindler, I figured that following the business trail from his shop—the one he didn't really own—was the way to find out who would have wanted him out of the picture.   It was obvious the funeral flower business hadn't been taken over by the Shaws.   I was going to have to go back to the source of the sales.   It was time for another trip to the mortuary, and this time I wasn't going to be stopped by the gatekeeper; I would go to the funeral director himself.

I stopped at my trusty local fast food restaurant on the way home. I was in no condition for healthy eating. What did I care if I gained a few pounds?   I didn't have a boyfriend to impress.

When I arrived home, I looked around extra cautiously for arsonists, polygamists or reckless drivers.   The coast appeared to be clear, but I still rushed in to my house, locked the deadbolts and peered into every closet, nook and cranny to make sure nobody hid in wait for me. I lifted the phone receiver and heard that I had at least one message. The first was from my mother's number, I skipped it for the time being. Maybe I'd skip it all together, I was pretty sure I didn't want to deal with anything she had to say.

The last message was a surprise, as it came from Danny Barnes' cell phone. It was unusual for him to call my home. I waited impatiently for the recording of his message to start. "Dolly, hello. I called your home phone because I didn't want anyone at your shop to over-hear any of this. I hate to leave this on a message, but I needed to tell you something as soon as possible. My brother has a buddy at Hillside Police who knows I own a flower shop. So, a few days ago, he asked if I could come and look at something and give my expert opinion.

"I'm sorry I didn't tell you about it earlier, but I just plain forgot about it with our wedding trauma today, and then I didn't want to mention it in front of Mr. Hottie Pants when the two of you came in the other day."

I made a mental note to ask him about the "wedding trauma" the next time I talked to him. It probably amounted to someone thinking his prices were too high.

"My dear, they had me come and look at the casket spray that was on top of Derrick's casket. I went down there and had a look...and I don't quite know how to say this, but... it looked like one of yours. The flowers look like your style, but Quincy dear... it was the ribbon with that tacky old gold lettering on the banner. You're the only one around here who has that kind."

Danny was talking about the lettering we put on a ribbon to recognize the deceased. Typical banners might say "Beloved Husband," "Loving Wife," or something similar. It was either write with glue and glitter or use the adhesive gold lettering. I didn't think my lettering was tacky, and Aunt Rosie had left a ton of it at the shop. I didn't see any point in buying new just because Danny didn't like it.

"Now, I'm not saying you did anything, and don't worry, I told them I couldn't be sure, due to the fact it had been a few days since it was made. But you and I both know it looks like you made the flowers. I recognized your style instantly...just as easily as I can tell a Louis Vuitton knock-off from a mile away. Oh, which reminds me, you have got to see my new carryall. It's like a purse, but it's for a man, so I call it my murse. Oops, I got off track. Anyway, I thought you needed some warning. I had to give them some names—I was *forced* to! So I just gave them a list of all the florists in the area, and unfortunately you were on it. Sorry to be the bearer of bad news, but better to come from me than a police detective. Call me, dear. Bye."

I couldn't expect Danny to lie to the police for me, and I'm glad he thought to list other suspects. It was the same as looking at the listings in the phone book. But, eventually the police would go down the list until they eliminated everyone but me. Even *I* knew it wasn't likely anyone else had that old-fashioned banner lettering.

I decided to torture myself a little more by drilling down my own list of things that had happened to me in the space of the last week. A call from a psycho cop, a hit-and-run, a flaming bag of stink on my porch, a burning bush, an arrest, a car chase and Alex.

Alex. My heart hurt in my chest at the tiniest whisper of a thought of him.

So I thought about something else.

I thought about how I might look in orange.

Orange, because that's what prison inmates wear on TV. Or maybe the women prisoners wore those drab blue smocks—I didn't want to wear a smock.

I needed to pick up the pace on my own investigation before the police made it down Danny's list. This wasn't just about sales anymore. This was about finding the real killer on my own, so I wouldn't wake up in my denim blue smock in a bunk below a roommate named Crazy Sal every day for the rest of my life.

CHAPTER SEVENTEEN

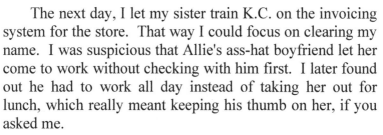

The next day, I let my sister train K.C. on the invoicing system for the store. That way I could focus on clearing my name. I was suspicious that Allie's ass-hat boyfriend let her come to work without checking with him first. I later found out he had to work all day instead of taking her out for lunch, which really meant keeping his thumb on her, if you asked me.

I wanted to find out who really owned Artful Blooms flower shop, and to know how or if that owner was connected to the mortuary. Doing a computer search hadn't led me to the owner, but I remembered that my cousin Jeff worked for the State Office of Corporations. He had access to all the information about corporations in the state, which were public record, and he would probably know how to get the information I needed.

"Looks like the name of the principle officer is L.D. Stanwyck." Jeff said.

"What do the initials stand for?" I asked.

"Actually, it's just L.D.," he said. "That's all I can see anyway."

"Thanks Jeff, I owe you. Come in to the shop and pick up a bouquet for your wife sometime, on the house."

L.D. Stanwyck was the same name that appeared on the paychecks from Artful Blooms, according to Derrick's designer. I needed to find out the identity of this L.D.

person, to see how he was connected to Derrick. My next visit would be to the Hansen Mortuary, where I would ask about the mystery owner's identity.

I turned into the mortuary parking lot around eleven-thirty a.m. Interior lights glowed behind the glass entrance doors. A silver Audi I didn't recognize was parked in the main customer lot. I parked in the back, near a beat up burgundy mini-van. Gaylen Smith's beat up mini-van. Gaylen Smith was the glad-handing, backslapping manager of the Hillside location of the mortuary.

I carefully opened the flower door, looked both ways, and walked past the no-florists-allowed sign. I snuck into the secret hallway that links the back room to the front offices and eased open the door leading to the main foyer. Gaylen hovered in his office stuffing bridge mix from the glass bowl on his desk into his mouth.

"All right Gaylen! What gives?"

"What are you talking about, Quincy?" he said through a wad of chocolate.

"I want to know why nobody will answer my questions about Derrick around here. It's bad enough you guys just dropped off the face of the earth when it came to ordering from me, but now you don't have a florist and I want to know what you're going to do about it." We wouldn't broach the subject of my murder investigation just yet.

"I don't see as how it's any of your business, Quincy."

"You don't see? You don't see how trying to get back almost half of the sales I used to make is any of my business?" I took an aggressive step toward Gaylen. I used my height to my advantage; he was only five foot six at most. He shrunk back; I had him cornered.

I softened my voice and my approach. "Listen, Gaylen. You and I have known each other for a long time. You know my parents, and I know yours. In fact, your parents are customers of mine, unless they're buying funeral flowers—the way things are now. I know that you guys have a need for a good, reliable florist, and I need more sales to stay afloat. So what do you say we help each other out?"

"I wish I could help you, Quincy, I really do, but my hands are tied. Greg Schilling is the boss, and he's the one you'll have to talk to about flowers, and even I have a hard time getting into to see him these days."

"Bull." I said.

"What do you mean *bull*?"

"You've managed this location long enough to have some say in which florist you use. And can you honestly tell me you would have let a close family member go through Derrick's shop, and pay him the exorbitant amount of money he wanted for shoddy, ugly work? Can you honestly say that to me Gaylen?"

"Well, no...I...listen, Quincy, no matter what you think, I don't have any say in who we use for vendors. I can't do a thing about it."

"You've given me no choice, Gaylen. You want to play that way? I'll play that way. What if I told you that I happen to know of a certain mortuary that has recycled expensive floor model caskets, putting the bodies in a cheaper casket once the family has left the graveside service?"

Gaylen was red in the face and he was sweating profusely.

"How could you possibly know that? What is it about florists and blackmailing? First Derrick and now you?" Gaylen whined.

"Blackmailing? How did Derrick blackmail anyone?" I opened my eyes and did my best Bambi impression.

"Ohhh, Quincy I've already said enough."

"Recycled caskets Gaylen," I said in a singsong voice.

"Okay, okay. It's not like I do it all the time, by the way. The casket the family had picked out was a special order, and that stupid Doug was supposed to order it, or the secretary, or one of the two, but they were too busy...fooling around to get it ordered in time. So when it came time for the family viewing, I had to use one that I had on display, until the new one arrived."

"Wait," I said, "you know about Linda and Doug?"

"Of course I do. Everyone around here knows about it." He sounded like I was the only one who *didn't* know. "So anyway, I didn't really recycle a casket that someone had paid for, it just bought me some time. No one ever knew about it, at least I thought—how did you know about it?"

I had actually put a lot of faith in a hunch that ended up paying off. I thought I had seen a scratch on the casket when I placed the flowers on top of it before the viewing. About two weeks later, I thought I saw the same scratch in the same place for another viewing. I didn't know if Gaylen was being truthful, but I thought it possible he wasn't lying. I told him about the scratch in hopes of a mutual exchange of information.

If my information got out to the public, the mortuary would be in big trouble. They would probably be sued by every family that had ever used their services—well maybe that was a bit of a stretch. But it probably violated some kind of state law to reuse caskets.

"So what were you saying about Derrick and blackmail?" I asked.

Gaylen sighed, then wiped his brow. "Okay, Quincy, but you have to promise it doesn't leave this room."

"I promise."

"Derrick knew about Doug's affairs."

"You mean with Linda?"

"And Mrs. Powell."

"You mean..."

"*That* Mrs. Powell."

"Great gossip fodder, without question, but who at the mortuary would care?"

"Doug's not just any employee. He's Greg Schilling's stepson."

"So, his stepson is a dirt bag. So what?" I asked.

"Doug is the only one to carry on the family business for one thing, and it wouldn't be such a good idea to have Mr. Powell on our bad side. That's all I can tell you about it, Quincy."

I assumed Gaylen meant it was bad to have a high-ranking political official on your bad side if you wanted their business, but then I realized they were probably high ranking officials in the church together too. It would have been too much to try to wrap my head around the depths of hypocrisy reached by this lot of people.

"Okay, okay, I won't ask anymore about the Powells, but what did that have to do with Derrick?" I asked.

"Derrick and Doug were two peas in a pod. They went to school together, lifted weights, drove their stupid trucks down in Moab together, all of that. Derrick knew about Doug's...relationships, and he came and told me about it. I didn't really care too much when it was the secretary, I could fire her any minute, but when he started talking about Mrs. Powell, I talked to Greg about it. We worked out a little arrangement with Derrick for flowers. Now that's it, Quincy, don't ask me anymore, I've already told you enough. And if I hear that someone else knows about this little secret between you and me; there will be hell to pay. Mark my words."

He looked at me with evil eyes. I didn't want to ask him who the new florist would be. It finally occurred to me that I didn't want to have any type of involvement with these corrupt men. I thanked Gaylen for his explanation, and told him my lips would be sealed. I didn't intend to share this information with anyone. I wondered if Derrick had said too much to the wrong person and it ended up getting him killed. And who better than morticians to know how to embalm someone? In fact, there really couldn't be anyone else—could there? Placing the body in their own mortuary was a brilliant idea. No one would suspect them for putting him there.

It was time to leave, tout de suite.

As I walked toward the exit, I saw a Porsche pull up next to the Audi in the customer parking lot. It was Derrick's Porsche. I recognized it well after the paint-keying incident. A woman got out of the passenger side, just as Linda pulled up in her black Lexus.

The mystery woman wore a camel colored dress suit with a three quarter length skirt and matching jacket with pleated shoulders. She had a pastel pink blouse with ribbons attached at the neck meant to tie a floppy bow. It was office wear from the early nineties. The two strips of fabric of the untied bow flapped in the breeze.

The loose ends of fabric fell at odds with the rest of her image, especially the dowdy pumps and just-so helmet of dark brown shoulder length hair. Those precisely parted and feathered bangs weren't going anywhere in the breeze. She looked like the librarian at the county headquarters and not someone who had just stepped out of a Porsche.

Linda got out of her car. The icy glare coming from her eyes was deadly—if looks could kill, the librarian would have had icicle daggers protruding from her chest. The mystery woman used her own set of keys to unlock the Audi. As soon as she got into the car, the Porsche screeched out of the parking lot.

Linda walked toward the mortuary, passing me without saying a word. I don't think she saw me, her eyes were practically glowing red and it looked as if steam would start spraying out of her ears.

I needed nourishment after the intense confrontation with Gaylen. I drove to the Bulgy Burger. I had contemplated Skinny's, but I knew Elma would ask about Alex, and I didn't want to see her, or her blue-eye-shadowed-lids emphasizing her deliverance of the stink eye in my direction.

As I sat, ploughing my way through a large Coke and double bacon cheeseburger with steak fries, I compiled a list of things I would need to figure out:

Murderer?
#1 Suspects- Hansen Mortuary-not Gaylen/who else?
Who is L.D. Stanwyck?
New $ for shop

The first thing was the list of murder suspects. I was fairly confident in moving the morticians from the Hansen mortuary to the top spot. Maybe not Gaylen, but he definitely knew something he was afraid to tell me. Usually I could get Gaylen on a roll and he would talk about anything ad infinitum. But this time he wouldn't say any more. The next thing was to find out the true identity of L.D. Stanwyck.

The last thing I added to my list was the need to find some new income. I had to face it. I wasn't going to get any funeral work referrals from the Hansen mortuary ever again. The upcoming gala would be even more important than I had thought. I had to impress the attendees.

I returned to the shop with a bag full of doughnuts from Bulgy's.

"Oh you should have," K.C. said when she saw the distinctly designed paper bag.

"Have a doughnut, Allie," I said. "Since you won't let me pay you enough, I'll make it up in doughnuts."

She laughed, "Thanks, but no thanks. I'm watching my weight."

K.C. rolled her eyes. "I'm watching my weight too. I watching it go right into my mouth with every bite, and I'm exquisitely pleased every time that I do. That's okay Kiddo," she said to Allie, "it just leaves more for me and the head honcho here."

"It looks like you guys have been busy," I said.

"Indeed we have," K.C. said. "I decided I should be able to help around the shop and not just do deliveries. I've been washing buckets and keeping things stocked. I thought I might be able to start arranging flowers soon, or at least learning how. Allie here showed me how to do a bud vase with a rose and baby's breath."

"Really?" I said. "How did she do, Allie?"

"She was great for a first-timer."

"Oh pah-lease. Boss, I owe you two an apology. I thought to myself 'K.C., how hard could this be?' and now I know. This is hard stuff."

"Don't worry, it takes time. We can practice a little every day. You'll get the hang of it." I said.

"Quincy, if you don't mind I'd like to take off soon," Allie said.

"Sure, no problem. Are you going to go help Mom get ready for her book club group?"

"How did you know about that?" Allie asked.

"She left a message for me last night inviting me to come. She's invited Ned Bunchkin to be there, I'm sure it's in hopes of setting us up."

"Eww, Nasty Ned from down the street?"

"That's the one."

"Who is Nasty Ned from down the street?" K.C. asked.

"He's this guy that lives in his parent's basement in our old neighborhood," Allie said. "He's six years older than our older sister and he plays video games all day. He used to have a booger collection he would show to all the neighborhood kids."

I shuddered at the thought of sitting on the loveseat at my mother's house next to Nasty Ned.

"I somehow doubt that Ned has taken a sudden interest in "Diary of a Pioneer Wife," I said. "She thinks she's helping me find a husband. You didn't have any part in this great idea did you, Allie?"

"No, I swear. In fact, I was going to tell you I want to leave because Brad called. He's coming home early and we're going to go out shopping together."

"Oh, great. Have a good time." I said. It wasn't a gleaming endorsement, but I wasn't going to fight with Allie about Brad, especially since she had come in early to work for me.

"K.C.," Allie called from the back door, "you were excellent today! You'll be our head designer in no time."

"Thanks, Kiddo."

The ringing phone interrupted us and K.C. went into the back room.

"Rosie's Posies, this is Quincy."

"Oh good, Quincy, it's you."

I recognized the voice of Linda, from the mortuary.

"What's up Linda?"

"Are you somewhere private?"

"Um...yeah, let me move into my office."

"Quincy, I'm calling you from home."

"Why?"

"I couldn't risk anyone overhearing me. Besides, I left the mortuary. I can't go back there," her voice cracked on the last word.

"Linda, what's wrong? What happened?"

"It's Doug, my boyfriend. I caught him with someone else yesterday."

"I'm so sorry." I didn't know why she was calling me about this, but I didn't mind.

"If it hadn't been in our regular spot it wouldn't have been so bad. But I walked in on them in the embalming room."

Eww. I shuddered involuntarily at the thought of anyone doing anything there, but especially *it,* and at the thought of walking in on someone doing *it* there and I shuddered again at the thought of someone calling the room their regular spot—for *it.*

"Linda, I don't know what to say." That was no lie.

"I guess I'm just telling you this because I don't have anyone else to tell," she cleared her throat, "and because I know who he had up on that embalming table."

Ahhh!

Linda's voice was not so sobby anymore. Now, it was steeled with anger. "That whore Lucinda Powell was giving it like a porn star when I opened the door."

"Linda!"

"Quincy, when I passed you earlier today in the parking lot, the other woman that was leaving was the whore. They were just flaunting their relationship in my face today. Yesterday, I had just bought a new tie for Doug on my lunch break and I put it on to surprise him, you know..."

Oh please don't tell me the rest.

She continued. "Gaylen had gone to lunch, so I turned off the hall cameras and snuck downstairs, and then I took everything off and tied the tie around my neck. I wanted it to be like I was a big present all wrapped up in a bow."

"Uh-huh," I said feebly, knowing she wasn't going to stop.

"So I opened the door," her voice got shaky again, "and I yelled 'untie this package hot stuff,' and," her voice cracked and she bawled out the rest almost unintelligibly, "there they were. He stood with his bare ass facing me with a pair of naked legs and sensible shoes wrapped around him."

"Linda, this is awful." Awful to listen to. "I'm so sorry."

"Quincy, I called you because you came around before and asked me about the mortuary's involvement with Derrick. I've just had it with all of them. The only reason I didn't tell their secrets before is because I've been protecting Doug. I thought we had a future together."

He was twenty years younger than Linda and it sounded like he boinked everything in sight, but she thought they had a future together. *Foolish woman.*

"You've always been good to me and my family, and you've put up with a lot of crap from that mortuary, so I'm going to help you out."

"Linda, I appreciate your wanting to help me, but I'm confused. Why are you telling me about your boyfriend?"

"Well, I've heard about the trouble you are in, Quincy."

"What trouble?"

"The arrest and how you're in trouble because of Derrick and his car and the argument."

So she knew a few things about me. I shouldn't be surprised. For some reason the people at the mortuary know everything about everyone. They probably had my mother and her network on the payroll as consultants.

Linda went on. "Well okay, there are a couple of things that I haven't told you. First of all, my boyfriend…I mean my ex-boyfriend Doug works for the mortuary. I didn't want to tell you this then, but when you came before, he and I had just been…together. But he had to leave to take care of an emergency." The afternoon tryst, I remembered it well, cringing at the memory of my unfortunate groping incident apparently occurring at the same time as Linda's much more invited groping incident.

"Anyway, Doug went to school with Derrick Gibbons, and Derrick's father always knew Greg Schilling very well. A few years ago, the mortuary opened their little secret business and they made Doug the manager. He and I had been seeing each other for about four months then. He used to work here in Hillside with me and then they transferred him up there to manage that location, just when we were starting to get to know each other."

"Wait, which location was he transferred to? The secret business?"

"It's a discount mortuary that caters to people who don't have a lot of money for services."

"Isn't that most of the people who live in Hillside?" I

asked.

"Well, the Hansens don't really advertise, they mostly just refer people there when they know people aren't going to be able to pay the regular rates for services. They basically provide a pine box and a small room where the next of kin can say goodbye for an hour. There's no graveside service or viewing or music or anything like that."

"So the mortuary wasn't satisfied with being the only gig in town, so they decided to use the new place to provide services that they would have provided for almost nothing in the past, but now they charge enough to run another location."

"Pretty much." Linda said.

"Where is this place? I never knew they had another location."

"Like I said, they don't advertise it. It's about three miles south of their main location in Ogden, on the same side of the road."

"They're on the same street? That seems bizarre. Why wouldn't I just stop in at the cheaper mortuary if I lived in Ogden?"

"It's not named after the Hansens, its called Lawson's. And that's all that's printed on the sign. Nothing else. Like I said, they only work with referrals. Most people don't even know it's there." She had a good point, I'd driven past there a hundred times and had no idea it existed.

Lawson's? Why did that name sound so familiar? "Why Lawson's?" I wondered out loud.

"It's Doug's biological father's last name. The Hansens let him name the business since he would be running it. He doesn't run it anymore though. His jerk stepfather demoted him. I was going to go be Doug's secretary, but his stepfather said they needed me more here. Not that I care anymore, the lying little prick."

"Who is Doug's stepfather?"

"Greg Schilling," she said as if I should have known.

"Isn't Doug's last name Lawson? That's why he named the new business Lawson's...right?"

"No. Doug's mother always used her maiden name for the family until she married Greg. Greg Schilling is Doug's stepfather," she said impatiently. "The Hansens take care of their family, even if they're not blood related, or if they don't like them very much. Greg hates Doug, but he tolerates him. In fact, I'm thinking that's why they stuck him in the new location at first. They probably wanted to get him out of their hair, but Greg's wife makes sure that Doug still has his hand in the family business."

"How is Greg Schilling related to the Hansen's?"

"His mother is a Hansen. She's a daughter of the original founder."

"I'm confused. So, do they provide flowers at the new discount mortuary too?"

"No."

Argh! "So what does this whole extensive genealogy chart have to do with Derrick?"

"Oh yeah, the reason I called was to tell you about Derrick. I wanted to tell you earlier, but I couldn't because I was afraid someone would overhear me. Anyway, now that I don't care if I lose my job, I'm going to tell you. About a year ago Greg had a staff meeting with all of us. He told us we were supposed to recommend Derrick's flower shop and no one else's period. If we were caught recommending someone else, we would be fired."

After talking with Gaylen I knew why. It must have been part of Derrick's blackmail deal.

"After you left that day, I got to thinking about things, and I remembered something I saw one time. I got to looking through some of the files and found a large deduction in the new location's bank account right about the time that Derrick opened his shop. I don't know this for sure, but I think maybe the mortuary provided the startup money for Derrick's business."

I didn't want to reveal everything I had learned from my conversation with Gaylen, so I played along until I learned more. "But you would think Derrick would be paying it back somehow, especially with a percentage of his sales."

"I thought of that, Quincy, but I can't find record of payments anywhere. And believe me, I've looked."

Derrick hadn't been giving a percentage back because of his blackmailing deal. The connection between the mortuary and Derrick's murder appeared to be growing more obvious. The mortuary was sick of paying Derrick to keep his mouth shut about Doug—Linda's boyfriend who was also schtupping with the politician's wife and who was the stepson of the mortuary's main manager—so they just got rid of Derrick. I might actually have figured it out.

"Linda, I had just finished a meeting with Gaylen when I passed you coming out of the mortuary earlier. He told me they worked out a special arrangement with Derrick for flowers." I didn't tell her it was due to Doug's dalliances with Mrs. Powell, Linda would have had a melt down.

"Oh Quincy, don't you believe a word that comes out of that fathead's mouth. He still thinks he's next in succession to take over any new manager positions that come up. The Hansen's keep it in the family and Gaylen refuses to see that. He's an ass-kisser and he'll say whatever Greg Schilling tells him to."

I expressed my condolences to Linda about her boyfriend's infidelities and thanked her for all of the insider information. After hanging up I was left with more questions about the mortuary than had been answered. And now I had two different versions of the story regarding Derrick and his flowers. I tended to believe Linda, since she was willing to give me all the gory details, whether I wanted them or not, but I had made Gaylen squirm enough that it seemed he was giving me details he would have preferred to keep to himself.

It was time to take a look at the ledger I had borrowed from Derrick's box of leaf shine. I walked to the bathroom and opened the little closet where I kept an extra supply of toilet paper, tampons and paper towels. This seemed like the place least likely to be explored by a certain male detective that might make up another reason to arrest me and search my shop while I sat there waiting to be rescued.

I opened the ledger, and stuck to the front page was the little sticky note with the phone number from Derrick's designer.

"That's it!" I was so excited at remembering the forgotten connection I couldn't help saying it out loud.

"Hey Boss...you okay in there?"

I had forgotten about K.C.

"Stanwyk. L.D. Stanwyk," I said as I came out of the bathroom. K.C. looked at me with concern.

"The D. stands for Doug! He owns the flower shop; it's on the corporate papers that my cousin looked up for me."

"Boss, I'm old and batty as a belfry, but I think you just might have passed me up in the cuckoo of the year contest."

I explained what I had been told about Derrick's flower shop and who owed what to whom. She nodded her head in understanding.

"So, this frisky young buck used money from the business he was running to pay for Derrick's flower shop, and nobody has made any type of payments back to the mortuary?"

"Right."

"It sounds to me like someone was made to pay up." K.C. gesticulated while she spoke and the bucket brush she still clutched bounced through the air. "Derrick couldn't pay back the bill to his friend, who risked being kicked out of the family business. I can see where the friend might take offense to that situation."

"Linda told me there was a large withdrawal from the business Doug was running. It happened around the same time as Derrick opened his shop. I thought Derrick was getting the referrals from the mortuary to help him have enough money to pay back the investment in the flower shop. But according to both Gaylen and Linda, Derrick didn't pay anything back. Why would any business person, smart or not, just give the money to someone to finance a business, without receiving any payments?"

"He was a charitable guy?" K.C. said.

"Doubtful," I said.

"Blackmail?"

"Probable. That's what Gaylen Smith said." I helped stack the clean, dry buckets on a shelf. "K.C. what do we know about Derrick?"

"Let's see. He was a buddy with the guy that was sleeping with the secretary and the real estate developer's wife."

"The real estate developer who is also a powerful politician," I added.

"Derrick was also sleeping with the politician's girlfriend," K.C. reminded.

"Did the politician know that his wife was doing the deed with someone?" I asked.

"That's a good question. If I was that mortuary I would try to keep every thing that stallion did in the stable. It wouldn't be good to have the guy who's in charge of everything in this state mad at you. The guy is a real estate tycoon. If there's anyone who pulls the strings in this town it's the guy who controls the land." She put her wrists against her hips with elbows out and scratched at the ground with her "hoof" while making neighing sounds.

"K.C., you're right," I said through my laughter, "a little strange, but right."

"You're probably right about that, Boss," she winked and laughed along with me.

I called Linda back. First I asked her what Doug's mother's maiden name was and she confirmed it was

Stanwyck. I also asked her if the mortuary was involved in any real estate ventures. She told me they had been working on a plan to build a brand new mortuary and a cemetery somewhere on the east end of Hillside, whenever the right piece of land came up. She said the drawings were beautiful if they could ever get the right zoning to go through.

"Linda, I have to apologize ahead of time for this, but it would really help me to figure something out. Do you think Landon Powell knew anything about his wife and Doug?"

"Well I didn't even know about it, Quincy, so I can't imagine he did. I'm sure she told him she was going to some church meeting every time she met up with Doug. I'll tell you one thing I do know. Doug was an embarrassment to Greg. Greg did everything he could to push Doug into the background and hide him from people."

I thanked Linda again and apologized for bringing up such a delicate subject. She was very gracious, but made it clear she wouldn't be talking about Doug Stanwyck Lawson Schilling ever again.

I gathered some jewelry tools and sat at the back design table cutting lengths of decorative wire that I would later curl into funky shapes for use in the gala arrangements. K.C. grabbed a towel and some window cleaner to polish the few remaining pieces of new glassware she had unpacked. "Well?" She blurted out.

"Well, what?"

"What did you find out?"

"Oh, sorry. I got lost in thought about what Linda told me. Doug was Derrick's buddy. Gaylen told me they were two peas in a pod. They must have bragged about conquests to each other. We can probably assume Doug bragged about sleeping with two cougars at once. Linda, who would have been a great conquest for him because he was sleeping with his stepfather's secretary who knew everything about the entire mortuary's business, and Mrs. Powell, who is married to one of the most powerful men in the state."

K.C. flipped the towel over her shoulder. "He would have crowed like the cock in a hen house to someone." I waited for her to put her hands on her hips again and crow. She refrained.

"Right. But we also know from what Mickey at the restaurant told us, that Derrick was dating Camille LeFay at one point, who was a mistress to Landon Powell. Why would Derrick, who had previously been dating the Shaw's *son,* suddenly want to date the mistress of a very powerful man who must have a huge ego, and huge connections?"

"We're back to blackmail aren't we?"

"Yes, I think we are," I said. "Derrick knew Powell's wife was sleeping with Doug. He knew how much this would embarrass the mortuary, who probably wanted to keep good relations going with the guy who could make influential real estate deals including the space for a new cemetery. He got a new flower shop with guaranteed customer business in trade for him not going to Landon Powell with his findings."

"Boss, you're one smart cookie."

"I don't know how smart. I can't figure out why Derrick would risk the sweet little business arrangement of his by dating Landon Powell's mistress. You'd think he'd want to lay low and make some money."

"Unless he was completely crazy," K.C. said. "Or…unless there was a bigger whale to fry."

"Yeah. I think I know who that whale is—I just need to figure out for sure why Derrick and Doug would risk messing with him."

The bells sounded on the front door. A seventy-ish year old woman came in. "Hi, how can I help you?" I asked her as I approached from behind the counter.

"I'm just looking!" She shouted at me.

"Okay, well feel free to let me know if you have any questions." I said politely then retreated to the design room.

"I don't know; I don't see anything I like." She waited

until I had reached the back counter to start talking.

I rolled my eyes, then painted a smile on my face and turned to go back to her.

"Can I help you to find something, or would you like to look at some pictures?"

"Well I don't know how else I'm supposed to order anything."

Great. I took a deep breath and walked over to the table with the big selection books from the wire-service companies with photographs of flower arrangements in them.

"What's the occasion?" I asked in a sweet as molasses voice.

"I need a funeral arrangement for my neighbor. We took up a collection from forty people in the ward and we want it to be nice."

"Okay, let's look at some of these pictures and see if there is something you like."

I opened the book and we looked at the pictures. All the photographs of arrangements had price stickers below them.

"How big is this one here?" The woman asked.

"It's approximately 24 inches high and 18 inches wide." I explained, even though the dimensions were printed next to the picture.

"Is that a nice one? I don't want to send something small, I want it to look, well, you know."

What she meant to say is that she wanted it to look big. She wanted it to look bigger and fuller than everyone else's, but she didn't want to pay more than everyone else.

"How much will twenty-five dollars get us?" she asked.

I showed her a very small planter that cost twenty-five dollars.

"Is that all?" she said incredulously. "How about this one, I like this, how much would it be?" she asked, pointing to a large picture in the book.

"That floral spray would be two hundred dollars." I told her nicely, even though she was pointing right at the price with her index finger. I could tell by her grimace she thought the price was too high.

"How about this," I said, "since you took a collection, tell me how much you have and I'll make something that looks similar for whatever amount you collected. It might be smaller in size, but we'll use the same colors and shapes of flowers."

"I've collected thirty-five dollars." Interesting, she collected from forty people and only came up with thirty-five dollars.

"Okay then, we'll make a spray for thirty-five dollars. What day will you need it for?"

"Well the viewing is on Sunday, the funeral is on Monday. Will you get it there on Sunday?"

"Yes we can get it there on Sunday for the viewing."

"Now I don't want you making this ahead and delivering it on Saturday, I want the flowers to be fresh." Of course, none of the wholesalers are open Saturday, so no matter which day the flowers were actually put into a container, they would be the same age, and would have been sitting in the cooler for the same amount of time as the flowers I didn't use. But it would be a waste of time for me to try and explain.

"I would be happy to deliver these flowers on Sunday afternoon for you," I said sweetly.

"Oh, I forgot. How does that work?"

"How does what work?" I plastered the most patient look on my face that I could come up with.

"I'm sure you don't work on Sunday, so how will you get the flowers there?"

"I'll have to come in and make them and then deliver them on Sunday," I said.

"Oh, no. I'll not have flowers from the ward being made on the Sabbath," she shut her eyes and set her lower jaw.

"Well ma'am, if I don't make them on Sunday, I'll need to make them on Saturday, which you asked me not to do."

"Oh. I suppose if you make them up on Saturday, late on Saturday evening, but then you'll be working on Sunday by driving. And I simply won't pay for something that will break the Sabbath day, I won't."

"How about this? I won't charge you for delivery, and I'll make the flowers on Saturday. When I come down to the shop on Sunday to pick up my newspaper, I'll just run in and grab the flowers and take them to the mortuary on my way home."

"I suppose that would work. But if anyone were to ask, you wouldn't tell them you delivered them on Sunday?"

"My lips are sealed."

"All right then."

We finally finished the transaction and I pulled the money from her cheapskate grip of steel and put it into the cash register. I watched the customer walk all the way out to her car before I turned to K.C.

"Can you believe that?"

"Oh I can believe it. I went to high school with that shrew."

"Why didn't you come out and talk to her? You could have rescued me."

"Heck, as soon as I saw her get out of her car, I hid. That old hypocrite. I could hear her telling you not to break the Sabbath on her account. That woman nearly runs me over every Sunday after church when she drives down to the grocery store to buy things for Sunday dinner."

"Speaking of hypocrites," I said, "I keep thinking about Landon Powell."

"What about him?" K.C. asked.

"We know he's got a girlfriend on the side."

"He's a politician, what do you expect?"

"He's also one of the higher ups in the church."

"Nothing new about that either, Boss. People can behave badly, make mistakes…sin, even, at every level of the human hierarchy."

"There's something missing. What's the connection between Powell and Derrick?"

"Oh Boss, don't make me be vulgar. The connection is the woman between them. Well I don't literally mean between them. I couldn't assume that they were into that kind of kinky stuff. Anyway what I'm trying to say is they both dated the same girl."

"Yeah, what does Camille LeFay have to do with all this? And why would Derrick risk everything and switch from a boyfriend to a girlfriend under such suspicious timing?"

My cell phone interrupted our musings. I answered and couldn't hear anyone on the other end.

"Hello? Helloow!" I said impatiently.

A whisper voice replied, "Quincy, can you hear me?"

"Allie? Where are you?"

She whispered again, "I'm at Brad's condo."

"Allie, why are you whispering?" I was afraid to ask, because I knew the answer.

"You were right, Quincy," her voice sounded on the verge of crying, but there was too much fear present for her to give in, "he hasn't changed."

"Is he there in the house?"

"No he said he was leaving for 15 minutes. He has my car keys. He doesn't know I have this phone. I haven't used it since we've been back together. I hid it just in case."

Deep in her heart she'd known he wouldn't change.

"I'm coming to get you. Try to go to a safe place and barricade yourself in."

"He said he was going down to the store for a minute. But he said not to try anything stupid like leaving because he would catch me."

"I'll be right there."

I turned to K.C., "It's Allie. Her boyfriend has beaten her up again. You stay here while I go and get her."

"Hold on, Boss. I'm not sitting here while you go running head on like a bull with a bee-sting at a wife-beater. I'm coming with you. I know a thing or two about his type. My husband never laid a hand on me, but his brother used to go after his own wife, until we showed up one day and surprised him. After that my husband made sure I knew how to take care of myself." She hurried over and grabbed her purse. "I'll drive, you just give me directions and get yourself ready."

"Okay," I said with uncertainty.

We hustled out and I locked the door behind us.

When we got into K.C.'s car she opened the glove box and reached in. Her hand came out with a little canister. "Here, take this and use it when the time comes." I took it from her and read while she started the car and tore out of the parking lot.

It was a can of pepper spray. I had the feeling things were going to get ugly.

"How will I know when the time has come?" I held the can carefully, afraid it would spray me.

"Oh, you'll know. Trust me, and yourself."

K.C. and I arrived at the gate in front of the "community" of condominiums where Brad lived. We had to stop at the guard shack and tell him why we were there. I hadn't thought about this before we left my store.

"Afternoon, how can I help you ladies?" said the guard.

My heart jumped into my throat, I'm not a good liar and all I could think to say was, *We're here to rescue my sister from the jerk that lives here*. But that probably wouldn't get us through the gates. We could ram through I supposed.

K.C. piped up without missing a beat. "We're here to visit my granddaughter Allie McKay. She's staying here with her boyfriend..."

"Brad" I whispered.

"Brad. You'll have to excuse me, I'm used to her calling him Sweetie all of the time. I guess you don't have a Sweetie that lives here do you?" She smiled coyly at the guard.

He blushed and chuckled. "Not that I know of, but I know who you're talking about. I don't call him Sweetie though."

K.C. and I laughed along with him.

"Go on ahead. Have a nice day ladies." With that he waved and we waved and the automated gate slowly started to swing open.

We pulled up to the condo and as I went to open the door, K.C. grabbed my arm.

"Wait!"

"C'mon, K.C. we've got to go while Brad is gone."

"Just hold your horses. I need you to reach into the back and grab the Enforcer for me. It hurts my bursitis to reach over the seat like that."

"The what?"

"Just reach down on the floor there behind the seat."

I thought it was a strange time to go searching around in the car, but I reached down and lifted up a Louisville Slugger.

"The Enforcer?" I asked.

"Do you think I would go on those out of town field trips on the bus without protection? This has been my constant companion for years."

"I am not rushing into that house toting a baseball bat. I just want to get my sister and get out of here."

"Suit yourself, Boss. But I'm bringing my old pal."

"Fine."

We went up to the door and knocked. No one answered for what felt like forever. Just as I started to think about what to do next, the bolt on the door opened and Allie peeked out.

"C'mon, Allie lets go," I said.

She stood there not saying anything, her eyes were huge and she stared at me strangely.

"Allie! Come on."

The door swung open. Brad stood behind Allie. He must have left her car somewhere else, because it wasn't in the driveway or anywhere near the house when we pulled up.

"Quincy, this is a surprise visit. We weren't expecting you," Brad said.

"I'm sorry we didn't call ahead," I said. "K.C. and I just wanted to take Allie out shopping with us on the spur of the moment."

"Gosh, well we're busy, so it'll have to be some other time."

"We can't..." I wanted to say something to stall but couldn't think of anything.

"We can't wait to see your place," K.C. blurted out. "Allie has told us all about it."

"She has?" He wasn't buying.

K.C. pushed past me and I could see she had stuffed the bat into the back of her pants, down one leg. The little handle peeked up above the waistband of her comfort stretch jeans.

"Oh yes! Once I saw you drive up with that fancy car of yours to drop Allie off at work, I thought to myself, this man has got some taste. I bet that car was expensive." K.C. knew exactly where this man's motivation came from.

"Yeah, it was very expensive," Brad said, as if he had been complimented.

"You know, my grandson has one just like it, and it was ex...pen...sive! It cost a pretty penny."

He closed his eyes and a crooked smirk checked one side of his face. "I don't think so, I had it specially made. Nobody has one just like it."

"Oh, really?" K.C. sounded like a doting grandmother, enchanted by his every word. "Is this it in this picture here?" She reached for a framed photo from the sideboard table just inside the door. She had worked her way inside the house without Brad realizing what she was doing.

"Don't touch that!" Brad yelled, then left the doorway and rushed over to the table. "I mean, yeah that's me with the car." Brad let go of Allie to make sure K.C. didn't touch his prized possession.

Before I knew what was happening, K.C. slid the bat out of her pants. Bursitis my ass.

"Run Allie!" K.C. yelled.

Brad wheeled around and looked up just in time to see Allie's back as she ran out the door. He lunged toward us and I felt the swish of air as the bat swung past my ear and landed in the middle of Brad's left rib cage. I thought I heard a crackling noise. K.C. had swung that bat like it was full-count in the bottom of the ninth. Brad collapsed to the floor.

K.C. ran out the door and I followed. The bat hung from K.C.'s right hand and as I leapt down the first step, the bat and my back leg crossed paths. I fell sideways off the stairs, about four feet to the ground. K.C. kept running.

My back hit the flowerbed, knocking all of the air out of me. I tried to get up but I couldn't breathe. I gulped and wheezed, willing myself not to panic while it felt as if I might die of asphyxiation. I could see Brad above me looking out the door. His eyes flashed with rage as he watched K.C. and Allie get away. Then he looked down and saw me.

He came down the stairs, crouched next to me and spoke very calmly. I expected him to drag me by the hair up the stairs, but then I was reminded by memories from the past about what would happen next. He needed to keep up appearances in the neighborhood. The pain wouldn't happen until we were inside. I was furious and petrified at the same time. I had to think of a way out of the situation, but my brain was frozen along with the rest of my body.

"You stupid bitch. You don't know what a huge mistake you've made," he hissed, quietly, through gritted teeth. "You're going to get up, and we're going to walk into the house just as nice as can be. Don't even think about making a sound. Do you understand?"

I nodded then slowly got up, barely having found enough air to breathe again. I felt the pain of the impact setting into all of my joints as we walked up the stairs. Brad pretended to assist me by holding my forearm and resting a stabilizing hand on my shoulder. In reality he was squeezing hard enough that his fingers seemed to be digging into my bones.

"You think its okay to make me look bad?" he yelled once we were inside with the door closed. He shoved me toward the coffee table. I hit my shins on the edge and fell forward onto the couch.

"You don't need any help looking bad, you've got that covered on your own," I said.

"What did you just say?"

"You heard me," I said.

"You just don't get it. I gave you plenty of warnings to stay out of our business, but you didn't pay attention."

"You mean the fires."

He said nothing, but the self-satisfied grin on his face told me I was right. My previous experience had taught me that when in this situation, the best thing to do did not involve adding fuel to the fire. I ignored experience. Bad idea.

I stood up gingerly and tried to make my way to the door.

"Sit down! Where do you think you're going?"

"I'm leaving. I don't want to be here and you can't keep me here."

"Oh yeah? You know, you're just as stupid as that

sister of yours. You're not going anywhere." He slid in front of me and blocked the front door with his body.

"Get out of my way Brad." I tried to push him out of the way and unintentionally pushed on his torso, probably where the bat had hit. I don't remember what happened after that.

CHAPTER EIGHTEEN

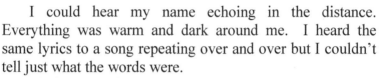

I could hear my name echoing in the distance. Everything was warm and dark around me. I heard the same lyrics to a song repeating over and over but I couldn't tell just what the words were.

"Quincy! Wake up. Can you hear me?"

I opened my eyes and the brightness made them water and slam shut. They weren't open very long, but long enough to make the insides of my skull whirl around like I was on a ride at the amusement park.

"Quincy, c'mon, wake up." I recognized the voice. It was a voice that made me want to open my eyes again even though I knew it would hurt.

I barely opened them in a squint and in the center of the gauzy edges I saw a beautifully shaped pair of lips saying my name, and then a strong cleft chin under those lips. So I opened my eyes a little more and saw two warm brown eyes looking at me.

"Alex?" My voice sounded foreign as it left my mouth.

"Hey. There you are," he said softly.

"What…" I couldn't finish the thought. I reached up to press on my forehead from where the ringing seemed to be emanating. "Ow." I had touched my eyebrow, which sent a shock wave of pain through my skull and down my spine.

"Careful, Quince. You took a pretty good shot to that eye."

I was still groggy but managed to look around. I was propped up against the La-Z-Boy recliner in Brad's living room.

"Where's Brad?" I asked as I struggled to stand up.

"Hold on there. Where are you going?" Alex asked.

"I have to find Allie."

"Allie is fine. You need to just sit for a minute."

"How do you know she's fine? Do you know where she is?"

"She's at your shop with your driver."

"She's with Nick?"

"Wow, you really did take one to the head, didn't you?"

"Huh?"

"Allie is with the lady that's your new driver. She's the one that called me and told me you were here. When your mind gets clear we've got a lot to talk about."

At this point I had come to enough to realize where I was, and what had happened, up until the part where I pushed Brad. I could pretty much guess what happened after that, even though I didn't remember. But, I knew Alex was not going to appreciate the reason I ended up in this situation, no matter how noble my intentions.

"Do you feel okay enough to walk out to my car?" he asked.

"Yeah, I'm fine. I want to get out of this place."

Alex escorted me out of the house to his car. It felt wrongly comforting that he placed his arm on my back as we walked.

As we approached the curb, angry yelling echoed throughout the neighborhood. I looked back to see an officer escorting a handcuffed Brad to a police car.

"That bitch and her crazy friend break into my house and hit me with a weapon, and *I'm* being arrested? It was self-defense. I'm suing all of you into oblivion. Especially you." Brad was staring directly at me. "I'd watch my back if I were you." He said it in a way that made my flesh crawl.

I sat in the passenger seat of the car Alex had directed me to. It wasn't a black and white, but it wasn't his Scout, either. It had a radio and computer in it just like the police cars I had ridden in before. My mind felt fizzy, like soda pop. I sat there for what seemed a long, long time, looking around at the inside of the car, and outside the window. The air conditioner was blowing full bore into my face, and I was alone. Alex had left me to go talk to the other officers. I was completely aware of my eye now. It felt like something had been drilled into my skull through the socket.

Alex came back to the car and asked how I was doing.

"How am I doing?"

"Oh. Sounds like you're not so foggy anymore," he said timidly. "Quincy, I know what you're probably going to say, and I don't blame you for being upset with me."

"Upset? What is it I should be upset about, Alex? Besides my sister being kidnapped, I mean."

"Okay, now I know for sure that you're mad. And I don't blame you, but…"

"Can I have a ride to my car please?"

"Fine. I'll give you a ride to your car."

Not a word passed between us on the ride to my store. When Alex pulled into the parking lot I pulled on the door handle, but nothing happened.

"Could you unlock the door please?"

"Nope."

"Alex, come on. I am in so much pain right now, and I've got a business that should be open."

"We're not leaving until you hear what I have to say, Quincy."

I was trapped. It was a recurring theme in my life, being trapped with a dangerous man. And danger could present itself in different forms. I clenched my jaw, balled my fists on my lap and closed my eyes, prepared to endure one more wrenching of my heart.

"First of all," he said, "it was an extremely stupid thing

you did going to Brad's house."

"Someone had to do something."

"Yes, the police. You should have called the police."

"It hasn't helped calling the police so far. In fact, any contact I've had with the police has been enough to put at the top of my list of the worst things that have ever happened to me. Including, and especially you."

Alex's mouth dropped open then snapped shut and formed a straight line. His jaw worked as if he were chewing on his next sentence. He took a deep breath.

"I know you're mad at me, but don't use that as justification for acting crazy. If something happens, you call the police."

"You know what, Alex? You're right, I am mad at you. You come into my shop after disappearing on me the first time, you make up some story about a note, you manipulate me enough to get a few thrills for the road—I guess, and then you leave me again."

"Manipulate you?" he shouted.

"Well, what would you call it?" I shouted back. My head felt like a bell in a church tower on Sunday. I couldn't help grimacing.

"Okay, lets just calm down. Quincy, I'm so sorry I had to leave like that. I wasn't manipulating you. I tried to tell you..." He sighed and gripped the steering wheel hard enough to turn his knuckles white. He looked straight forward, through the windshield, "I'll be able to explain it all to you really soon."

"Explain all of what? You abandoned me. You made a fool out of me. It's bad enough that I've got psychos chasing me and I just got punched in the face by another nut job, but you've hurt me more than all of those other things combined."

His eyes softened and the tension left his face. He let go of the steering wheel, and reached for my hand. My first instinct due to previous experience was to jerk away from him when he reached out, since we had been arguing. But he gently cradled my hand in his.

"Quincy, when I left the other day—I shouldn't be telling you this—I left because I got an emergency page about Arroyo."

"Arroyo? I thought you were dealing with gangs. Wait…you still have a pager?"

"Yes I have a pager, in case my cell phone isn't working. It's a backup, which is a good thing, because like I told you, my phone was broken. I had to leave immediately. I can't tell you any more. I told you I was on a special task force and that is it. You have to take my word for it."

"Take your word for it? You couldn't have left a note, or stuck your head into the other room and said…anything?"

"It was a code red. I was supposed to leave right away, but I did look into the front and saw you were dealing with Cindy. It looked like you were involved in something important and I didn't think I had time to explain things to you. I didn't want to interrupt what looked like an intense conversation between you and your employee." He let go of my hand and softly brushed his thumb over my cheek just below the swollen part of my eye, then winced. He looked into my eyes and sighed. "I'm watching out for you, Quincy. I'm sorry I can't give you any details now. I'll be able to later, I promise. Until then I just need you to trust me."

"I can't. I'm sorry. Thanks for the ride, Alex. Goodbye."

CHAPTER NINETEEN

I managed to go to work the next morning. My eye was puffy, swollen and looked as if it had been painted a lovely combination of chartreuse and lemon.

"Oh Boss," K.C. exclaimed, "you look like a sock-eyed salmon that didn't make it upstream. You shouldn't be here today!"

"I agree, but someone's gotta be here. It looks worse than it is anyway. I'll be fine."

"You shouldn't have refused treatment, Boss."

"How did you know about that?"

"Oops. A little bird told me. Anyway, don't we have an early delivery today?"

"Nice subject change. Actually, we do have one, I'll hurry and make it and you can take it right away."

"Okey-dokey."

K.C. left with the delivery once the flowers were arranged. I refused to let myself think of anything having to do with Alex, and I didn't need to worry about Allie anymore, since she went and stayed with a trusted family friend. I needed something to occupy my thoughts, so I finally started the bookkeeping I had managed to get distracted from several times before.

After almost an hour of bookwork, the phone rang. LaDonna Shaw's voice was on the line. I shook my fist in the air at no one, having forgotten we were going to meet soon so I could show her all about how to use her new system. She had just barely wrapped her mind around the concept of email, and I didn't want her to lose the momentum. We arranged to meet after work.

The phone rang again. This time it was Linda.

Phone wedged between my ear and shoulder, I divided my attention between the paperwork and her call.

"What's up? I'm surprised to hear from you so soon."

"I know, I told you I wouldn't be talking about those guys again, but I just had to tell you this. I made a bunch of copies of documents on the computer at work before I left, just in case those jerks at the mortuary tried to accuse me of anything."

It seemed like a smart thing to do.

"Anyways, I came across these plans for a cemetery that I've never seen before. They have a date from not too long ago, and no one ever said anything about this to me. I know you were asking about anything unusual going on around there so I thought I'd tell you about this."

Yeah, nothing else unusual was going on at the mortuary besides some plat maps Linda didn't know about, I thought to myself. People having affairs on the embalming table wasn't odd at all.

I got the address of the property from Linda and thanked her for thinking of me.

What a coincidence the two mysteries I was trying to solve just presented themselves to me in phone calls mere seconds apart. Coincidence or not, the two parts could possibly be related. First I had to figure out just what the relationship was between Irwin Shaw and Derrick Gibbons. Irwin had been so enraged about the farm investment. Who were the other intended investors? And where was the farm supposed to be located? Speaking of land, what was with the top-secret nature of the cemetery plans Linda found? I knew someone who might at least be able to help me learn a little more about the land.

I called my mom's first cousin Jack's wife, Tammy. She worked at the county courthouse in the county Recorder's office. I gave her the coordinates on the plat map so she could look up the address. A few minutes later, she called back.

"Quincy, this really is kind of strange. Do you remember that farm land LaDell Williams sold to the National Nature Land Preservation Society?"

"Not really. Did he own the land in the address I gave you?"

"Well, he used to, but he sold it to the NNLP Society. His land was up in East Hillside. He's a friend of your grandpa. Anyway, he sold to the Nature Preservation Society, because they supposedly buy up land from people like farmers and ranchers who need to sell, but don't want to sell it to housing developers. The Society is supposed to keep the land in a sort of national public trust, so it can't be developed. It's part of the deal they make with the landowner they buy the property from. They might pay just a little bit less than the developer would, but it keeps the land natural."

"What does this have to do with the cemetery?"

"The coordinates you gave me show the cemetery on the land LaDell Williams sold to the Nature Preservation Society. I'm no lawyer, but my dad was approached by the Society for the same kind of a deal, and they assured us that if we sold them our land, they had to keep it as natural habitat, and that it wouldn't be sold for development of any kind. This map shows the new property owners as the Hansen Family Trust. I don't know how this got recorded without someone knowing about it. Heck, not just knowing about it, but raising a stink about it. I don't know, Quincy. It's a mystery to me, I hope I helped."

"Absolutely, thank you so much."

"Hey before you go, I heard you were out drinking the other night at Skinny's with some hot guy. What's that all about?"

I explained to Tammy she had been a victim of my mother's political machine. I was surprised she hadn't heard of my black eye yet. She wouldn't have heard that one from my mother though. Allie and I agreed we would not be talking with our mother for a while about Brad, the police, K.C.'s bat or my black eye Maybe not ever.

K.C. rumbled through the back door. I looked up at the clock and realized she had been gone a long time. Her down-turned mouth suggested someone had taken away her birthday. She dragged herself to the front counter, and put her delivery ticket into the wicker basket with a sigh.

"K.C., did everything go okay on deliveries?"

"Well," she paused, "no."

"Why? What happened?"

"Boss, I think I may have gotten myself fired."

"What did you do?"

"I was coming back from the delivery out to the Anderson's and I thought I would take the old road out to the bottoms and cut across the West side, so I could miss the busy traffic up on Main Street." She shuffled over to the design table and plopped down on a stool.

"And?" I asked.

"I was driving down the road, singing along with Old Blue Eyes, and I got so caught up in singing, I didn't notice anyone following me."

I got a queasy feeling inside. "Don't tell me. A red truck was following you."

"How did you know?"

"I'm a psychic. Then what happened?"

"At first I thought I would flip them the bird, but then I remembered I was in the company vehicle. So I kept driving. I tried to speed up some, but it's a washboard road out there and I didn't want to spin out. That little truck kept right on my tail and they were honking their horn and waving their arms out the windows and flashing the headlights. So I figured they must want me to pull over for some reason."

"Oh no, K.C. you didn't."

"Well yes I did. I thought maybe some part was hanging off of the car or something dangerous like that. So I pulled over and I made sure my purse was handy and I rolled down the window. This young man came up to the side of the car. He had a beard and he was wearing a plaid shirt. He reminded me of a lumberjack. Anyway, he came up to the car yelling and screaming. He said 'Are you Rosie?' and I said who wants to know? And he said none of your business."

My stomach tightened. "And then what happened?" I said.

"He said 'My boss says you better watch out or you just might get yourself hurt.' So I said 'Who is your boss? And what the heck are you talking about?' Then he yelled, 'I'm the one in charge here, you just make sure you watch out because we have our eyes on you and you're gonna end up wishing you had listened.'"

"Did anything else happen?"

She nodded. "I have never had a young person talk to me like that and live to tell about it. I asked him if that was a threat and he said 'Yes.' Now, Quincy, nobody threatens physical harm to Karma Clackerton even if they think I'm somebody named Rosie. I said to him 'Young man, let me make sure I heard you right. Did you just threaten to harm me?'

"And he said, 'Well what do you think Grandma Genius?'"

She pulled a taser out of her purse and held it up. "I reached into my purse just like that, and grabbed this thingy and gave him what he had coming"

"You tased someone?" I thought my eyes would pop right out of their sockets. "You just happened to have a taser in your purse?"

She smiled broadly. "Yes," she said fondly, "it was a gift from my granddaughter, Emma."

"So then what happened?"

"When he fell over, his buddy came out of the truck. He was blathering on about how I'd killed his cousin and how I must be a devil woman. He sounded like he was about to cry. So I got out of the truck and brought the Enforcer out with me."

"You carry that thing around in the van?"

"I do now. I've gotta be ready for anything."

"So what did he do?" At this point, I almost thought she was telling me a tall tale, except that she described the truck and the drivers perfectly.

"I said 'Young man stop your blubbering. I want to talk to you.' And he just paced around his cousin's body with his hands on his head, crying 'What am I gonna do?' over and over. I said 'Young man' again, and he ignored me. So I said 'Listen up you little shit, if you know what's good for ya.' And I slammed the bat down on the ground so he could hear it real good. Well, that got his attention. I asked his name and he told me it was Rusty and then I asked his cousin's name and he told me Dusty Stephens. I told him I didn't believe him. I mean Rusty and Dusty? Come on. But he insisted that's what their names were. I swung the bat up onto my shoulder and then I tapped it now and then, just to keep him on his toes."

"What was the other guy doing?"

"He just laid there kinda twitching. I asked the kid who was still standing up who his boss was and he told me Mr. Powell. It didn't register with me until later that Mr. Powell could be the same one we've been talking about. Anyway, I took the taser thingy and aimed it at Rusty or Dusty, whichever one it was and I marched him to the back of the little truck so I could keep an eye on him while I memorized the license plate number. Then I told him 'I'm sorry but I'm gonna have to tase you too.' And I tased him in the butt, cause it seemed the least harmful way to do it, then I got in the van and drove down the road until I was out of sight and called the police."

"You just left them there?"

"Wuhl yeah, what else was I going to do with them? Drag them into the car? They're fine. I made sure both of them were still breathing when I left. The first one was starting to come-to I think."

"K.C., I'm speechless."

"Oh good, I like to do that to people."

"What did the police say?"

"Oh." Her face changed from the animated storyteller to the bearer of bad news. "This is the reason I think I might be fired."

If tasing two men and driving off in my marked van didn't strike her as a fireable offense, then what did, and how bad was it?

"I had the phone number for your...friend on my phone. I thought it might be better to call him."

My face felt the temperature of molten lava at the mention of Alex. "Why do you have his number on your phone?"

"Well, yesterday he called me and told me to keep an eye on you because you wouldn't go to the hospital and he was worried about you. He said you were mad and wouldn't talk to him. Sorry I didn't say anything before, I thought it best not to make you feel worse. And I'm sorry to have to tell you but, after I told him everything that happened today, he asked if I was okay and I said I was, and then he said not to mention this to anyone, including...you."

"Why didn't he want you to tell me?"

"I don't know. I thought maybe you two were an item, until he said that and then I thought I had made a terrible mistake. I thought maybe I would call the police station, but he told me not to. I'm awful sorry, Boss, I just didn't know what to do."

"K.C., you did the right thing by telling me. Are you really okay after all that?"

"I'm just fine. I got to use my new toy, and put some young punks in their place. I don't think we'll be hearing from them again."

"Huh, yeah." I gave her a courtesy laugh.

"Hey Boss, tell me again about this shindig we've been getting ready for all week."

K.C. was referring to the county Gala. It was a giant job, and it would provide a needed shot in the arm to my bank account. In fact, it would be more than a shot in the arm. With the way things were going, the future of Rosie's Posies would hinge on whether the gala was a success or not. I would do everything in my power to make the event a hit and keep the business alive.

K.C. and I finished up at the shop. She offered to mop the floors and sharpen the tools, which was great for me because I was tired and unfortunately, I still had an appointment at the Shaw's.

The drive to the Shaw's was extra spooky now that the red truck stalkers were back. However, after the treatment they got from K.C., they probably needed to recover more than I did from my head injury. I hoped the Shaws were especially fast learners this time. I didn't want to spend more than an hour at their place. After I was done there I would go home and eat ice cream in my tube socks and maybe let myself stew about Alex until the pain killer sleepiness kicked in.

When I walked into the Shaw's shop, LaDonna was finishing up a bridal consultation with what looked like a twenty year old girl and her mother. Irwin worked on the fan inside of their walk-in cooler. I peeked in and asked if I could borrow some sticky notes from his desk.

"Sure, if you can find them under everything."

I moved a pile from the chair so I could sit down. I hoped to find a sticky note pad so I could mark everything in the office with step-by-step instructions. I saw something bright yellow under a pile of envelopes from the phone company and reached for it. When I did that, I knocked over an adjacent mess and a gleam of metallic gold caught my eye. I took a closer look and saw it was a cell phone. A gold-plated cell phone. I had seen one of those before hadn't I? No, I realized, I hadn't seen one, but I had heard Gaylen Smith comment about one once. A lump lodged itself in my throat. I searched for and found a Rolodex that matched the antiquity of the roll-top desk in technological advancements in office products. If my hunch was correct, I was about to need to get out of there.

I found what I was looking for. I used the phone on the desk to dial the number on the Rolodex card that said, "Derrick's cell." As I listened to the dial tone the cell phone didn't ring. I must have been wrong. In an attempt to replace the pile of papers to its original state of chaos, I felt something move. The phone vibrated on top of the stack of envelopes. The display window read, "Shaw Phone." My heart leapt to my throat.

"What's going on here?" I heard directly above the back of my head. I jumped in the seat and my legs froze. I craned my neck to the left to see Irwin Shaw standing over me with only two inches between us.

"Oh, I couldn't see the sticky notes, I'm sorry if I disturbed anything. I was just calling to retrieve my messages while the two of you finished up." I was almost sure the pounding in my chest would betray the fear coursing through my body.

"You're sure you didn't move anything on the desk?" Irwin had an intense glare in his eyes, the eyes of someone who wanted to strangle the life out of the woman sitting in front of him.

"No!" I stood up and my hip knocked an entire stack of papers to the floor. "Oh, I'm so sorry...I...I've got to go. I just got a message from my mother, and it looks like we'll have to postpone this meeting. Sorry about the mess." I backed up slowly, feeling behind me with one hand so as not to trip over something and get knocked out only to find myself waking up on an embalming table in the basement. "I'm so sorry, I just, have to leave." I had made it to the doorway between the back room and the showroom where LaDonna was still talking to the girl and her mother.

"Quincy, wait, I was just teasing. You cant' find anything on that desk without moving things around. Come back."

I rushed out of the store without saying goodbye to LaDonna and I had the van in reverse before I even realized I had started it. Irwin Shaw had the cell phone of a dead man on his desk and I didn't want to stick around to ask him why.

CHAPTER TWENTY

For the next two days, I kept a low profile. I showed up at the shop, made sure the display cooler was stocked and that our hospital account was ready every day. K.C. made sure the deliveries were made and that the people receiving them were happy.

I had considered calling the police about the gold cell phone—for about a nano-second—and then remembered how successful all my attempts at involving the police had been before. Besides, my only focus then had to be on the Gala.

Pre-ordered fresh product began to arrive for the event and we spent the afternoons taking flower bunches out of their plastic wrappers, stripping the leaves and thorns, cutting the ends and then placing them in buckets of water combined with floral food. All of the bunches would hydrate in buckets for a couple of hours and then be placed in the walk-in cooler.

The Gala was happening in two days, and the day after that would be the Pioneer Day holiday for the State of Utah. All the banks and stores would be closed, and I could hide out all day long and sulk. Until then, K.C., Allie and I would get ready for the big event. Floral foam bricks had been counted and set aside and would now be soaked. Longer lasting flowers like carnations, orchids and chrysanthemums could be placed in arrangements a couple of days in advance, and the remainder would be placed the day before. On the day of the Gala, we finished everything that could be done at the store, and then K.C. and I delivered the arrangements, containers and props to the conference center in three trips.

We finished the tall cylinder arrangements with colored water and dripping crystal garlands on-site on the dinner tables in the ballroom. Once everything was finished, we returned to the shop and closed up to get ready to attend ourselves. Allie decided she didn't want to go, and I wanted to join her in the boycott, but K.C. wasn't having any of it. She was going to the Gala, and one of us was too, she insisted. She was right. I just had a sour attitude, and a green and purple eye socket, but in reality it was very important for me to go and mingle with potential new clients.

I was on my way to lock the door and go home to shower when the phone rang. It was a few minutes shy of closing time, so I ran back to the design room and picked up.

"Hi, Quincy, this is Bryce."

"Oh hey, thanks for returning my call." Bryce had been a floral wholesaler once upon a time, now he grew crops, floral and otherwise.

"No problem, I've been out of town doing some consulting. It's been awhile since I saw all you folks in the biz, what's new?"

I didn't have time to fill him in on the sordid details so I got right to the point. "Not much. I just ran across some information on switch grass, and I knew who to call with my questions."

"Great. That's one thing I love to talk about. That's the consulting I just finished doing. What kind of questions do you have?"

"You grow your crops for fuel not for cut crops is that right?"

"Actually both. I started selling it at Flowertown wholesalers. Is that where you heard about it?"

"No, not at first, although I called them for your number. I heard about it as an alternative fuel source in a little pamphlet that I...was given."

"Oh no. It's not that "Fuel of the Future" thing is it?"

"Um yeah, actually it is."

"Quincy, I'm telling you, stay away from that Derrick Gibbons. He is poison. He is a rotten apple, and I mean to-the-core rotten."

Bryce obviously didn't know what had happened to Derrick. I filled him in after he told me how he knew Derrick's father really well, and when Derrick decided to go out on his own, he came to Bryce with the idea of investing in Bryce's farm as a backer. The only trouble was that Derrick didn't plan on doing any of the work, and he was really secretive about where his money was coming from.

"I knew he didn't have any money from his Dad and he didn't want to share any financial details with me about where he got his money, so I told him thanks but no thanks. A little later on I heard about a pamphlet that was circulating. I think he went about getting investors assuming I would come around. But I never did. In fact, I told him that if he ever came onto my property I would shoot him for trespassing."

"I wonder if one of his investors wanted to collect their money back and he'd already spent it." I said.

"I wouldn't put it past him to do that. He drove here in a new car every time that he came."

I thanked Bryce for the information and told him I would say hello to Aunt Rosie when I saw her again. The list of Derrick's potential killers had just become substantially longer, and I think I was still being considered a member of that club.

###

I climbed into the van wearing a full length, pewter evening gown with an empire waist and full-length sleeves. *Eat your heart out Alex*, I had thought to myself as I donned the dress borrowed from Allie. She'd never worn it because she had ordered it online and discovered the skirt too long and the bust too tight for her figure. I lucked out by mentioning my lack of an outfit to wear to the gala before she sent it back. It fit my bust and my length just perfectly, thank you very much.

I imagined I had just stepped down into a limousine rather than up, into a van. No offense to Zombie Sue, of course. But somehow the positive imagery didn't change the fact that I felt like a truck driver hopping into the cab of my eighteen-wheeler. No matter. I wasn't going there to show off my ride. I was going there because I had provided the flowers for the event, and because I had a pretty good idea that Landon Powell would be there. Bigwigs from all-around the state and surrounding areas would be attending to show off how "charitable" they were. And since this wasn't a local family diner on a weeknight, it didn't hurt that there would be a cash bar one hour prior to the silent auction. It always helps to get people liquored up to open their wallets a little wider. I was going to have a talk with Mr. Powell about his goons following me around and making threats.

When I looked in the rear view mirror of the van I caught the full view of the sickly mustard yellow and pea green skin surrounding my eye socket. The black eye delivered courtesy of Brad was coming into full bloom just in time for the Gala. Foundation and powder make-up could only go so far.

I drove to K.C.'s apartment to pick her up. I had been given two complimentary tickets to the gala, and since I wouldn't be going with Alex, K.C. would use the other ticket. She and I could tear down the arrangements right after it was over. I warned her to bring a change of clothes and comfortable shoes in order to clean up the event. She walked out of her apartment as I pulled into the driveway. A red beehive of hair towered on top of her head. She wore a tea-length gown of leopard print fabric with a plunging v-neck, and la piece de resistance, bright gold, glittered slippers with a wedge heel and a matching gold sequined wrap. She also hefted a giant zebra-print shoulder bag accessorized with klunky silver hardware.

She opened the sliding door of the van and tossed her bag onto the floor. It landed with a thud. Seconds later she plopped down in the seat with another thud.

"Hello Boss! I'm ready to par-tay! I'm so excited for this shin-dig tonight!"

"I'm glad one of us is." I said as I turned and looked at her.

"Holy cow that's still some kind of shiner!" She yelled as she lurched backwards for dramatic effect. "You should be proud a that one kid. You showed some real moxie in earning it."

"Not really," I said, "I just tripped as I ran away from Brad's. I don't even remember him giving me this." I absentmindedly reached up and touched the swollen area around my eye, which reminded me how much it still hurt.

"Oh come on now. Cheer up! We're going to a gala. Who wouldn't be excited to go to a gala? I feel like Cinderella going to the ball, and you look great, Boss. All you need to do is sweep that long hair of yours across your face to cover your eye—like the Hollywood actresses do. You'll be right in style. But wait until you finish driving though, you're gonna have to cover half your face to hide that beauty."

"Thanks for the tip." I said sarcastically.

"Anytime." She replied. "So what's got you so down little camper?"

"Sorry K.C., I don't mean to be a downer. It's just that I know Landon Powell is supposed to be there and he's…"

"He's the snake in the grass who hired those two goons to follow your van around!" She interrupted. "Well don't you worry about him. Those politician types don't think about anyone else, especially not at a fancy wingding like this gala. He'll be concentrating on shaking hands and plastering on a fake smile for all those folks he's rubbing elbows with. He won't even notice you're there. Besides, have you ever met him, Boss?"

"No I haven't."

"Well there you have it. He probably doesn't even know who you are in person. Just follow my lead and lay low."

No easy task, when my dinner companion was dressed like a jungle cat in a foil candy wrapper costume.

We arrived at the venue ten minutes later. The conference center was a brand-new building attached to a hotel in the restaurant row area of Hillside. The theme for the event was "Moonlight Serenade." We had produced spheres made from genetically modified purple carnations and a variety of arrangements composed of various purple and silver materials. My favorites were the Blue Vanda and Chanel Blue Dendrobium orchids imported from Thailand. K.C. and I had come earlier and placed all of the arrangements in the large dining room and the lobbies and silent auction room. We even put small arrangements in the bathrooms.

The ballroom looked spectacular with the draped ceiling and suspended spheres of different sizes and materials. We arrived early just to make sure everything remained in place. Carol Murphy, the gala coordinator, was there to greet us as we walked in.

"Hello, Quincy and..." she paused to take in the entire picture that was K.C. Clackerton. "You both look so...festive." Carol would make a good politician.

"This is K.C., you may have seen her earlier today while we set-up."

"Oh yes, K.C., forgive me, I didn't recognize you. You look—breathtaking." Carol was quite literally correct and K.C. beamed. I tried to take in the view of all of our work with the perspective of a newly arriving guest. And even though I could only see through the one eye that wasn't covered by my sweeping hair, I felt a great sense of accomplishment. The flowers and décor created a spectacular scene.

"The flowers look absolutely fantastic," Carol said. "There are a couple of ladies on the committee who have walked through already and they would love to talk to you about flowers. One of them has a daughter who just got enDerrickd. I'll introduce you tonight."

"Thank you, I would appreciate that." I would just have to pretend that it was perfectly normal to have my hair covering half of my face. Like an eccentric artist. Yes, that was it. I was an eccentric floral artist.

We stood at the entrance to the main ballroom where the catering staff buzzed around the tables. We spoke with Carol until we were interrupted by the sound of crashing glass. We both jumped and looked over at one of the waiters trying to right the arrangement he had just knocked over on a dining table.

"Excuse me Carol." I walked over and offered to help the waiter as he frantically tried to put everything back in place.

"I am so sorry." He said. "I don't know what happened."

"Don't worry about it. I know how to fix them." I straightened the tablecloth and the dishes around the centerpiece, picking petals and pieces of purple statice off of the salt and peppershakers and the butter dishes. He had bumped a cylinder vase enough that the water sloshed out of it. He said he would have to go get replacement dishes from the kitchen and I asked if I could follow him to find some water and a pitcher to replace what was spilled.

When I stepped into the one-way door leading into the kitchen, it smelled like disinfectant and sour dishrag. I followed the server into a secondary kitchen with rolling metal shelves full of dishes, carafes, rectangular metal boxes full of silverware, and rolled up napkins. The nearest sinks had trays of glasses in them, so I walked around the corner looking for a place to fill a carafe with water. As I walked around a brick wall partition, I heard angry whispering voices. I stopped, thinking I was intruding on a catering staff conversation. I quietly pivoted to find my water elsewhere when I heard a male voice say Landon.

"Exactly what is it then, that I'm paying you for? I had to resort to using those two idiots you hooked me up with to keep the pressure on, because you flaked out on me. You know you wouldn't have a job in the department if it wasn't for me."

"Lan, would you just listen to me?" the second voice said.

"No. I will not listen to you. You will listen to me. Things could get really rough for you around the department if I'm not happy. Do you know what I'm saying?"

"Yeah, I know."

"Alright. Now you've got to take care of that big mouth out there. She's flapped her jaw too much. We need to shut her up. Do you know what I'm saying?"

"Yeah. I've got an idea."

"Good. Now get out of here, I can't be seen with you."

I took that as my cue to get out of the way. I took a giant step back the way I had come and then turned and rushed to the other side of the kitchen and out the one-way door.

Even though I hadn't seen the two men, I had heard them planning a crime. One of the voices seemed vaguely familiar, but not enough to recognize the person it had come from. That same speaker had called the other Lan. Probably short for Landon Powell. Who was the big mouth

Powell talked about? I knew it was a woman. Me? But I hadn't flapped my jaw. Much.

I also hadn't murdered Derrick, but that didn't stop people from considering me a suspect.

I hurried back without the water and luckily, K.C. was taking care of the problem. My heart still pounded while I looked over to the front of the room. Carol smiled politely and nodded while talking to a curvaceous woman with fake blond hair, who wore a body-hugging sapphire floor-length dress. She waved her arms around as she spoke to Carol. It made it easy to spot the enormous diamond bracelet on her wrist. It was a solid four-inch band of sparkle. I noticed Carol gesturing to me to come over.

"Quincy," she said as I arrived, "this is Camille LeFay. She has been looking for you. Excuse me while I go check with the band." She looked relieved and practically ran away. I had never met Camille, but her name was familiar.

I took a steadying breath and tried to set aside the fear I was experiencing from what I had just overheard. I scrutinized Camille's face hoping to find some clue to help me remember who she was. She looked beautiful in the way that people who are meant to be arm candy look. She wore bright red lipstick, lots of eyeliner and mascara, and she had a fake beauty spot penciled in on her upper lip. She had enormous basketball-shaped fake breasts. If the wind were to change direction suddenly she would tip right over.

"Hi, you wanted to see me?"

Her reply came in a throaty, sexy voice. "No, but my boss does." She eyed me up and down, her expression finally suggesting I wasn't much worth looking at.

I tilted my head, confused at what she had just said. "Who is your boss?"

Her eyes zeroed in on my newly exposed black eye. My expressive head tilt had caused my hair to betray me.

"I hope the pay is good." Camille said.

"Pardon?"

"That shiner. I hope it's worth it—putting up with the guy that did that to you. He must be rich."

"Oh." I quickly placed my hair to cover the eye. "No, I tripped and fell and then…it's a long story."

"Uh huh. All I can say is that you can find another sugar-daddy. They're a dime a dozen honey. You don't have to put up with one that hits you."

"Thanks for the tip."

"Take my boss, for example. I got this just for listening to him whine." She held up her wrist and the bracelet. She slurred her speech and I could smell the source of her confidence. She must have taken a wine bath before the event.

"Now who did you say your boss was?"

"I told you. Landon."

"Landon Powell?"

"Well duh. Of course, Landon Powell."

"And he's the one who wants to see me?"

"Oh yeah, that. Yeah he told me to find out who you are and point you out to him."

"Why?"

She paused to think for a long time and then she started to sway on her feet. I reached out to steady her.

"Whoa," she giggled. "I guess I had a little extra wine before I came here. What were we talking about?"

"Your boss. Why does he want to see me?"

"I don't know, something about Derrick. Derrick!" She shouted the name. She held up her pointer finger and closed one eye. She shook her finger at me. "Now that's someone who liked to hit. I got these out of him before I dumped 'is ass." She brushed back her hair to display M&M sized diamond stud earrings in her lobes. It occurred to me then, that this was the woman Mickey had talked about at the restaurant.

"You knew Derrick Gibbons?" I asked.

She laughed. "Yeah I knew him, in the biblical sense,

if you know what I mean." She began to laugh hysterically. I couldn't help but notice her eyelids drooping heavily and the skin on her face emanating a layers-deep ruddy red.

"Did you and he...have a relationship when he was murdered?"

"I don't know. We were off and on for a while there. I think he was with me just to use me. I mean besides just for...you know."

"What else did he use you for?" I was hoping this conversation didn't turn out like the one I'd had with Linda, but seeing as how liquid truth had freed Camille's tongue, I needed to ask as many questions as I could get away with.

"He was always asking me stuff about Landon's business. He wanted to know about different projects and land and boring shit like that. Oops," she put her hand to her mouth and giggled, "sorry about the swear. He didn't turn out to be anything special. There wasn't much going on down there, if you know what I mean." She wiggled her fingers below her waist, oblivious to the disgust I struggled to conceal. "I mean he started juicing and lifting weights more and more and things kind of quit working in the man department."

"Why did you start going out with Derrick in the first place? I mean, didn't you say you got that from...you know...with your boss?" I pointed to the diamond bracelet.

"Landon started having trouble keeping up...if you know what I mean. It happened after he found out his wife was sleeping with someone. I guess what was good for the goose wasn't good for the hen...I mean the chicken, you know?" I nodded my head to give the appearance of understanding. "Anyway, Derrick used to visit Landon at the office all the time and he started asking me out. It took awhile but he promised me these so I said yes." As she said this she cupped each hand under a basketball and lifted up. "Double H's, baby."

"Whoa..." I let slip. "Did your boss know you were

seeing Derrick?"

"Are you crazy? Landon would kill anyone if he knew they were sleeping with me."

"Did Mr. Powell know who was sleeping with his wife?"

"No. He heard some rumors though. He told me about it. He was going to have his cop buddy look into it."

"Any idea what that buddy's name might be?" I asked innocently.

"Yeah," she said too loudly, "of course I remember. I know everything about everything. Le' me think." She stopped and stared into the air in front of her for a long time, then appeared to be falling asleep. "I don't remember his name, but it starts with an A. For sure I know it starts with an A."

"Was it Arroyo?"

"Nooo. That's way off."

A...Alex? My breath caught up in my throat for a moment. "It wasn't Alex, was it?"

"That sounds right," she said. "Who's Alex?"

"Never mind."

I'd had my suspicions, especially lately, with what Alex had said to K.C. He was in league with Landon Powell. He had been sent to spy on me from day one. The more I thought about it, the more obvious it was. Showing up at the hit-and-run had put him right where he could keep an eye on me. He'd known all about my snooping at Derrick's place and the mortuary.

My chest tightened and an invisible boa constrictor wrapped itself around my left arm. Was I having a heart attack? My stomach knotted into a baseball and my chest burned, deep inside. It wasn't a heart attack; it was reality hitting me, telling me I had been made a fool.

Looking back, it occurred to me why he had been *so* attracted to me. No one falls for someone that hard and that fast. He was merely playing a part. I couldn't believe I hadn't seen it coming. And that I had been so *stupid*. I had kissed him and thought about doing much more, while the whole time, *he* had just been enjoying the physical perks of the job. I'd hoped I would have been a better judge of character. But then, my track record should have told me I wasn't.

"Heeyy!" Camille's slurred voice woke me from my heartache-induced trance. "I'm s'posed to find somebody named Candy…no…Clancy. Do you know anyone named Clancy?"

"No, sorry."

"Oh well. My boss wanted me to find out what Clancy looks like. He's really mad at her for some reason…wants to see her. Oh well, I don't care. He's bringing his stupid wife to this thing and making me sit at a different table. Like his wife doesn't know about us. She's no dummy. She just decided to get back at him the way he did with me. What's good for the hen is good for the gander you know? Hey what's your name? I forgot."

"It's Quinella."

"Oh. That's an ugly name. I like you anyway, Stella. You're all right. I…don't feel too good." She put her hand to her stomach.

"One more thing, Camille, did Derrick mention who he was seeing before you?"

"No, he said he hadn't been with any women in a long time." A wicked smile curled her lips. "I'm all the woman he needed."

"I was kind of thinking it wasn't a woman he was seeing before you." I braced myself in case she didn't like my accusation.

"I don't get it."

"Someone told me that he had quite a close male friend, like maybe even a boyfriend." I winced and leaned back in case she had a quick first step leading into her right cross.

"Oh. Did he have money?"

"That's what I hear."

"Oh. Probably then," she shrugged. "My stomach really doesn't feel good. I've gotta go."

"The bathroom is over there." I pointed to the left. She hustled out of the room in the same direction.

So Landon Powell was trying to shut me up.

Alex had to have told him everything I knew about Derrick. The only thing he could want to shut me up about was my innocence. He must have killed Derrick or had Arroyo or...Alex do it. I had to get out of there. I could hardly breathe. I wanted to crumple into a ball in a dark corner.

"There you are, Boss!" K.C.'s enthusiastic greeting pulled me out of the depths. "Oh, Quincy, thank you so much for bringing me to the ball. I haven't felt like this in years. I feel like a storybook princess. I don't know the last time I felt so alive. Not since my poor husband died, God rest his soul. This party hasn't even started and I've already met some swell folks. I think I might even have found a gentleman friend to take me out. Fred over there is the hotel manager, and I think he's sweet on me. I invited him to sit at our table. I hope that's alright with you."

K.C. beamed. She was having such a good time. Maybe I could just leave and come back and help her clean up. But I couldn't leave. I'd heard Landon Powell telling someone to shut me up. If I went home, someone could be waiting for me. Powell had told the other person to get lost during their kitchen conversation, so he wouldn't be here. I was in the safest place possible; a crowded place where no one could shut anyone up without 500 of the most influential people in the county or even the state knowing about it. Besides, K.C. was radiating joy. If I let on about any of the danger I was in, she would deflate like a helium filled Mylar balloon that had been put in the flower cooler.

I told K.C. I was very happy for her and her new friend and that she was having such a good time. I told her I wasn't feeling so well, and I wouldn't be socializing too much before the event started. People were already filling the auction room for a preview. Dinner would start in twenty minutes. She decided to wait with me at our table. We talked about our strategy for taking things down after the event, so as to avoid seeing anyone at the silent auction.

The dinner began later but my stomach was too nervous to tolerate much food. The lights were dimmed and the entertainment began. Women and men in striped and swirl-print leotards hung from ceiling to floor drapes of fabric. They twisted and slid through the fabric from which they hung. Mystic music encircled the room.

K.C. looked over at me wide-eyed at the performance. "Boss, you really must not be feeling too well," she whispered. "I've never seen you turn down food since I've known you." She'd only known me for a few days. So I liked to eat.

"I'm still not feeling too well," I said, while grimacing and grabbing my stomach. I wasn't lying! I was sick at the thought of being murdered if I left the room.

The fabric dancing finished and the M.C. took to the podium. "Wasn't that beautiful and exciting everyone?" The audience applauded. "Before we continue, we would like to acknowledge our distinguished guests. Mayor Jefferson," the M.C. said as a spotlight flooded the table where the Mayor sat. "Senator Powell," said the M.C. The light found a table where a good looking man in his fifties sat next to the woman I had seen in the mortuary parking lot with the untied blouse. She did her job well, sitting next to her husband, looking at him admirably in her very modest dress, appropriate for a devoted Mormon housewife. Of course, Camille LeFay wasn't sitting at their table, but she wasn't sitting at any other table that I could see. She didn't appear to be in the room at all.

The M.C. continued.

"We would also like to extend our thanks to all of the

wonderful people who have made this event possible. L and M lighting, the event center catering, Dragonfly Dance Company…" As each name was ticked off the list, the spotlight found the table where the holder of the name sat. I realized I was on that list and that Landon Powell wanted to see me.

"Oh my stomach," I bent over then looked at K.C., "I think I'm going to throw up." I dove under the table just before I heard the M.C. say "Rosie's Posies." I could see the flood of light pass across the table as it illuminated the tablecloth. I waited a few seconds to make sure the M.C. directed everyone's attention to another table.

"Boss, are you okay?" K.C. whispered loudly under the table. I crawled out and got back in my seat.

"False alarm," I said. "Did anyone see me duck, do you think?

"I don't know, I was looking down here for you." It suddenly occurred to me that K.C. was lucky she ducked, too. The wrong someone might have assumed she was me.

The event finished with the silent auction, giving us time to tear down and load the van from a rear service entrance. K.C.'s new acquaintance was a great help. Not only did he help us move everything, but he became another possible witness, which would be a deterrent for a murderer who wanted to make me disappear. We moved into the silent auction room after the crowd left and picked up the few arrangements there.

I drove the van to the shop and K.C. and Fred rode together in his car, and then met me to help unload.

Tearing down an event is in some ways just as difficult as producing one and getting it delivered. Besides the special events contributing to the no life factor for the florist, usually you're so tired at midnight or two in the morning, you just want to leave everything there and hope that the elves magically appear to clean everything up. K.C. and I didn't see any elves, but Fred did have a certain twinkle in his eye, and his ears were slightly pointed.

As the nose of the van reached the curb, the ache in my shoulders demanded my attention. My legs felt like lead down to my ankles, where the lead turned to burning molten fire under my feet. I couldn't bear the thought of working any more that night.

K.C. came over to my window. "Let's head 'em up and move 'em out," she said.

"You know what? I'm exhausted. There's nothing in here that we need to worry about keeping fresh. We can leave it and deal with it in the morning. Let's just go *home*." I realized as soon as I said it that I couldn't go home. Someone had been assigned to shut me up. I would be a sitting duck at home. "Oh, crap. Never mind." I paused to think about where I could sleep that night.

"Boss, you've been acting strange all night. Tell me what's really going on."

I explained most of what I had overheard at the party, and told her about Camille LeFay and how she was sent to find me. I didn't tell K.C. I suspected Alex. I didn't want to hear why I was wrong about him, or that I should have known better. Either way, it would require thinking about the times I had spent with him, and my heart just couldn't handle it.

"I would offer a spot at my place, kid, but my apartment's too small. How about I come stay over with you? I've got the Enforcer and a few tools in the car. We'll show those pansies who they're dealing with!" She pumped her fist into the air and her face reddened, matching the beehive on her head.

"You know what K.C., you're right! This is my life and I am going to stay at my own house! I'm not going to let a low-life dirty cop dictate what I will and won't do."

"Right on sister!"

Fred took us to K.C.'s apartment where she gathered some clothes and her cache of weapons. Fred didn't say much, but his eyes widened at every new piece of equipment that emerged, revealing how impressed he was with K.C.'s arsenal. We drove to my place in K.C.'s car and went to bed after checking the locks and the blinds several times.

I won't say it was the best rest of my life, but having K.C.'s weapons within reach at any moment made it a lot easier to relax. I let myself sleep in, since the shop was closed for the holiday. When I finally opened my eyes, my alarm clock said 8:47 am. The aroma of bacon hung in the air. I followed the scented trail to the kitchen where I found K.C., wearing one of my grandma's frilly aprons, flipping pancakes in between shimmies with the spatula held aloft, playing air percussion. The small radio on top of the fridge played "Rockin' Robin." Her red beehive still towered atop her head. It hadn't moved a centimeter since I picked her up at her apartment the night before.

"Morning, K.C."

"Good morning to you, Boss. You're just in time for breakfast."

"Where did you find all of this breakfast?"

"I went to the store after my morning constitutional."

"What time did you wake up?"

"Oh I was naughty and slept in until five."

I wiped my bleary, sleep-heavy eyes. "Slept in?"

"Yes, Fred left so late after we necked on the couch that I allowed myself a little extra snooze time. I hope you don't mind."

"Why would I mind that you slept in—wait, did you say you and Fred…"

"Oh yes, he's a real tiger, that Fred." She giggled. "But it wasn't very thoughtful of me, Boss, having a gentleman caller leaving your house so late."

"Of course I don't mind, K.C." At least someone in

this house was getting some action.

"Well, I've made us a nice breakfast, so we'll have plenty of energy to go back to the shop and clean up our mess."

Breakfast was wonderful, and probably a shock to my system since my first meal of the day usually consisted of a piece of bread followed by the Coke that I bought on the way to the work in the mornings.

The prospect of cleaning up after a big event like the gala did not inspire enthusiasm, but K.C.'s gung-ho attitude did. We arrived at the shop ready to get busy and get out.

I unlocked the back door and walked through each room turning on the lights. K.C. volunteered to take the garbage boxes to the dumpster, while I put the supplies away that were left out on the counters in our haste to finish before the gala started.

"Boss, I'll open the van and start putting things out on the black top, and then we can both bring everything inside."

"Sounds good, I'll start bleaching the buckets, and then I'll meet you outside."

I turned on the water and poured a little bleach and soap into each bucket. My bruised eye twitched and I reflexively reached up to brush it with the back of my wrist. Ouch. It was still as sore as it was colorful. The painful touch reminded me of the day I received the injury. Of all the events of that day, the one that repeated over and over in my mind was that of Alex's arms wrapped around me, comforting me after my entrapment by Brad. I pushed that picture to the corners of my mind, knowing that the more I let myself think of Alex, the more it would sting in the realization that everything had been a nasty hoax.

"Boss! You need to come out here. Right now!" K.C.'s voice was drenched in panic.

"K.C., what's wrong?" It was the van. Maybe someone had vandalized the van, or worse.

I ran outside to see the damage.

"It's—it's inside the van. You have to look in the van."

Before I leaned in, I could smell something strange. It wasn't familiar and it was horrible. I started to gag and had to turn away and take a deep breath. I leaned against the side door and peered inside. It took time for my eyes to adjust to the change in light. The air felt thick and hot on my skin. Once my eyes were used to the light, I saw a glimmer in the dark where the light from the late morning sun shone past my shoulder into the van.

I crouched down and took a step inside, kneeling next to a mirrored pedestal. I reached toward the shiny thing, and as I touched it, I realized it was jeweled, I leaned further still and as the realization hit me that I had seen this bracelet the night before, I lost my balance and fell forward with a scream. Tumbling glass vases clanged and crashed and I landed on a solid surface with no give. I was lying on top of the lifeless body of Camille LeFay.

CHAPTER TWENTY ONE

As one might expect, my first instinct after discovering Camille LeFay's dead body was not to call the cops. I had my cell phone with me and I did what any well meaning, upstanding, *innocent* person would do—I called my lawyer. I explained to Cal, as briefly as I could (seeing as how he would bill me by the hour, and possibly the word), why I could not call the police to report the crime that I had *not* witnessed or been any part of. Like any great attorney and friend would do, he took care of it. Having a well-known and respected hotel manager stay at my house most of the night before had proven to be a great alibi too.

I left my lawyer to take care of the police and my van, which was now a crime scene. I just hoped things would be cleared up soon and that I wouldn't have to be involved any more than I absolutely had to regarding our gruesome discovery. Cal told me I could leave once I had talked to the police—none of whom I knew—thank goodness. He said he would take care of everything and let me know what the next step would be.

At home, K.C. and I went over any of the facts we knew of, which might link me in some way to the new murder and the old one.

"We have to think about all these puzzle pieces," K.C. said. We have to put them together. Find a pen and some paper. We're going to connect the dots." She put on her cat-eyed reading glasses, carefully adjusting them with the palms of both hands until they sat just-right on her nose. "By the way, where was this Camille LeFay sitting last night? Maybe I would remember seeing her and who she was with before she was killed," K.C. said.

"You were preoccupied with the spilled centerpiece when I talked to her, so I don't know if you saw her then."

K.C. shook her head.

"She ran to the bathroom, sick, after we spoke. That was the last time I saw her," I said.

I retrieved something to write with, and on a fresh sheet of paper wrote Derrick's name at the center and circled it. I then drew lines like spokes of a wheel coming from the center circle. "We know that Derrick had a relationship with the mortuary," I wrote Greg Schilling at the end of one of the spokes. "From what we've learned, we can draw spokes to Landon Powell, or at least Camille LeFay. We can connect Derrick to Bryce and his switch grass farm. We can connect him to the Shaws too because he was partners with their son and they had the switch grass pamphlet that Derrick created. We might be able to draw a spoke to Detective Arroyo because he's the detective over the murder case. Of course, there's Alex."

K.C. tilted her head down, peering at me over the tops of her reading glasses. "What about Alex? Boss?"

"I have reason to suspect Alex, by something Camille said."

"Suspect him of what?"

I hunched over and put my head in my hands. "Everything."

"Quincy, are you sure?"

"I'm not sure about anything, K.C. But think about it. How perfect for an undercover spy to infiltrate by getting the girl to fall for him, then report back her every move to his bosses? He has the perfect cover."

"Boss, you've been watching way too much TV."

"Trust me, K.C. It makes me sick to think of it, but we can't rule out any of the puzzle pieces."

K.C. sighed. "Okay," she said with reluctance, "I think you're batty, but lets just try to see where he fits." She took the pen from me and wrote down "Alex." She looked at me and raised her eyebrows, "Where exactly do I draw his spoke?"

"To Landon Powell. I think he's working for him."

"Alright and how is he linked to Derrick?"

"Oh. Well, I haven't figured that out yet."

K.C. peered at me and shook her head. "Love is the pits sometimes kiddo, but lets get serious here."

My heart ached but I knew Alex was up to something. All of the mysterious disappearances, and then re-appearances with no good explanation were not normal. I should never have trusted that man.

"Who else is left?" I had to change the subject.

K.C. looked at me as if to tsk-tsk me with telepathy. I ignored it and carried on.

"We can draw a spoke to Doug Stanwyck because he and Derrick were buddies. We've talked to everyone except Landon Powell and Stanwyck. We can't talk to the boyfriend obviously, but I've talked with his parents—the Shaws—and Powell...well I'm not going to be talking to him due to the fact that he tried to have me shut up."

"Hold on a minute to them there horses, Boss. Did you actually hear Powell telling someone to shut *you* up?"

"Well...no. He just said her. That 'she knows too much.'"

"Well didn't you say Camille LeFay was blabbing everything to everyone at the party? I mean if anyone needed to be shut up in Powell's eyes, it was probably her, don't you think?"

I paused a moment to think about what K.C. had said. "I'm an idiot."

"Oh no kid, don't be so hard on yourself."

"Obviously he was talking about Camille. She knew everything about Powell and Derrick and she didn't seem to care with whom she shared that information. Wow, what a relief we didn't have murderers outside the house all night. Oh, poor Fred!"

"What about Fred?"

"I got up to use the bathroom and then went out on the porch to get some air early this morning—before you were awake. He was asleep in his car. He must have been out there in his car all night watching out for us."

"Oh he wasn't out there all night." K.C.'s expression became coy.

"Is that so?"

"We necked on the couch for quite a long time, Quincy. I didn't exactly tell you the whole story about this morning before breakfast. We heard you stirring around in the bedroom and so he sneaked outside. He must've been pretending to sleep like I was. Teehee."

"Well, well, well. Congratulations K.C. You kids *do* be careful won't you?"

"Oh, Quincy!" she laughed. "You don't need to worry about me. It's you that I'm worried about. You and Alex I mean."

"There's no more me and Alex. Remember the whole pretending to be someone he's not—in league with Landon Powell—thing? Anyway, let's talk about something else.

"You know you haven't talked to that Stanwyck character. He was supposedly a good buddy with Derrick. Maybe if you talked to him you could shed some light on things and see where all of these spokes are connected."

"Good idea. I'll call Linda and see where I might be able to find Doug Stankwyck today."

"Do you think I could tag along, Boss?"

"Sure. We'll be incognito in your car in case anyone sees us there. Lets go."

Doug Stanwyk's rockin' bachelor pad turned out to be a two-story house in the middle of a suburban cul-de-sac. The grass on his front lawn was gray-green with large patches of dead yellow splotches covering all the corners. A couple of overgrown dwarf pine trees stood poor watch on either side of the front porch, where empty beer bottles and cans surrounded the legs of a couple of plastic lawn chairs. Yard work was not a priority for this household. It looked as if fancy cars were, though. The bright yellow Hummer, Derrick's Porsche and a couple of other sports cars I didn't recognize were parked on the street and in the driveway. The garage door had been left open, leaving visible all the junk piled and crammed into every available nook and cranny. Tools and motorcycles and snowmobiles were recognizable forms amongst the rest of the flotsam.

I reached to knock on the door but K.C. interrupted me with a nudge from her elbow. She opened her purse and showed me the taser, winked and patted the purse then nodded at the door, giving me the go ahead.

I might have rolled my eyes at this in the past, but currently I wasn't feeling so cavalier about the danger we might be bringing upon ourselves. I knocked then stood back.

The door was opened slowly by a shirtless man in boxers with his hair sticking out all over his head.

"Come in ladies," he said.

"Are you Doug Stanwyck?" I asked.

"The one and only. Come on in, I was just popping open a brewski, you want one?" He held a brown bottle aloft.

"Um, don't you want to know who we are before you ask us into your house?" I asked.

"Not a couple of hot ladies like you. Why would I question my good luck?"

I glanced sideways at K.C. with her goddess hair. She shot a look of disbelief back at me and my eggplant-colored eye socket.

"Well don't just stand there, you fine young buck, show me to that brewski you were talking about." K.C. said. I looked at her and raised my eyebrows. "What?" she whispered as she walked past me into the house. I shrugged and followed her in.

The furnishings had seen better days. At least the blinds were open to let in some light, but a smell pervaded the entire place. It was the aroma of unwashed sheets mixed in with sweaty gym clothes chucked into a pile in the corner to cover up the last week's uneaten pizza.

"Good thing you ladies came when you did," he said, "I just finished a mega workout session in my gym downstairs." He looked over at his flexed right arm and kissed his bicep, then repeated on the left side. "You two wanna see my gym?"

No, but thanks for clearing up the mystery of the smell.

"No, thank you. Actually, my name is Quincy, and this is my partner K.C." I wanted it to sound like we were private investigators.

Doug perked up and sat up straight. "You two are lesies? I knew it. This is so hot. I had a dream about this last night. It's coming true." He waggled his eyebrows. "When are you guys gonna kiss?"

"Um, we're not those kind of partners," I explained.

"Damn." Doug deflated like the blow-up doll that was probably in the corner under the clothes and the pizza box.

"We're investigating the death of Derrick Gibbons, and we were told that the two of you were good friends."

"Yeah, Derrick and I were amigos since high school. We were on the wrestling team. The only loss he ever had was to me, and the only loss I ever had was to him. We were an even match. We competed 'til the day he died."

"You mean you still wrestled each other?" K.C. said.

"No man, I mean in everything. We kind of had this competition. He would snag a hot chick, so I would. He got a sports car, so then I got one. We shared the cars most of the time." That explained why I saw Derrick's Porsche at the mortuary after he had been found dead. "We even competed in business deals."

"What kind of business deals?" K.C. asked.

"Oh, all kinds of—wait, I shouldn't be telling you guys this stuff."

"Why not?" K.C. tapped Doug on the knee. "We're just friends getting acquainted. We heard about two cool dudes who like a good time, and we thought we would investigate. That's all."

Doug looked at K.C.'s hand, still on his knee then looked up at me and winked. "Aw what the hell. Chicks are always gossiping with each other. If there's one thing I know my way around, it's chicks and how to get what you want from 'em. I'll tell you what you want to know. Just get ready to return the favor." I looked at K.C. and cringed. She just shrugged.

"So, did Derrick live here too?"

"Yeah, most of the time, when he wasn't hanging out with a chick. He didn't like to live alone though. He liked to have someone around in case."

"In case of what?" K.C. asked.

"Oh, in case he took too much insulin, or not enough. Especially when he would work out. If he wasn't real careful with his diet, he could have problems." I wondered what affect all the steroids had on his diabetes.

"So, didn't Derrick own a flower shop?" I asked.

"Yeah, when I got my job, he had to have his own place too."

"You mean he opened the flower shop just to compete with you?" I asked.

"Yeah, pretty much."

"I got a gig running a mortuary for my step-dad's

company, so Derrick figured he needed to do the same thing, only he didn't have any money and his old man cut him off from any funds, so I gave him the money to start it up. It was going great until they kicked me out of my job."

"Now, why would they kick you out?" K.C. asked with mock disdain.

"I know. Right? They didn't like us owning a flower shop, especially since I didn't ask their highness' permission. But I got back at them."

"How'd you do that?" said K.C.

"I let them know that I knew what they were up to and I got a little somethin' extra on the side. You know?"

"No, we don't know," I said.

"My step-dad was always kissing that politician's ass because he pulled some favors for them."

"What kind of favors?" I asked.

"You ladies aren't going to tell anyone what I tell you right?"

"Of course we won't—Dougie." K.C. said.

"You girls are all right." He took a swig from his beer. "Powell got his friends in the legislature to swap some land rights. So my uptight step-dad got his precious cemetery for dirt-cheap on some land that was supposed to be part of some nature preserve or something. My step-dad must have something on the guy."

The secret cemetery. Landon Powell broke the rules for the Hansen Mortuary using his political power. Doug was right; Greg Shilling must have had some real damaging information on Mr. Powell.

"How were you involved?" I asked.

"I could show you now if you're into it." He stuck his tongue out and circled the top of his beer bottle with it. It was meant to be seductive, but it was in fact, disgusting.

I glanced over at K.C. She appeared to share my sentiments about Doug's tongue action, looking as if she were suppressing a gag. "I'm scared to ask, but what do you mean?" I said.

"I seduced his wife. Seduced, that's a cool word. I heard it in a movie."

"You seduced Landon Powell's wife," I said, "and did he know about it?"

"Oh hell no. But my step-dad sure did."

"And Derrick had to do the same thing for the competition." K.C. said. "He seduced Powell's mistress, Camille."

Doug got a smile on his face, "Yeah. Seduced. She had huge knockers."

"Yeah, she told me that Derrick paid for those huge…um for those," I said. "I thought he didn't have any money."

"He didn't for a while, but he was getting paid for the funeral flowers by people referred by the mortuary. Then the mortuary paid his rent and didn't know it. And then he was getting money from that little boyfriend that he had, and Powell was paying him. Powell's girlfriend came last."

"Wait a minute. Hold on there," K.C. said. "He was doing the horizontal tango with Powell's mistress and getting paid by him? That doesn't make sense."

"He wasn't getting paid for her," he said as if we were stupid, "Powell was paying Derrick to keep his mouth shut about the land deal. Derrick knew some things, thanks to me, that Powell was willing to pay for not sharing them with anyone else."

"Ooh, that's smart Dougie." K.C. said. Doug looked at her and pursed his lips in a fake kiss.

We had to get the rest of the facts quickly before Dougie's advances became more intense. "What about the boyfriend?" I said. "Was Derrick really bi-sexual?"

"Who really knows, dude? I don't think that he was though. That kid just needed someone to hang out with. He was lonely. Derrick told me the kid inherited a bunch of money from some old guy but he had almost spent it all by the time Derrick met him. Derrick just let him cry on his shoulder until the money was gone. Then it was time to move on. The dude took it kind of hard I guess."

"Yeah, you could say that." Doug's description of Derrick's callousness angered me. I could see why Irwin would want to kill Derrick. But, Derrick obviously had so many other enemies with their own strong motives. "Well, Doug you've shared a lot of information with us. And we do appreciate it," I said. "But, we've got to get going now."

"Wait up. I gave you what you wanted, now it's your turn to give back to the Dougster." He shaped his hands in a "V" and pointed them down to his lap.

"Yeah, about that…"

"Dougie, we are so sorry, but we have to go now. Maybe another time," K.C. said. "We promise we won't tell anyone what you told us."

"Who cares, you're chicks. What are you going to do about it? No one will take you seriously."

"Good point," I said as I grabbed K.C.'s wrist before she could hit him.

"Hell, you know you're just turned on by my sophistication," he said, then bit his bottom lip in an attempt to look like a male fashion model.

"Did you hear that one in a movie too you little twerp?" K.C. growled.

"Well, we've got to be going now," I interjected. "We've got girly pedicure appointment's to get to."

"Chicks," Doug said. "When are you coming back for some Doug love?"

We were out the front door before K.C. had a chance to answer.

"Boss, I'm surprised he wasn't in the coffin with Derrick. The line up of people who had good reason to rid the earth of the plague named Derrick is getting longer and longer, but I don't think Doug did it. He needed someone to brag to about his conquests."

"I think you're right. Blegh, I feel like I need a shower after being in the same room with Doug."

"Oh I don't know Boss, if it doesn't work out with Fred, I might go get myself some Doug love."

"Ugh."

When I got home I thought I would check on the health of my hydrangea plant. Even though it reminded me of Alex, it also reminded me of Aunt Rosie and Grandma so it wasn't completely unpleasant. I looked around my yard and realized what a mess was left after all of the microbursts we'd had lately. Broken branch tips and loose papers from the neighbor's garbage cans had collected in the corners against the fence. I walked around and gathered them. A multi-colored square caught my attention. I picked it up and felt the weight of heavy card stock. It looked like a greeting card, decorated with a floral print. I turned it over. My name was written on the other side. I opened it and read:

"Dear Quincy McKay, I've only known you for a few days, but I have a serious question to ask:"

Beneath the words, two little squares were drawn, the word "yes" written above one of them and the word "no," written above the other. I smiled at the memory of such notes passed around in elementary school.

"Do you like me? Check Yes or No," was written below the boxes. I drew my hand to my mouth as I let out a giggle just as when I received one of these notes in school.

"Sorry, I haven't written a note to a girl since the third grade so I had to go with what worked in the past. I hate to tell you I have to leave for a special assignment and I won't be able to talk to you until I get back, so please try not to get into any trouble while I'm gone. I'll be thinking about you the whole time. I can't wait to see you and your orange-striped tube socks again. Be safe!! Like*, Alex"*

So he hadn't lied about the note and the plant. But that

didn't mean it wasn't all part of the act. I didn't know anything about him, really. Only what he'd told me about his family and his past. I knew that he was good, very good at his job. He was good at other things too. I mean, cleaning up my porch, mountain hikes with dinner…making out under the trees... So good.

I felt someone watching me from behind and looked up. My suspicions of Alex took a back seat to the more immediate danger. I turned and looked up the street but didn't see anyone. No one was hiding behind the sunset orange rose bush growing against the front fence. I crept around the corner of the house to make sure nobody waited for me on the back patio. I walked to the other side of the house and peered across the driveway at Sarah's kitchen window. Her sunflower yellow curtains flapped in the breeze, but she wasn't there.

Everything looked normal in the neighborhood. Down the street, I noticed the silver car that had been parked in front of the Ragsdale's house for the last week, but Mrs. Ragsdale had mentioned her sister was coming in from out of town to help with the new baby.

I guessed I wasn't being watched, I was just feeling paranoid. Hard to imagine why.

CHAPTER TWENTY TWO

The desktop printer whirred, filling my soul with joy as it printed the invoice I would send off to the conference center. I took a celebratory swig of my Coke and enjoyed the sweet burn as it traveled down my throat. The payment for that invoice couldn't come too soon, and I said a little prayer that they would pay it before the due date. One can always wish.

K.C. skipped in from the back entrance of the store whistling a happy tune.

"What makes you so chipper today?" I asked.

"Oh nothing. It's just a grand day outside. I think big things are going to happen for us today, Boss."

"Big things huh? You wouldn't happen to have gone out with Fred last night would you?"

"A lady doesn't kiss and tell, my dear."

"Who said anything about kissing?"

"Oh boy you got me. We had a hot date last night. I think I'm in love." She started singing "Love is a Many-Splendored Thing."

The front door chimed and a little old lady walked in.

"Hello, how are you today?" I asked.

"Oh I'm fine honey." She slowly made her way to the front counter. She was steady on her feet, just slow. "I need to order something to put on the grave of my husband. It's his birthday coming up."

"Would you like us to make a nice wreath for you?"

"That would be lovely, but listen dear, I don't want it too fancy because one time my son and I bought this beautiful, expensive hanging basket and one of those nice shepherd hooks to hang it on. We spent a small fortune on it. Well no sooner than my son had helped me into the car—I'm ninety two you know and—where was I?"

"You said no sooner had your son helped you into the car…"

"Oh yes, well we were just driving away and we saw a grown woman sneak over to the basket and she took it off of the hook and ran off."

"She stole it right in front of you?"

"She certainly did."

"What did you do?"

"We just kept driving. We were worried she might hurt us if we confronted her. We called the police and reported it, but there isn't a lot they can do."

After her terrible story, I showed the woman a very simple grapevine wreath that would mostly be decorated with ribbon and would cost less than twenty dollars. She left the store and I could see a younger man of maybe sixty, who had waited for her in the car, get out to help her.

"K.C.," I said as I walked to the back room, "you will not believe what I just heard. Stealing a wreath from a ninety two year old woman before she has driven out of the cemetery. It's sickening."

"I used to put nice little mementos on my husband's grave, but people steal everything, even bits of ribbon. I'm surprised they don't steal the gravestones out of the ground."

I was truly angry for a good hour. I imagined a gravesite covered in freshly cut sod, with funeral flowers resting nearby, the "Beloved Husband" banners floating in the breeze. *Honestly, who would be disturbed enough to steal useless pieces of ribbon…*A chill spread across my body.

"Stolen ribbon...stolen ribbon! That's it, K.C. They stole my ribbon."

"What in tarnation are you talking about, Boss?"

"Danny called me to say that the casket spray on top of Derrick's casket had a banner on it with the same type of tacky lettering that only I have."

K.C. placed her hands on her hips. "Well that was rude of him."

"The point is—that ribbon was a link between me and the murder. K.C., someone stole that banner from the cemetery after a graveside service that we provided the flowers for. The murderer stole my design identity to frame me."

"Why would anyone do that...I mean why did they choose you?"

"They had to have known about my fight with Derrick."

"That sounds like a definite possibility," K.C. said.

"This just helps me to prove my innocence. I've been taking pictures of all of the funeral work that I do before it goes out the door. I'll just look at whose funeral we did a day or two before they found Derrick, and match the flowers and banner to the ones that were on Derrick's casket. I'm going to call Danny. He can tell me what color the ribbon was, and I can share my pictures with his brother."

K.C. clapped her hands and danced a little jig. "Way to go, Boss. I told you big things were going to happen today."

Before I clicked off the electric sign and reached for the light switches, I remembered I had left my cell phone on the desk. I walked back to retrieve it and saw the blinking voicemail message light. I hadn't heard my phone ring; it must have done so when I went into the cooler.

I looked at the caller ID, and there it was. Alex's

number. Thumb hovering over the keypad, I stood still for about twenty seconds staring at the phone, trying to decide whether or not I wanted to hear what he had to say.

I'd had enough time to think about things since the night with Camille LeFay. I had entertained the possibility that maybe I'd jumped to conclusions about Alex's involvement with Landon Powell. I wasn't completely convinced of his innocence, but maybe there was more to Alex's story than I knew.

After taking a deep breath, I dialed the code to my voicemail as fast as I could—no stopping allowed.

"Quincy, I know you're mad at me, but you need to listen. I can't talk long...I shouldn't be calling you now. I know about them finding Camille LeFay's body in your van. Powell and Arroyo had alibis for that night but I think they were involved. I'm only telling you this so you'll stay away from them. They're dangerous. Do not go snooping around. Be careful, stay close to home and work. You're safer that way. I miss you. I'll talk to you again as soon as I can."

"I miss you." That's the only thing I retained from the voicemail. I missed him, too.

I had to play the message back. He'd said something about danger, something, something and that he missed me.

The phone rang before I could push replay. My heart jumped in my chest in anticipation of hearing Alex's golden-honey voice once again.

"Hello?" I answered expectantly.

"Quincy, is that you?" It was LaDonna Shaw and she sounded upset.

"Yes, it's me. LaDonna, what's wrong?"

"Oh Quincy, its Irwin. He's stormed off. I'm really worried he might be mad enough to come back here and hurt me. We argued about Bobby and the store and...everything." Her voice began to sound hysterical. "Quincy, we drove in together and he took the car. I didn't know who else to call."

"LaDonna, you should call the police if you think Irwin might be violent."

"I don't want to call the police. This is a small town. The neighbors will know and we'll be ruined. They won't come to our store anymore." I could see what she meant. Everyone knows everyone's business in a small town. "Can you help me, Quincy? Just come and give me a ride. I can figure out where to go, but I need you to get me out of here first."

"Okay. I'll be there as fast as I can. It's a twenty-minute drive. Make sure to lock the doors. Lock yourself in the office with the phone."

"Okay, dear. I'm such an old fool. I'm so sorry to drag you into this."

"Nonsense, LaDonna. I'll be there as quick as I can. Stay safe."

###

As I entered the highway I checked my rear view mirror. Two cars had turned onto the road behind me. Ten miles later, the second car, a silver sedan still followed me. I told myself to calm down. I was on the way to help LaDonna and I needed to stay focused. Smooth asphalt gave way to bumpier travels as I turned off the highway onto the narrow country road leading to the Shaw's. After a glance in the mirror I was relieved not to see the silver car.

Until I turned the corner.

The silver car was still behind me. Fingers strangling the steering wheel, I scrutinized my options. I had to get to LaDonna, but if these were the two morons that worked for Landon Powell, I couldn't lead them to the Shaws. Who knows what they were capable of?

I knew just what to do. I had the zombie van and I knew my way around the back roads. I took a sharp right at the next intersection that took me to an old cattle farm.

The gravel road faded into dirt with the ruts carved into the roadway over years of use. Between the ruts grew tall, thick thistle and cheat grass that rattled and whipped the undercarriage on the van. I knew the dirt road would eventually return to gravel and empty out onto the main road. I looked in the mirror.

Tall grass and weeds slowed the silver car, but not enough for my comfort. The distance between the silver bloodhound and Zombie Sue could easily be closed when we reached gravel.

I was banking on something I remembered from high school joy rides. At the junction where dirt led back into gravel was a massive divot in the dirt side of the road. It was more like a sinkhole and had the reputation for eating up the kinds of little cars you would drive in high school. I came upon the sinkhole, full of water left over from wicked microbursts that dumped on the higher elevations as they curled around the mountain ridge.

Zombie Sue and I whizzed through the dip as fast as we dared. Muddy water splashed as high as the top of the van. The water resistance on the van was powerful and it made a deafening sound on the bottom of the car. I slowed down on the way out on the gravel side of the road. I anticipated the impending splash out with fear and glee.

The weeds were high enough that driver of the shorter sedan couldn't see over them well enough to stay on my tail. That little silver car took a nosedive into the sinkhole and never came out. I shouted out loud and then drove as fast as I could to LaDonna.

I pulled up and got out in front of the store and knocked on the door. As I leaned on it, I realized it was loose, it wasn't locked. I pulled it open and called out.

"LaDonna?"

"I'm back here, dear." Her voice came from the office. I ran back, rounded the corner and found my nose smashed into the barrel of a revolver.

"Thanks for coming so quickly. Dear."

"LaDonna I..."

"Wasn't expecting such a cold greeting? It was a heck of an idea having me back in this office. No way for you to see the gun. I didn't even have to hide it."

"LaDonna, I don't understand." My legs felt like they had been wading in a spring-cold river. They were numb. The only thing I could feel was the pounding of my heart.

"You have been more than helpful, dear and I hate to impose, but I do need your help just one more time. Now you walk yourself outside to your van, and don't you try anything funny. I may be a shriveled old prune, but I'm a sharpshooter champion in my age division. Father made sure I could hunt and fish like any of the boys and I was better than all of them. When you get to the car, you get in to the driver's seat and wait for me to get in the shotgun seat. Oh ho," she giggled, "shotgun. I've made a pun. Now move it! And don't you think you can drive off without me. I can fell a deer a mile away. A thin little windshield is nothing."

I walked to the front of the store. LaDonna had the gun jabbed into the small of my back and she walked along side of me like I was helping her. The charade really wasn't necessary; there was no one within a two-mile radius. No cars passing by. Nobody.

I got in the drivers seat and she trained the gun at my face like a gangster in a movie while she slid around the front of the car and got in. This Grandma didn't have any trouble in the feeble broken hip department; she hopped into the elevated van seat like she was doing the high jump.

"Back out and drive that way." She waved the gun indicating west. I was sweating so much my palms almost slipped off of the wheel.

I tried to talk to her, to calm her down and get any type of information I could.

"Shut up and drive where I tell you to."

I did exactly as she said.

CHAPTER TWENTY-THREE

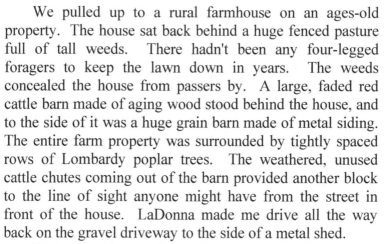

We pulled up to a rural farmhouse on an ages-old property. The house sat back behind a huge fenced pasture full of tall weeds. There hadn't been any four-legged foragers to keep the lawn down in years. The weeds concealed the house from passers by. A large, faded red cattle barn made of aging wood stood behind the house, and to the side of it was a huge grain barn made of metal siding. The entire farm property was surrounded by tightly spaced rows of Lombardy poplar trees. The weathered, unused cattle chutes coming out of the barn provided another block to the line of sight anyone might have from the street in front of the house. LaDonna made me drive all the way back on the gravel driveway to the side of a metal shed.

"LaDonna, please tell me what you want. I just want to help you."

"Oh dearie, I know it. You're a regular Florence Nightingale," she said in a sarcastically sweet voice. She sighed heavily. "Let me tell you something, sister," her voice was no longer light and sweet. "There's nobody in this world you can trust, and that includes your husband." She waved the gun at me indicating I should get out of the van.

"Uh, uh, uh," she said, as I turned off the ignition. "I'll take those keys."

Fingers trembling, I handed her the keys and got out of

the van. She zipped right up next to me and jabbed the gun into my side.

"Go in that door over there."

I walked toward the side door of the barn. I heard the distinctive click of the van doors locking and then the clinking of keys as they hit the ground. LaDonna mumbled unintelligibly to herself. I couldn't think of anything to do to distract her besides talk.

"I know what you mean about not being able to trust your husband," I said.

"Oh is that so?" She ordered me to wait and she twisted the door handle, all the while skillfully pointing the gun at me. She swung open the door and motioned for me to go in.

Once inside, I saw old stacks of hay bales, a big tool bench, pulleys hanging from the ceiling, and lots and lots of different kinds of tools hanging on the wall; most of them looking like they could slice someone's head off. A strange, out-of-place stainless steel box, the size of a cement truck, took up almost one complete side of the building. It looked like a big walk in cooler but it had drawers in it. A stainless steel table stood to my left, in the center of the room. Much like the one I imagined Linda found Doug and Mrs. Powell using. It occurred to me this was an embalming table, and the big metal chest of drawers was the place where they kept the bodies of people after they went to the big refrigerator in the sky.

"How do you like it?" LaDonna asked proudly. "Looks pretty darn professional don't you think?"

"For what profession?" I asked.

"We told you that Irwin kept up his licenses. He taught me everything he knows. After the kids were grown we took the job as rural undertakers. We went all over to the different farms when people went belly up and we transported the bodies to the morgue."

"They let you have a mini-morgue in your barn?" I

asked, astonished.

"No. That, young lady, was the bargain of a century. The school district surplus manager called us when we were looking for another cooler for the shop and told us he had this. It was just the thing to have on hand. We can store an elk in there after the hunt, or pheasants. Or we can store bodies. And since I sent Irwin on an errand, you're going to need to help me with one of those bodies."

Her words didn't immediately sink in.

"Over there." She jerked her head in the direction of the metal table. Just beyond the table on the ground was a long black bag. I recognized it as similar to the one I fell on at the mortuary. Seeing the bag helped the reality of the word "body" sink in. The room started to move, and my stomach started churning. I focused on breathing. In, out, in, out.

I'm not usually the type to become sick at the sight of something gruesome, but this wasn't like when I cut my finger open. This was gruesome in an entirely different way. Knowing how this person had become a body in a bag was enough to unsettle me to the core. I continued my makeshift plan to try and talk to LaDonna to stall until something happened. I didn't know what, but something.

"LaDonna, who is this?"

"Who?"

"The person in the black bag!"

"Don't get snippy with me, young lady." She said this like a regular grandma would say it. "It's that damned JoAnne, if you have to know."

She responded every time I asked a question, so I kept going. "JoAnne. You mean the florist?"

"Yes, yes," she said impatiently, "from JoAnne's Flower Basket."

"Why did you kill her?" I asked, as if it were as common as asking where she bought her shoes.

"She was just plain mean, that's why. And her arrangements were terrible."

I couldn't disagree with either of those statements.

"But doesn't she have a family or loved ones who are worried about her?"

"Family!" she shouted. "My family is ruined, my poor boy is gone! No one cared about my family. I don't give a hairy rat's patoot about Jo...Annnnes family. Besides, if she didn't want to get herself killed, she shouldn't have been so rude to me."

This woman was crazy, there was no telling what might set her into a rage, but the talking kept her from aiming at me as attentively so I kept going.

"LaDonna?" I kneeled down next to the bag, "Did you kill Derrick Gibbons?"

Her face grew pale and all expression washed out of her face. She stared into space for a moment, and then, as I watched, her face grew redder and redder and began to screw up, growing tighter with every moment.

"I had to protect my son. I've had to protect him his whole life. He thought he was in love with that...common thief. Bobby wanted to sign away his money, his land. That idiot Derrick fancied himself some kind of developer. Thought he was going to get rich off of some kind of plant they use to make gasoline. I've never heard anything so stupid in my life."

I wanted to keep her talking to stall. I needed to think of something while she talked. "You mean switch grass?"

"Whatever it's called, it's all a bunch of hooey if you asked me. There's plenty of oil in the ground. Besides, farming doesn't bring the kind of money that the land underneath the farm does. That politician offered double what it was appraised for."

"You mean Landon Powell?"

"Yeah. See this land here is valuable. I've had all kinds a people out here nosin' and askin' around."

She still had the gun trained on me. You'd think the old gal's arm would be getting tired by now. I desperately needed something or someone to intervene.

"Why is this property so valuable?" I asked.

"You know what? You really are a stupid young thing.
Just because you know how to work on a computer doesn't
give you any smarts." She looked at me in a way I
imagined she had probably looked at her husband a million
times; disgusted and annoyed. "You've seen all the
development out here. Mr. Politician told me he was
building a ski resort up here; a mega-resort is what he called
it. He said they were gonna have the Olympics here again,
and that he was going to build the finest European ski
village in the country. He showed us pictures and
everything. He said he had some eye-talian designer
coming out to draw up the plans after we sold it. I told
Bobby this is just what we had been praying for, but no. *He
wanted to be a farmer*," she mimicked in a childish voice.

"Why didn't you just sell the land? Why did Bobby
have to be involved?"

LaDonna let out a sigh that suggested the years of
fatigue she had been carrying on her shoulders. "When
Irwin and me got married, Daddy didn't come to the
wedding. He hated Irwin. Said he would never amount to
anything. Daddy died after we had moved away and had
our kids. When we came back for the funeral we found out
that Daddy left his house to me in his will, but he left all the
land to Bobby. He was named after Daddy, and I guess
Daddy thought that meant he should have all of his land."
Her voice betrayed her tough exterior. The disappointment
was apparent.

"So you killed Derrick because he wanted to be a
farmer with your son?"

Her eyes lit up and the sadness and fatigue left her. She
straightened up and looked as if she peered through me
rather than looking at me.

"I had to *protec*t him! A mother must protect her
offspring. It's the way of nature. That detective came and

told me about Derrick's girlfriend. He told me that Derrick wasn't gay, and that he was running around town with some tramp. I tried to convince Bobby to break it off with him, before he found out the truth. Bobby thought he was in love. Can you believe that? Bobby was always in love with the first man he'd run into that showed any kind of interest. The guy he was with before Derrick used to beat on him," her voice cracked, "he threatened to leave Bobby all of the time, but then Bobby found out he had been infected with HIV. The son of a bitch gave it to my son. He knew he had it and never told Bobby. Too bad that man died suddenly." LaDonna's eyes grew dark and distant. A wicked smile slowly spread through the wrinkles around her mouth. "Quincy, my dear, did you know that they can't trace a murder by insulin, not if the bastard was a diabetic? He had a lot of money hidden away too. Thought Bobby didn't know about it."

Sweet little old LaDonna had revealed herself as a cold-blooded killer. It wasn't likely she was going to let me go after telling me all of her dirty secrets. I had to think of a different approach. I needed some way to distract her. If I could just knock the gun away, I had a size advantage, and maybe I could knock her over, long enough to get away.

"You were just protecting your family, LaDonna. Anyone would do the same. Derrick was out for himself. I hated him too. He stole my business away just because he wanted to compete with a buddy. A guy from the mortuary—he told me how he and Derrick would compete with each other. When Derrick started dating Camille LeFay, the politician's girlfriend, Doug started pursuing the politician's wife. It was all a game for them. When Doug got his own mortuary to run, Derrick had to have his own shop—it didn't matter that he didn't know how to run it properly, he just wanted to be one up on his buddy. LaDonna, I'm on your side. I found out that Derrick was dating the last woman because she had information on the politician's land dealings. He thought that he would get investors for the switch grass farm and develop it and then sell it to one of the huge energy companies for a profit. He was using your son, just like you said."

She swayed almost imperceptibly. I thought maybe her gun arm was dropping slowly. "No one is on my side, Quincy." The arm holding the gun popped back up, steady and sure, training the barrel right at me.

"Was Derrick a diabetic?" Another wicked smile curled the corners of her mouth. I didn't need a verbal answer. "The casket spray looked an awful lot like my work, LaDonna."

"I know, dearie. What a wonderful coincidence it was that your aunt and I trained at the same place."

"And the banner with the lettering?"

"Everyone steals bows and banners from a warm grave, Quincy. Don't be naïve."

"Funny you chose that particular person's final resting place to defile. I checked my records. That person truly was someone's '*Beloved Son.*' I made three banners for that family; I did guess correctly about which one you chose to use, didn't I?"

"You did," she said, cold as ice. "I had to get rid of him, Quincy. He caused my little boy to hurt himself. My little baby! That good for nothing husband of mine wouldn't do it. He never understood Bobby. He never accepted the fact that Bobby was gay. I knew it from the day he was born. He was different than my other kids. I knew that, but I loved him. How could anyone think that my precious little baby was anything less than perfect? How could his own father turn away from him?" Tears tracked down her face and sputtered on her lips as she yelled. "Enough!" She looked at me with rage behind her eyes and she pointed the gun at my face.

"Quincy, it's too bad that we met when we did. I would have liked getting to know you. You've been so helpful.

You're going to help me now. You need to drag that bag over to the middle of the floor underneath that big hook. Then we'll hoist it up with the hook and send it over to the drawers in the fridge. I would have had Irwin do it, but he was driving me nuts. Besides, you're a strong young woman, it's better to have you do it."

The panic set in.

The bag would probably be heavy, I could buy some time dragging it slowly. If she complained, I would tell her I needed help and when she came over I would try to knock the gun out of her hand.

I tried to drag the bag but it was heavier than I could have ever imagined.

"Put your back into it, girl."

"It won't budge, LaDonna. Are you sure just one person can do this?"

"Irwin manages. He is built like a bull though. You sure you can't do it?"

I conjured up some tears. "Please, LaDonna, I'm trying to h-h...help you," I sobbed, "but it's too heavy!"

Her face softened a little, but it was probably due to the inconvenience of it all rather than any feelings of empathy.

"Oh for hell sakes, I have to do everything around here. Move over."

When she came within two feet of me, I crouched and lunged at her while letting out a primal scream, like I'd seen when football players pushed the tackling dummies on TV. I lowered my shoulder and plunged into her sternum. We tumbled to the ground.

She lay still beneath me. I lifted my head slowly. Her eyes were closed and her arms were splayed out wide, above her head. She must have hit her head on the ground and been knocked out. The gun rested a few inches from her hand. I got up and kicked the gun away then crouched over her and made sure she was breathing and had a pulse. She did, thankfully.

I picked up the gun and thought I would put it under my waistband like I had seen in the movies. I tucked it in but I was afraid it would go off. I tried to think of a place where I could stash it that no one would suspect.

The Body Bag.

I reluctantly unzipped the bag, knowing that mean old JoAnne would be staring back at me. I held my breath and tugged on the zipper. The opening revealed a bulging burlap bag of sand. The body bag was full of sand bags. I felt a surge of relief, glad—in a sad way for LaDonna's confusion and hope for JoAnne, even though she was a nasty woman. I stashed the gun and zipped up the bag.

While LaDonna laid there on the floor like a lump with a gray curl and set hairdo, I had time to slow down my thoughts and think about my situation. I became aware of a loud droning noise that I hadn't noticed while I was fearing for my life. I heard a big clunk in the direction of the body drawers, and then the constant noise stopped. The sound was familiar, it was the motor of the cooling system of the refrigerated drawers cycling off.

I paused for a moment to look at my surroundings and decide what to do about LaDonna. I didn't have my cell phone, maybe I had left it in the car; I wasn't sure. Besides, I didn't have my keys to the van. LaDonna had tossed them into the gravel after she locked the van doors. I didn't dare leave her; she could die there because of me. Yes, she was a murderous criminal, but I didn't want her death on my hands or my conscience.

I searched the walls of the building for a telephone. If I could call 911, I could tell them where we were. If LaDonna woke up and gave me any trouble, I could hold her gun on her until help arrived. But if she woke up, I would know she was okay, and then I could just run. She couldn't outrun me, could she?

I didn't see a phone anywhere. I thought maybe I would just take off and find help somewhere, but LaDonna was looking kind of gray. I couldn't just leave her.

I heard a faint sound coming from inside the big metal box. I paused and listened carefully, and I heard it again. It sounded like a muffled voice. I followed the direction of the sound to one of the drawers and fumbled with the handle until I figured out how it worked. The chest-high drawer finally opened and I looked down into the red, scowling face of JoAnne from JoAnne's Flower Basket.

Her mouth had been gagged and her hands and feet were tied with old shop rags. She had been stuffed into the drawer, and it looked like she didn't have any room to move. I pulled the gag down, out of her mouth.

"JoAnne, are you okay?"

"AAAHH, AAAHH!" JoAnne screamed, over and over again. She screamed, then took a breath and then screamed again.

"JoAnne! It's me, Quincy. I'm here to help you."

"AAAHH, MURDERER! AAAHH!" She stopped making noise long enough to spit in my face. I had more than enough to deal with without this treatment, so I yanked the gag back into her mouth.

"I'm here to help you if you'll shut up long enough!"

"Who's here? What are you doing?" A voice shouted from the side door.

I spun around to see Irwin Shaw at the door.

"Who are you talking to? What—what did you do to my wife?" Irwin rushed over, trying to overcome his old man limp.

I wasn't sure if Irwin was a co-conspirator with LaDonna or not. My guess was yes. I leaned my back against JoAnne's drawer and slid it almost shut.

"It's not what you think," I said. "She tried to kill me!"

"She's an old woman! What have you done?" He crouched slowly and with great effort until he kneeled next to his wife.

"Me? She's the one that drove me down here at

gunpoint and threatened to kill me if I didn't help her move a body!"

"What body?"

"J..." I started to tell him, but I decided not to on account of JoAnne not really being dead, but also on account of me not knowing Irwin's level of involvement in Derrick's murder, and what he thought was JoAnne's murder. "Just some body. I don't know whose."

"Who?" He said questioningly. "Don't you mean what?"

"Huh?" These people were animals. They didn't even refer to their victims by name. I was in a barn out in the middle of nowhere with two geriatric serial killers. My impulse by now was to drop to the ground and roll up into the fetal position. But I knew I needed to keep my wits about me to try and get out of this barn of terror alive.

"C'mon, Mother wake up." He slid one hand under her head and shook her shoulder with the other. "What the hell did you do to her? Is she alive?"

"She's alive. I checked her breathing and pulse. She just hit her head while we were trying to move the body." I left out the part about me playing defensive tackle. "We need to call for help."

"No!" he yelled. "We'll do no such thing!"

"Irwin, your wife needs medical attention. She's had a head injury."

"Oh she'll be just fine. I don't need any police here poking around. LaDonna's been busy, and I haven't been able to keep up."

I swallowed and it felt like my heart was sitting at the bottom of my esophagus. My legs were frozen into the ground. But I couldn't wait around any longer and chance being shoved in a drawer like JoAnne. Irwin kneeled over his wife, and with his aged hip joints I knew I could easily escape. But I also knew JoAnne was still in a drawer and any minute the motor from the cooler that had clanked back on would be cycling off and then Irwin would be able to hear her. I ran to the other side of the barn to the body bag where I had stashed the gun.

"Where do you think you're going?"

I had already made it to the bag and unzipped it. I grabbed the gun and pointed it at Irwin.

"Don't move!" I yelled.

"Quincy, what the—"

"You and your sadistic wife aren't going to kill anyone else."

"What are you talking about? We haven't killed anyone."

"You said LaDonna's been busy."

"Yes, busy with hunting."

"Hunting! That's what you call it? It's called murder you monster." I kept the gun aimed at him even though my finger wasn't on the trigger.

"You're not one of those animal rights activists are you?"

"What?"

"Hunting is a perfectly natural thing to do. Our ancestors have been hunting for food and clothing since Adam and Eve. It's a God given right and Mother and I have been harassed by the fish and game everywhere we've lived. A God fearing man or woman shouldn't have to get a license to provide for their family. I don't need any cops down here snooping around and getting the Fish and Game in our business."

I couldn't tell if Irwin was just in a state of shock or if he had some form of dementia. "I'm talking about Derrick Gibbons, Irwin."

His face darkened. "What about him?"

"Your wife murdered him."

"You're lying! You really did kill him didn't you? And now you're trying to blame a couple of senior citizens. You're a murderer!" With perfect timing the motor to the drawers clanked off and the sounds of a muffled stuck pig emanated from JoAnne's drawer that I had left ajar. Irwin looked behind him toward the drawers and then back at me with a confused look on his face.

"Quincy, what's going on here? Who's in the drawer? What have you done?"

I could see he was genuinely confused, and his eyes glistened with what looked like tears. Maybe he really didn't know about Derrick's murder. My arms were getting tired from holding up the gun. I lowered it and Irwin didn't move.

"Irwin, I don't know how she got there, but JoAnne is in the drawer. Your wife forced me in here at gunpoint, and she let me think that JoAnne was dead in this body bag. She came at me with the gun and I knocked her down and she hit her head. LaDonna told me she killed Derrick Gibbons because of how much he hurt your son."

"Oh dear." His voice grew frail and tender as he looked down at his wife. "I'm afraid it's all unraveling now. Mother. I'm sorry." He looked up at me, his jaw trembled. "She hasn't been quite right lately. She's been imagining things and misplacing other things. She probably put something in that bag thinking it was something else. She's always been a great markswoman and hunter, she's got all kinds of trophies. I started to worry about her using guns when she started with her stories, but she always snapped out of it. She loves hunting and camping and fishing, it reminds her of time she spent with her father and me and the kids. I just wanted her to be happy. But she's been real bad lately. She would see a story on the news and think it was about her. I'm afraid that's what happened when she told you about Derrick. But she's carried it much further this time. I'm so sorry, Quincy. I don't want to lose her. She's been my sweetheart for sixty years."

I put the gun down on the bag and walked over toward Irwin who kneeled, holding his wife. They both looked very small on the floor of the giant barn that surrounded them.

"We've got to get JoAnne out of that drawer." I said. I extended my hand and helped Irwin up from the floor. LaDonna was still out cold but she looked okay. She wasn't turning blue or anything. We both pulled on the top of the drawer and rolled out a wide-eyed, red-faced JoAnne.

"JoAnne, I'm going to take the gag out if you promise not to scream," I said. She nodded, still looking scared out of her mind. I slowly reached down and gently pulled the gag out of her mouth. I cringed in anticipation of the squeals she might produce. Thankfully, she said nothing; in fact she made no noise at all. Irwin and I helped her sit up. I started working on the knots that tied her hands together, and once those were undone I helped JoAnne bend her knees up, so she could get her legs out of the bottom of the drawer. It took some doing, her movements were stiff and her legs were rather large in diameter and difficult to lift. We finally managed to get her turned around. I knelt and began the work of untying her feet. She said nothing the entire time; she just followed my directions.

"There," I said, once I conquered the final knot. "You're finally free. Can you move your feet?"

"AAAUGH, Murderer!" She screamed and kicked me in the chest sending me flying backwards. JoAnne had the leg strength of a Clydesdale once she got her range of motion back.

When I opened my eyes, everything was dark. I wasn't sure where I was, but it was too difficult for me to care. I shut my eyes. The memories of what had just happened floated around the periphery of my mind like tiny little puzzle pieces that just didn't fit together.

I opened my eyes again. It was still dark. The surface under my back was hard and flat. The end of my nose felt cold like when I was a little kid and my mother had to drag me away from the sledding hill up the street. My fingers were tingling and when I moved them I became aware that my wrists were tied together. I knew where I was.

The first thing I thought of when I realized I was in a drawer in a mini-morgue was hypothermia. I had spent enough time in my walk in cooler to think that I might have a tolerance to the cold air. This was probably a false belief, but it helped me not to panic until I had my next thought. Air.

I began to cry. Now I really couldn't breathe, especially since I had a gag tied around my mouth. Crying while you're gagged is not conducive to helping you feel like you can breathe. I allowed myself the crying indulgence for a few seconds until I thought to myself, *No. Get yourself under control, Quincy.* Crying would probably use up more air. As my eyes adjusted to the dark, I realized the light was uneven around me. I tipped my head back and saw an illuminated line above and behind my head. The drawer hadn't been closed all the way. Okay, I could breathe.

My fingers weren't tingling anymore, they were numb. Would they have to cut my hands off when they found me? Would someone find me? I had to find a way to escape. I kicked my feet to see if they were tied together too. They weren't tied, but I hit my knee on the metal above. I kept my legs straight as a board, just like when we played the "Straight as a Board, Light as a Feather" game in junior high school. I flexed my ankles and tried to inch the drawer open by pushing on the metal ceiling with my toes. No traction. The tread on my cross trainers had been worn off completely. I kicked wildly at my cold metal tomb. Now my toes were tingling.

All I could do was yell for help.

"Help!" That didn't do any good. I couldn't even hear me yell with the gag in. I would just have to lay here until someone found me or until I thought of some other idea for escape. I lay there with my eyes open, because it seemed to help me think. Suddenly, the light in my drawer brightened. I tipped my head back and saw that the crack above my head was much brighter than before. I listened intently, but all I could hear was the groan of the compressor motor. Soon, I heard other noises. Someone was yelling. They were close enough that I could hear them over the motor. I kicked my legs robot-style so my toes made noise on the ceiling. It really hurt, but I kept at it, harder and harder.

I heard a loud rumble and my eyes were blinded by a flash of light. When I opened my eyes again, a beautiful pair of warm chocolate drops stared down at me. Alex scooped me into his arms and pulled me out of the drawer.

CHAPTER TWENTY FOUR

The emergency room isn't usually the first place that comes to mind when you think of romance. But I'm not the most usual person in the world, nor is my life. I decided to give Alex one more chance, partly since he rescued me and probably saved my life and all, but mostly because of what he revealed to me after the rescue.

"That ought to do it," said the nurse, as she finished wrapping my foot. "You'll probably need the crutches for a few weeks, but the physical therapist can give you more specific directions."

"All this for a toe?" I asked.

"All this for a *big* toe, yes. You'll be surprised how much you use that thing. Now tell me, did you really break your toe by kicking the ceiling?"

"Yep." I looked at Alex, who sat in a chair opposite the examining table. He winked at me.

"She kicked it pretty hard, that's how I found her."

"Uh-huh," the nurse said. I don't think she believed me. She turned to Alex. "The doctor will have to come back in and see you one more time before Quinella can leave." Stupid medical records with full names printed on them. "You've been given the care sheet for someone with a head injury, right?"

"Right. I'll keep a close watch. I won't take my eyes off of her." Alex gazed at me while he spoke to the nurse.

He flashed his melt-my-insides smile.

"She didn't sound too convinced," I said.

"She didn't have all the facts. As far as she knows you were messing around in the back seat of an old Scout."

"What?"

"Where else are you gonna be able to kick a metal ceiling?"

"You didn't tell her what happened to me?"

"Only the necessaries." He grinned mischievously. "I might have just made up the part about the Scout."

"Thanks for rescuing me while tarnishing my reputation."

"My pleasure."

"I'll forgive you for disappearing, since you made this one really big, unexpected appearance. But only if you tell me how you found me."

He leaned forward in the chair, elbows on knees and fist under his chin. "You know, you look pretty cute for a girl with a black eye and a broken toe."

"Flattery will get you nowhere. Well—maybe it will get you somewhere—we'll see. But don't change the subject. How did you find me?"

"Rusty and Dusty Stephens."

I gave Alex the do-you-seriously-expect-me-to-believe-that, look.

"The guys in the red truck," he said.

"It wasn't a red truck following me this time."

"I know. It was a rental car being driven by Rusty and Dusty..."

"What?" I interrupted. It made my head hurt.

He held his hands up defensively, "Hold on, let me explain. It was a rental car paid for by me, which *you* caused to bottom out. They had to haul it off on a tow truck. That's why it took so long for me to find you. You're really lucky, you know."

"I know. I'm sorry to have caused all that. And I hope

you bought the extra insurance."

"Very funny," he said

"But seriously, Rusty and Dusty work for the police?"

"Not exactly." Alex looked around then got up and shut the door to the hospital room. "Okay," he said in a hushed voice. "First of all, I need to tell you that I'm not a regular police officer." Well, duh. "I've been working in undercover affairs for the last nine months on a case involving a bad cop."

"Arroyo?"

"Yes. Until last night I was working undercover to find out if departmental suspicions were true about him and his involvement with a crime boss of sorts."

"Landon Powell." I said.

"How did you know?"

"I know many things. Continue."

An appreciative smile curled the corners of Alex's mouth. "I couldn't find anything on Rusty and Dusty until your delivery driver called me after she roughed them up."

I smiled, thinking about K.C. taking down those "Two young bucks."

"They were so scared of what would happen to them once Landon Powell heard how an old lady took them down, it was easy to convince them to help me out. I couldn't have you officially watched, because I was afraid Arroyo would find out. So I struck a deal with Tweedle-Dum and Tweedle-Dee, and I paid for the rental car myself. They still think they have diplomatic immunity for helping out the police."

"Diplomatic immunity?"

"So they're not the sharpest tools in the shed."

"So, basically, you're telling me that I evaded two men who were being instructed by you, to follow me around, and that I could have kept this whole concussion, broken toe thing from happening?"

"Pretty much, but you did solve Derrick Gibbon's

murder."

"Well, that's great, I suppose, but you had me followed by thugs."

"Nah, I checked them out. They're harmless. As a matter of fact, once they thought they were protecting you, they took their job pretty seriously."

"But why were they following me in the first place—I mean in the beginning, with the red truck?"

"After the murder, Greg Schilling figured people would be snooping around the mortuary, and that they would learn about the shady favors that were being traded with Landon Powell. Schilling knew about the incident between you and Derrick, so he told Powell about it. Powell then sent Arroyo to redirect the investigation toward you. We think it was a diversionary tactic until they figured out for themselves who had really committed the murder.

I shifted around on the examining table and grimaced when I moved my foot. The pain pill the nurse had given me wasn't working yet.

"Are you okay?" Alex said.

"I'll be fine, I just wish the doctor would get here so we can go." I squirmed on the table until I found a slightly softer spot for my bottom. "So what about Camille LeFaye and JoAnne and Irwin and LaDonna?" I asked. "What happened to all of them?"

"It looks like Camille LeFaye was hit hard on the head." He knit his brows and shook his head. "Poor lady. Her death is still an ongoing investigation." He leaned forward and reached for my hand, "Sorry I couldn't be there for you after you found Camille. I was watching Arroyo."

"I don't understand. If you were watching Arroyo, how did he slip a dead body into my van?"

"He didn't put her there himself. We think he's involved, and we have plenty of other evidence of wrongdoing in other cases, so he'll be locked up for a long time even before he's charged in Camille's case."

"It was a bit of a shock, landing on a body in my own van."

"You've got to quit falling on top of dead bodies. People are going to start to wonder..."

I threw a rolled up Ace bandage at him. "What about the others?" I asked.

"JoAnne is the reason we finally found you. She called 911 in hysterics and gave a description of you as her captor. She was at her shop when somebody knocked on her back delivery door, and the next thing she knew, you were opening her drawer."

"Is it wrong that I'm not sure if I want to thank her?" I said, as I gingerly put my hand to the sore spot on my head.

Alex looked at me sympathetically. "LaDonna's in protective custody upstairs, in the ICU. Irwin brought her here and turned her in."

"If Irwin turned his wife in, and JoAnne called 911, how did I end up in the drawer?"

"JoAnne. She said she ran away from the barn, but then waited around until Irwin left with LaDonna. She was still freaked out thinking you had put her in the drawer, so she returned the favor. I guess she was worried that if you died, she could be put in jail for murder, so she called for help."

"What a gal."

"Well, the end result was getting you back. So, I'm forever grateful to JoAnne." My heart fluttered in my chest as he flashed a smile at me. "You told me you got LaDonna talking. Did she tell you how she killed Derrick?"

"Not exactly. I asked her if Derrick was a diabetic."

He raised one eyebrow, "And?"

"And, her reaction told me I had figured it out." Alex looked puzzled. "Irwin is a diabetic. While I was standing there trying to stall, I remembered. LaDonna knew what would happen if she gave someone too much insulin."

"My sweet, clever Quinella."

I glared at him. "Ooh, if I had something else to throw…"

He laughed and held his hands in front of his face. "Okay, okay, sorry. Did you find out why LaDonna did it?"

"Derrick took advantage of her youngest son, which eventually led to his suicide. I think in her mind, Derrick basically murdered her son. She was avenging him."

Alex shook his head. "Wow, a mother's protective instinct…" He stood then came over and sat next to me on the examining table. "I was so glad to see you when I opened that drawer, Q." The nickname was much better than the real thing. "Let me take you home and take care of you. Just for a little while," he said softly, coaxing.

I started to protest but was interrupted when he caressed my cheek with the back of his hand and turned my chin toward him with his fingers. He brushed his lips over mine, then pulled back. It felt like a feather tickling my skin. I sat up straighter, and tilted my head to meet his lips again with my own.

"Quincy!" We were both startled enough to stop short of what I'm sure would have been the Greatest Kiss Ever, by the grating, high-pitched voice of a woman yelling my name. "Quincy, where are they keeping you?"

"Oh hell. Speaking of motherly instincts—Alex, you're about to meet my mother."

###

"Quinella Adams McKay, don't you dare step foot in that kitchen again. You're not supposed to be walking around, crutches or not."

"Mom, it's okay. They want me to start walking on it a little bit. Besides, we need to get all of this food outside on the table. Everyone will be here soon."

Mom pulled out a chair at the dining room table and pointed to the seat. I obliged her and sat down.

I had decided to show my thanks to everyone for

supporting me through the last tough stretch by hosting a barbeque at my house. Danny volunteered to plan the party so I wouldn't have to "strain" myself during recovery. Given his experience with event planning I was eager to see what he'd come up with.

"Quincy, I don't see any drinks in the fridge. Is someone bringing them?" Mom said.

"Yes, Alex should be here with them any minute."

Mom's hands flew to her hips. She wore "The Look" on her face. My sisters and I always knew that when the hands went to the hips and she did "The Look," our mother was serious. "The beer drinker is bringing the drinks to our party?"

I tempered my eye roll and kept it internal. "Everything will be fine, don't worry. If you keep fretting about it, I'll have to get up and help you. Besides, Danny made all the assignments, just let him do his job."

She held her hands up, exasperated. "Alright, alright." She went outside, where I assumed she would go searching for my sisters. She wouldn't want to waste a good conjuring of "The Look".

"Hey, Boss," K.C. appeared at the back door, "I bet that dog of yours is barking. How goes the healing?"

"Hi, K.C., it's going great. I just have to wear this moon boot around for a while. Thanks for coming. And thanks for taking care of things at work. I appreciate it."

"No problemo, besides, your sister does all the work. Now, where can I put these green Jell-o shots?"

"You brought shots? My mother is going to freak out."

"Oh don't get your knickers in a twist. They don't have any alcohol; they just look like something I had at a party once. You can't have a shindig in Utah without Jell-O." Hopefully K.C.'s creation would be the only incarnation of Jell-O to show at this party. I wouldn't be able to stomach Great Aunt Zelda's family reunion, special amalgam of orange Jell-O salad, with whipped cream, walnuts, mini-marshmallows, carrots, coconuts, raisins and her secret ingredient…mayo.

"I'm sure Mom will show you where to put them outside. I'll be out there soon."

"Well, if it isn't the Unsinkable Molly Brown." Danny had announced his presence.

"This is going to be a great party, Danny. Thank you."

"Don't mention it Miss Molly. Unfortunately, after this little event, I have to strike a wedding. I sure dread event take-downs don't you?"

"My last event strike resulted in a dead body being found in my delivery van, so I am slightly averse."

"Oh dear, that's right. Has Officer Hottie come in to say hello yet?"

"Alex is here?"

"He just got here, I followed him into the backyard. I got an eyeful of what makes you so fond of him." He gave me an exaggerated wink with a head tilt.

"Hey, eyes off!"

Danny looked at me devilishly.

My cheeks were already stoking and butterflies bounced around in my stomach at the mention of Alex. Danny was right. Anyone could appreciate Alex Cooper's physique, including his perfect posterior. And I hadn't had a chance to ogle it since it walked away from me at the hospital, after my mother insisted she drive me home and stay with me. Alex had since had to leave town for work, again. We'd spoken on the phone, but I hadn't seen him or been in his very, physical presence for two and a half weeks.

"Let's go outside, Molly." Danny offered his arm and I leaned on it for support. Alex stood next to the beverage table, trapped by my mother and a small crowd of her comrades.

"Quincy, could you come over here?" my mother said.

Absolutely, it was the only way I would get anywhere near Alex with all of the Red Hat Club ladies fawning over him. I stumped my way over to the group on my own; Danny left my side to perform his social butterfly duties.

"Hi," I said to Alex. I was so excited; the word came out more breath than voice.

"Hello, Beautiful." *One of my favorite nicknames.* All the nerves in my body tingled.

The Red Hat group let out a collective "aah" and "isn't that sweet."

"Quincy, there's no ice," my mother said, quietly so her friends couldn't hear.

"Who's assignment was it?" I knew the answer, I just wanted to torment my mother a bit.

Mom let out a sigh. "It was mine, I was so worried about everyone else's assignments…I forgot mine."

I smiled at her, "I know. I'm just giving you a hard time. Who can we ask…?"

"So, Alex," one of mom's cronies wedged herself between me and Alex, almost knocking me over, "I hear you're a police officer. Have you made any arrests lately?"

"Where is your gun?" another of the lady sharks asked, as she circled the prey.

Alex looked at me, over the top of the first shark, silently pleading for help with his eyes.

"I can't believe this," I dinged my forehead with the heel of my hand, "I forgot all about the ice. What should we do?"

My mother grinned at me.

"I'll go get some ice." Alex could hardly spit the words out in order, he volunteered so quickly.

"I'll go with you," I said, and took him by the arm, pulling him from the shark tank.

He put his hand on top of mine, "I would love that…"

My mother cleared her throat.

I looked over and saw "The Look" starting to brew. "But you better go without me." We took a couple of steps toward the gate. "If I skipped out on this party, my mother and Danny would fight over who got to strangle me first. You know—I'd kind of like to see that…"

"No more violence for you. I think you're becoming an addict."

"Hey, I'm just an innocent little florist who got caught up in the wrong place at the wrong time."

"Ha, innocent my a…"

"Quincy, will you let Alex alone so he can go and get my ice?" Mom said.

"Yeah, Quincy, will you let me go already? I'm trying to get ice for your mom." He winked at her and gave my hand a squeeze in lieu of a kiss before he left. It was no fair. The squeeze felt the same as if someone had placed a drop of water on my tongue in the middle of the desert at high noon, then taken away the full canteen.

I watched Alex leave, to see the feature Danny had teased about before, and Danny had been right. My gaze didn't leave Alex's backside until it walked through the gate. I turned to my mom. You know what, I forgot to take a pain pill. I'll just go in and take it real quick."

"Do you need my help?"

Mom? Really?

I swallowed my smart-aleck reply. "No, thank you." She really needed a distraction. "Oh, K.C., have you met my mother yet?"

I didn't feel one bit of remorse for that trick. I escaped while K.C. shocked and awed my mother with colorful stories and the language to go with them. I hobbled up the steps, dragging my boot toward the kitchen and my medicine bottles. As I reached on top of the fridge, I heard voices coming from the patio, through the open window of the laundry room.

"Brad, what are you doing here?" Allie said.

"You're coming with me. Lets go!"

I ducked into the laundry room to look through the back window. Brad stood face to face with Allie, right in front of

the window, away from the rest of the group. Brad's hand
grasped her upper arm. My head throbbed at the sight of
Brad, reminiscent of our last meeting.

"Let go of me," Allie said in a louder voice.

"Allie? Brad? What's going on here?" my mother said
as she approached the two. "Brad, I haven't seen you in a
while." Mom's face changed from surprise to confusion.
"Is everything alright, Allie?"

"Everything's fine," Brad said. "We were just leaving."
Brad yanked on Allie's arm.

My heart started pounding. I hid behind the washing
machine and peeked around the side.

"No, Brad!" Allie yelled.

The background noise from the party stopped.
Everyone looked in the direction of the commotion.

"What's going on here? Brad, you let go of her." My
mother reached out and grabbed at the arm that held my
sister.

He shook her off like a rag doll and shoved her to the
ground. There was a collective gasp from the crowd.
Danny rushed over and before I understood what had
happened, Brad had a gun pointed in Danny's face.

"Back off! Just back off," Brad yelled. Danny backed
up with his hands up. Brad held the gun with both hands,
his arms straight out in front of his body. He pointed the gun
at the partygoers and arced the gun from left to right like a
swath cutting a barrier between him and them.

"Allie, I told you we were leaving." His voice sounded
crazy. He'd lost the icy cold, in-control tone I'd heard and
hated before. "You shouldn't have left my apartment. I told
you that you would regret it. Now lets go." He reached for
Allie with one arm, while still pointing the gun with the
other.

"Brad, just calm down. We can work everything out,"
said K.C.

"You shut up!" Brad yelled as he swung and pointed

the gun at K.C. "I've been waiting to pay you back. You and Allie's bitch sister. Where is she, Allie? I've been waiting for my chance to beat the living shit out of her and then put a bullet in her head. And now's my chance. Where is she?"

That was the last thing Brad said before he hit the ground. I had crept behind him and knocked him upside the head with the fire extinguisher I kept in my kitchen. It didn't have any spray left in it from when he set the bag of poop on fire on my porch, but it had been very useful, all the same. "Always keep a fire extinguisher in your kitchen." *Best advice ever.*

"I leave for ten minutes…" Alex exclaimed, as he stood at the back gate. He looked at me, mouth agape, as I stood with Brad's gun pointing at Brad's head while five people sat on top of him. I shrugged and grinned sheepishly at Alex.

Sirens grew louder as the police approached the house.

I relaxed my stance once I saw Alex. I pointed the gun down then pinched it on the very end of the handle, trying not to have to touch it anymore than I had to. I held it out to Alex, who had apparently forgotten his arms were wrapped around four bags of ice.

"I'll trade you." I said.

Uniformed officers appeared behind him in the open gateway.

"Cooper," said one of the officers, who nodded at Alex then looked at the scene. He looked back at Alex. "What the hell, Cooper?"

"I have no idea," Alex said. His mouth fell open again.

The other officer peeled K.C., Danny, Allie, my Mother and my other sister off of Brad, checked to make sure he was alive, then handcuffed him and rolled him over. Then the officer called an ambulance.

After the police and the ambulance left with Brad inside, we all decided we should still have our party. Not even an armed crazy man could cause the wasting of perfectly good food as far as any of us were concerned.

We had a grand time despite the rough start. Eventually everyone cleaned up, gathered their things and trickled out.

Alex and I lingered in the backyard until the last person left.

He stepped behind me and sweetly caressed my hair away from my neck, then massaged the muscles in my shoulders. I could feel the tension I had stored there from holding the gun at Brad. Alex must have read my thoughts. I could feel the heat rise in my cheeks as I imagined him reading *all* of my thoughts. He leaned down and whispered in my ear, "How are you feeling?"

Exquisite! I shuddered with goose bumps when his breath hit my neck. I was at DEFCON 3. *Warning, Core melt down imminent!*

I hopped around on my good leg to face him. He placed his hands outside my upper arms to steady me.

"I'm doing *very* well, considering all things. Especially now. Actually, I could really use some pain relief. I went in to take a pill at the same time Brad crashed the party, so I never got to take it."

"Hey, that hop you just did reminds me—how did you manage to sneak down the stairs with that boot of yours, and not draw Brad's attention?" He looked down at my foot. I wiggled my sock covered toes, sans boot, at him, and then wished to heck that I hadn't.

"Ouch," I said.

"Poor baby."

He looked down at me and his eyes locked with mine. Just like that, I was back to DEFCON alert, but this time there was no use trying to resist, the defenses were not even switched on. He gently touched my nose with his index finger then kissed the same spot. Then, he barely brushed

I hope you enjoyed
THE FINAL ARRANGEMENT.

Visit www.annieadamstheauthor.com for information about
the author, more books in the Flower Shop Mystery Series
and Quincy's Flower Arrangement of the Month Club—
exclusive for members only who sign up on the website!

Coming soon:

DEADLY ARRANGEMENTS

Planning a wedding is murder.

the last, determined remnants of my black eye, on the very ridge of my cheekbone, with his thumb. His other hand wove through my hair and teased at the back of my neck and he feathered his lips over the sliver of purple on my face.

He swept me off of my feet, literally, when he picked me up as if I weighed no more than a child.

The feeling of electricity that flared up in my chest could have lit up the whole city.

He kissed my mouth, hungrily, matching what I felt inside. In a low, breathy voice he said, "I've been looking forward to that since we were interrupted at the hospital." He smiled at me and the tiny lines around his eyes crinkled, framing the melting drops of chocolate.

I bit my bottom lip. "Me too. I'm so glad you're here."

"Let's get you inside and feeling better."

I couldn't wait to see what that entailed.